M000291296

Doc Curtis fc managed to quick... ... p... shouting behind him and dared not look back, fearing it might slow him just that much more.

He made it through the field and emerged onto a rough access road running between the cultivated land on one side and the woods on the other. The doctor dashed across the dirt road and through the weeds and scrub bordering its opposite side. The trees stood twenty yards ahead. He would make it, find a thick trunk to hide behind, and fire a warning shot. If he could drive them off, it would be best. If not, he would do what needed to be done. Life had reduced itself to its most basic terms: kill or be killed.

Just five yards from the trees, a gigantic black beast bounded from the woods and landed before him. The doctor skittered to a stop, and his feet went out from beneath him. The creature stepped closer, looming. Its eyes glowed red, and the skin around its muzzle drew back, revealing a mouthful of sharp canine teeth.

The Klan had come at him in two directions, the doctor realized.

He raised his pistol and fired into the snarling face above him.

Praise for Robert Herold

"A terrific grasp for horror writing"

~ N.N. Light, Reviewer

~*~

"In company with Stephen King"

~Alfred Runte, Author & Historian

~*~

Praise for Moonlight Becomes You

1st Place: The Southeast Writers Association
Purcell Award for Best Novel

1st Place: The Southeast Writers Association
Hal Burnard Award for Novel

Moonlight Becomes You

by

Robert Herold

An Eidola Project Novel

Moonlight Becomes You

Cover Art by *Debbie Taylor*

The Wild Rose Press, Inc.
PO Box 708
Adams Basin, NY 14410-0708
Visit us at www.thewildrosepress.com

Publishing History
First Black Rose Edition, 2021
Trade Paperback ISBN 978-1-5092-3408-0
Digital ISBN 978-1-5092-3409-7

An Eidola Project Novel
Published in the United States of America

Dedication

To Devon, Colin, & Tasha.
And, as always, to Ruth,
whose love makes it all worthwhile.

Other Wild Rose Press Titles by Robert Herold

The Eidola Project
Johnny Appleseed

Chapter One

Doctor Joseph Curtis felt the gun against his back as Tom Garraty pushed him through the gauntlet of colored folks standing outside Garraty's mansion. Doc Curtis recognized everyone in the lantern light. He'd attended to all of them or their kin since arriving in Petersburg, Virginia, after the Civil War, twenty years ago. He spotted Fredrick, who had a hernia last spring. Ralston and Henrietta, whose baby he delivered just three weeks ago. Old Chester Cummings, whose boil he lanced. And many more.

Garraty received a chorus of sympathetic remarks as he shoved Doc Curtis through the crowd. No sympathy for him, he noticed, the guy with the gun to his back. *Didn't seem fair.* Several women stood off to one side crying. Even the preacher, Reverend Green, expressed his sympathy, though Garraty would never set foot in Green's church except to burn it down. All these people here to pay their respects. Bad news traveled fast.

An hour ago, the doctor and his wife, Dinah, had just put their two boys to bed. They sat on either side of a kerosene lamp, he with a copy of *Harper's Weekly* and she darning socks. Someone began pounding on their door.

Dinah looked at him and shook her head, sensing danger. "Don't open it," she whispered.

1

Instead, he'd gone to the door, thinking it might be an emergency. Just as he reached out to push back the bolt, the door crashed into him and nearly knocked him off his feet. Garraty grabbed the doctor's shirtfront, steadying him, while at the same time thrusting a revolver into his belly.

"Get your bag," the tall, muscular white man demanded. The doctor could smell the bourbon on his breath.

Garraty stood a good six inches taller than the doctor and had broad shoulders. His blond hair was so close-cropped on his tanned head, he appeared almost bald. He wore no jacket, only gray breeches and a white shirt, rumpled and stained with sweat. Disheveled or not, Garraty wasn't just any white man, but the grand wizard of the local Ku Klux Klan.

"No!" shouted Dinah, standing and spilling her straw basket of sewing materials from her lap. Spools of thread bounced on the floor, rolled across the pine floorboards, and banged to a stop against the wall.

Doc Curtis waved her off and shook his head. She should know better than to cross Garraty. He looked back at the man who still clutched him by the shirtfront and was still pointing a gun. The doctor attempted a smile. "What's this all about, Mr. Garraty?" His words sounded frightened, in spite of himself.

The Klansman looked surprised at the challenge. Instead of shooting him, Garraty took a deep breath and exhaled bourbon fumes. "My wife's giving birth. Midwife says the baby's breeched, and she can't right it."

"But why him?" asked Dinah, her distinctive almond eyes wide with fear. "Why do you want my husband?"

Instead of addressing her, Garraty stuck his face next to the doctor's. "Tried every white doctor in Petersburg. They're either out on calls or can't be found. Now get your things!" Garraty threw him across the room. This time he did fall.

Dinah screamed.

Doc Curtis rose to his feet. He hushed his wife and grabbed his black bag. Garraty shoved him through the door and into the night, where two bay horses waited in front of the house. The stirrups were set too low, and Doc Curtis struggled onto the unfamiliar mount, which snorted its disapproval. He fumbled around, searching for the reins, then spotted a lead rope that ran from his horse to Garraty's.

Garraty led them out onto the road then sent them racing through the darkness at an insane gallop. The doctor held onto the saddle horn for all he was worth, made more difficult by also keeping hold of his bag. Eventually, they arrived at the mansion and the crowd of colored people standing vigil.

Now, as they entered Garraty's huge house, the white man broke away, ascended the wide carpeted staircase at a run, and disappeared. The doc's first time in Garraty's place, its size and opulence gave him pause. The dark wooden floor to the foyer shone with a glossy polish. Here and there lay thick oriental carpets. Tables with painted ceramic statuary or vases decorated the room. Doors led off in every direction, and a wide central staircase rose to the second floor.

Instead of trying to make his escape, Doc Curtis followed Garraty upstairs and into a large bedroom crowded with white folk and a few colored servants.

3

The sweltering room stank of body odor, perfume, and the distinct scent of blood. Garraty pushed through them to a pale woman on the bed with sweat-soaked hair plastered to the sides of her head. He stroked the woman's face and said in a voice that cracked, "Elizabeth?"

Elizabeth's eyes fluttered open then closed.

A gray-haired and wizened white woman with a stout physique, who Doc Curtis knew to be one of the local midwives, came and presented a small bundle to Garraty. The man pulled back the blanket to reveal a bluish-colored infant.

"I'm sorry, Mr. Garraty," said the midwife. "I got the baby righted after all and got her delivered, but the cord had wrapped around her neck."

Garraty pushed the bundle away. "I don't want it." He descended to his knees before his wife's bed. "Is—is *she* all right?"

The midwife hesitated. "She's lost a lot of blood. I've managed to stanch it, but I can't promise you anything."

At that moment, the bedding around the woman's abdomen turned red. The spot grew larger, like a blossoming rose.

Garraty stood and regarded his wife in shock, then he swung around and grabbed Doc Curtis's upper arms in a vise grip. Garraty yelled at everyone else in the room, "Get out!"

Garraty threw Doc Curtis toward the bed and hissed, "Save her, or there'll be hell to pay!"

The doctor withdrew the bedding. A large pool of blood surrounded the woman's midsection. He glanced back at Garraty before he eased apart the legs. Fresh blood gushed from her vagina. The doctor grabbed the top sheet and shoved it between the woman's thighs. He looked over his shoulder again at Garraty and shouted, "Get me my bag! And have someone fetch me fresh towels and hot water!"

Garraty just stood there at the sight of him, a black man with his hand stuffed into his wife's privates.

"Now!" shouted the doctor.

Garraty complied.

The doctor worked for the better part of an hour. He sewed up what he could see but couldn't halt the bleeding to any great extent. In the end, the woman's eyes opened wide. She took a deep, rattling breath and did not exhale.

Witnessing this, Doc Curtis stopped his efforts. His hands came away from her, covered in blood. He stood and regarded the woman, seeing her as a person for the first time. She had smooth pale skin—something he *had* noticed from the first, his being the color of chocolate. Though untidy and plastered with sweat, her blonde hair framed her face and ran over each shoulder to her bosom. Now he noticed her eyes: bright blue, even in death. She had a delicate mouth and, based on what he could see of them, fine teeth. He wondered if she would have been a good mother.

The old midwife, the only other person in the room, approached the bed and folded the deceased woman's hands before closing the unseeing eyes. "God's will," she pronounced.

"If so, I should not be blamed," said the doctor, heaving a sigh. He stepped back from the body and regarded his bloody hands. He turned to the nearby bureau, on top of which rested several basins of water tinctured red from blood. He cleaned himself as best he could.

When he turned back to the bed, he saw the midwife draw a bloody sheet over the body.

The wrinkled woman looked at him and clasped her hands, as though in prayer. "I'll tell Mr. Garraty you did all you could."

"Thank you."

Shoulders slumped in defeat, Doc Curtis gathered his instruments from the bedside table and rinsed them clean. He packed them in his black leather bag and retrieved his coat. Outside the room, he descended the stairs and saw an old rail-thin colored butler rise from a chair by the front door to greet him. The man wore a blue velvet coat with large golden buttons.

"Is Mr. Garraty about?" asked the doctor.

"Don't know, sir. He left the house some time ago and sent all but the help packin'." The man looked up the stairs and back at Doc Curtis. "I'm a guessin' the news ain't good."

"No, it's not."

The butler shook his head in sympathy. He opened the door and held it for him. "I'm a sure you did your best. I hope Mr. Garraty sees it that way."

The doctor heaved another sigh and exited the house. He looked back at the butler, framed in the light of the doorway. "I do too."

"You watch your step on the way home. There's that critter we all been afearin'."

Doc Curtis nodded, recalling the young colored couple spooning in a field one night, about a month earlier, who had been killed and horribly mauled. It happened to other folks in the months before. People took to calling it the bogeywolf. "Thank you for your concern," he said as he stepped off the porch and continued farther into the darkness. The butler shut the door, making it darker still.

The doctor looked around as best as he was able but could see no sign of Garraty nor a horse for his return home. He'd have to walk.

His shoes crunched along the pulverized rock driveway in front of the mansion. He noticed the moon had risen in the last hour but provided little light where he stood. A stand of trees near the house blocked it, but the moon's position caused the outline of trees to shimmer.

Doc Curtis felt sympathy for Garraty's loss and couldn't blame him for being upset—a wife and child lost on the same night. The callousness Garraty demonstrated toward the infant was not unique. Doc had seen this before in men whose spouse died in childbirth. It might even be a blessing the infant too had died, instead of being saddled with the resentment and blame a surviving child often endured.

Of most immediate concern was that Garraty's hostility could be directed at him in this most intense time. He could well be blamed for what occurred before he even arrived. Though he tried his best to save the woman, Garraty threatened him with hell to pay.

The doctor reached into his bag and rummaged until he felt the cold steel of his service revolver. He had not used it since the war but kept it oiled, clean, and ready in his bag. He removed it, just in case. He walked along the road from the house, passed the copse of trees, and decided to strike out across a tobacco field, a shortcut, and off the road, which meant less chance of encountering Garraty. Now, away from the trees, the full moon lit the way.

Halfway across the large field of tobacco, he heard baying hounds. A coon hunt? He prayed it were so, but deep down, he knew he was the prey. Doc Curtis glanced behind him, and in the distance he saw the nightriders—a group of white-clad figures on horseback, carrying torches. One torch burned in the shape of a fiery cross.

The Klan.

The doctor stumbled over the leaf-clogged furrows, aiming for the woods on the other side of the field. If he could make it, he stood a better chance than here in the open. On he ran. His wet pants, heavy with dew from the broad-leafed plants, slowed him, as did the weight he put on since the war. While not far, the trees seemed an impossible distance away.

He ran as fast as he could, struggling for breath and fighting a stitch in his side.

It wasn't fair!

He had devoted his life to helping others. Could this be his reward?

Doc Curtis fought for every reserve of strength and managed to quicken his pace. He could hear them shouting behind him and dared not look back, fearing it might slow him just that much more.

He made it through the field and emerged onto a rough access road running between the cultivated land on one side and the woods on the other. The doctor dashed across the dirt road and through the weeds and scrub bordering its opposite side. The trees stood twenty yards ahead. He would make it, find a thick trunk to hide behind, and fire a warning shot. If he could drive them off, it would be best. If not, he would do what needed to be done. Life had reduced itself to its most basic terms: kill or be killed.

Just five yards from the trees, a gigantic black beast bounded from the woods and landed before him. The doctor skittered to a stop, and his feet went out from beneath him. The creature stepped closer, looming. Its eyes glowed red, and the skin around its muzzle drew back, revealing a mouthful of sharp canine teeth.

The Klan had come at him in two directions, the doctor realized.

He raised his pistol and fired into the snarling face above him.

Chapter Two

"Boy, I'm talking to you!" the white woman shouted. She looked to be no more than twenty, but indignation made her seem older. Her mouth twisted in distaste, as though chewing rancid meat, and her face reddened with anger.

Doctor Edgar Gilpin kept his head lowered and continued walking through the train station's covered outdoor platform, carrying his and Annabelle's suitcases. He had on his favorite suit, a natty dark-green plaid affair, well-tailored to his slender but muscular physique. The woman called to him again, but he pretended not to hear. Being one of the few colored men in the country with a doctorate in physics could not prevent white people in the South from addressing him as "boy."

A white policeman, shaped like a gorilla, appeared out of nowhere and stood before Edgar, bringing him to a stop. At the end of a long arm, the officer held a billy club in one of his meaty paws. "Hold up, you," he said to Edgar. The policeman looked back at the white woman who stood next to a small pile of luggage. "What seems to be the problem, ma'am?"

As the woman approached, she removed a lacey purple handkerchief from her reticule and dabbed the corners of her dry eyes for effect. She deposited the kerchief and looked at the officer with a doleful expression. "I can't tell you how upset I am by this boy's rudeness," she said, now using a lilting genteel voice. "I merely wanted this porter to fetch my belongings upon his return."

Edgar gave an indignant huff. "Do I look like a porter?" he asked as he raised his eyes to meet the policeman's, a rarity for a colored person in the South.

The policeman grabbed the front of Edgar's suit jacket with his left hand and swung his billy club over his head. "I don't give a good goddamn what you are, boy. You are going to treat this lady with the respect she is due."

"Please stay your hand, Officer," said a handsome dark-haired gentleman of about forty. "This is my man, and as you can see, he is already engaged in carting a few of my bags." It was Nigel Pickford who approached them, carrying two suitcases of his own. From Edgar's perspective, Nigel's flushed face, ruddy with drink, combined with a loose tie hanging around his neck, did not convey much authority. Nevertheless, Nigel was white and spoke with a Virginian accent— two important assets here in Petersburg that Edgar lacked.

Nigel set his bags on the platform, patted Edgar's back, and gave a patronizing smile. Edgar could smell the stink of whiskey wafting off Nigel, despite a promise to abstain. Nigel thickened his accent. "You were right, of course, in stopping him, as he should've respectfully declined the young woman's offer. I gave him direct instructions to proceed with all due haste to the front of the building. I'm afraid he took my instructions a little too literally. He's none too bright."

The policeman's weapon sagged, and now Nigel

patted the officer's arm that still clutched Edgar's jacket. "Please emancipate him." Nigel turned and lifted his hat, making a clumsy bow to the woman who started the row. "I do beg your pardon, ma'am. I shall order the very first porter I see to assist you."

"No need for a porter," came the cultured baritone of Professor William James, whose own accent betrayed his upper-class New England upbringing. The Harvard professor had just assisted two attractive white women from the train, dark-haired Annabelle Douglas and the younger redheaded Sarah Bradbury. In addition to Nigel and Edgar, the two women were part of Professor James's paranormal research group, the Eidola Project. Professor James tipped his top hat to the woman who had confronted Edgar, revealing his high forehead and salt and pepper hair. He stuck his valise under one arm and a small leather suitcase beneath the other. "Please allow me to assist you." He smiled through his beard and bent over. He managed to pick up all the woman's luggage. "Where to?"

The young woman, flustered by the changing course of events, smiled at last. "Well, thank you, sir. Judging by your kindness, the North has gone a long way toward healing the rift with the South."

"Delighted to hear it, as Dixie will be playing host to us for the next few days."

Professor James and the young woman moved past Edgar and the others to enter the station house.

Annabelle and Sarah flanked the policeman, Nigel, and Edgar. Both women smiled at the officer and batted their eyes.

"Might we all proceed, Officer?" asked Annabelle, the assistant leader of the group.

The policeman melted in the glow of the women's smiles. He let go of Edgar and lowered his weapon. "Certainly. I'm just glad we put things right," he said as he straightened himself. The policeman doffed his helmet and appraised both ladies in turn. "Perhaps, if either of you is free in the next few days, you might grace this station and me with another visit? In a social sense, that is."

"We would be honored. So nice to make your acquaintance." Sarah steered Edgar on while maintaining her radiant smile. Annabelle did the same with Nigel, who looked like he wanted to say something until Annabelle broke character for a few seconds to scowl at him. "Quiet," she hissed, "you're drunk!"

Which, of course, was true.

As they moved along the platform and entered the Petersburg station, Nigel decided to voice his irritation over the women interceding between him and the officer. "I believe I had things well in hand. No need for you ladies to have unleashed your feminine wiles."

Edgar turned toward Nigel with a scowl of his own. "I'm your man, am I?" growled Edgar. "And none too bright?"

Nigel made a sheepish grin. "I thought it rather clever."

"*I thought* after events on Nantucket," Edgar retorted, "you were going to embrace civility as well as sobriety."

"A child must crawl before it can walk. I'm here, aren't I? That's a big step, given my foreboding about this place. And considering I saved your life, both in Nantucket and possibly just now, you should be beholden to me."

Edgar huffed in response.

"You're welcome," said Nigel.

The group emerged from the station in time to see Professor James tipping his hat to the young lady as she departed in an open carriage.

At the end of the row of smart carriages, buggies, and other conveyances waited a shabby wagon with a colored preacher holding the reins. Catching sight of him, Professor James raised his hat and waved. The preacher smiled, tied off the reins, and came to meet them.

"Professor James?" the preacher asked as he approached. When Professor James nodded and extended his hand, the minister grasped it between the both of his and said, "I'm Reverend Green. Thank God you've come."

****

A short while after leaving the station, Nigel felt hot, dusty, and sore—which added to the litany of reasons why he didn't want to be here. Reviewing these reasons led to feelings of both gratitude and resentment toward this organization. They had lifted him from the gutter, where he'd sunk after the war, and given him a place where he could belong. Despite his bravado at the train station, he knew their generosity and bravery saved *his* life. Still, to be back here at the site of that terrible battle—which ended the war for him—filled Nigel with dread. On the trip from Boston, he attempted to exorcize the tremendous apprehension with his old standby, alcohol. He followed up with the airy bluster at the train station, but in reality, he wished to be anywhere but here.

Professor James and Annabelle rode next to Reverend Green on the buckboard seat, and the rest managed as best they could, bouncing around in the rear with the luggage. At least loose hay lay beneath them, which helped to cushion their ride. The three in front talked the entire trip, but Nigel couldn't discern their words over the wagon's noise and alcohol's waning effects, which left his mind somewhat foggy.

A surprising number of colored people roamed the streets of Petersburg, Virginia. In fact, they seemed to make up most of the city. Some even appeared prosperous. Realizing he might be a minority around here made Nigel uncomfortable in an altogether different way than being bounced by the wagon.

Despite his unease, every time Nigel glanced at Sarah, she had a smile on her face. "Why are you grinning?" he asked.

Sarah looked at him and lowered her eyes but continued to smile. "We are doing important work. That fact makes me happy."

"Frankly, I'd be a whole lot happier elsewhere," Nigel confessed.

"Had you a vision about our trip?"

"Not particularly. I just have a lot of bad memories hereabouts."

"The war?" asked Sarah with characteristic perceptiveness. She regarded him with sympathetic eyes.

"No doubt," said Edgar, insinuating himself into the conversation. "Some brutal fighting took place around here."

"Perhaps"—Sarah looked at Nigel and her eyebrows raised, showing her sincerity—"we'll be able to put some of those memories to rest."

"Rest in peace?" Nigel asked sardonically.

Sarah snickered. "Let's hope not."

The wagon came to a halt on the outskirts of town, and Nigel scanned the large warehouse, before which they stopped. Edgar and Sarah followed his gaze and surveyed the building too.

Weathered clapboards covered the windowless structure. A rutted dirt road ran from the main road to a pair of double doors, large enough to accommodate a wagon. Set into one of these large doors was a smaller door, the size one might have in one's house.

Everyone clambered off the wagon. Those from the back took a minute to brush the straw from their clothing.

Nigel spat the dust from his mouth and looked up again to appraise the structure. "I appreciate the fine accommodations the reverend has arranged for us." Nigel's voice dripped sarcasm. "I believe this is Petersburg's answer to the Willard Hotel."

Reverend Green chuckled. "No, I'm afraid not. You'd find these accommodations a might cold. It's our ice-house." He approached the smaller door, opened it, and ushered them in. "If you'll all step inside, I'll take you to the body."

"The body?" asked Nigel, incredulous.

Professor James nodded.

"Welcome to our fair city," said Nigel, "And over here is the body of which we are so proud."

Professor James motioned for Nigel to enter. "We're here at my suggestion," he said, "as it's on the way to where we're staying. It seemed an efficient use of time."

Upon entering, cold air washed over their faces. Nigel sighed, appreciating this, despite the grim reason for being here. A musty smell hung about the place. The minister took a lantern off a nearby peg and struck a lucifer against the thick wall. The resultant smell of sulfur tickled Nigel's nose, and he sneezed.

"I hope the place isn't giving you all a cold," said Reverend Green as he lit the lamp. He closed the door, which cut off all other light. The solitary lamp showed a wide aisle through the center of the room, flanked on either side by walls made from hay bales. The walls partitioned the building's interior into numerous bays that stretched off into the darkness. Within most of these areas were large mounds covered in loose straw. Rain appeared to fall from the ceiling from what the minister attributed to melting ice stored in the loft.

"Should have brought my bumbershoot," Nigel mumbled.

"Shall we proceed?" asked Reverend Green.

Professor James nodded again. "By all means."

"Watch your step," the minister cautioned. He led them along one side of the packed-earth aisle, avoiding the little stream of water in its center. "As I said in my letter, after the attack on Doc Curtis, his wife packed up the kids and took off, certain he'd run afoul of the Klan, and unwilling to risk further reprisals. We kept the body here, not sure if she'd return to claim his remains. Weeks later, the community decided to go ahead and bury him, but I got them to hold off 'til you arrived."

"Thank you," said Annabelle, who looked over for validation from Professor James. He nodded. Nigel noticed she always deferred to the professor when in his presence.

They stopped in the center of the cavernous room. Reverend Green handed the lantern to Professor James and entered a bay. He brushed hay from one of the mounds and drew an oiled tarp from a pine coffin. The oblong box rested on two bales of hay. Reverend Green reached into a space between the two bales and withdrew an object also wrapped in oiled cloth. A crowbar.

The minister struggled for several minutes, trying to pry off the lid. Edgar approached and put his hand on Reverend Green's shoulder, causing him to jump away from the coffin and drop the iron bar. Edgar retrieved the pry bar. "I apologize for startling you," he said and cocked his head at the coffin. "With your permission, Reverend?"

Reverend Green nodded, and Edgar made quick work of it. The boards groaned as if in agony when he pried them apart. The women flinched at the sound, and Nigel felt the hairs on the back of his neck stand on end.

When all sides were free, Edgar removed the top. The smell of rotting flesh rose from within, despite the refrigeration. Repelled, the group stepped back on reflex and fumbled for handkerchiefs to cover noses and mouths. Annabelle made a gagging sound but repressed anything further.

Once the group had done what they could to handle the stench, they stepped forward and crowded around the pine box. Burlap draped the figure within.

"Doc Curtis was beloved in our community"—the reverend's voice sounded muffled coming through his handkerchief—"but there's not much left of him. We identified the man from his nearby bag and the contents of his pockets." He drew back the cloth revealing the ruined body.

"My God," Annabelle croaked, giving voice to what Nigel felt. Everyone but Edgar and Reverend Green withdrew, but they all remained within viewing distance of the grisly remains, transfixed by the hellish sight.

The figure lay in pieces. It was difficult to recognize as a person, except for the remnants of clothing and the hair still clinging to the back of a crushed skull. Looking closer, Nigel could see the halves of the rib cage spread wide to reveal the empty cavity of his chest. Most of the flesh on the body was gone. What skin and muscle remained had turned a grayish brown. Someone had arranged the body parts to approximate a person, but the left leg and the right forearm were missing. Tattered fragments of clothes lay about the carcass, and a shoe remained on the surviving foot.

"The poor man," said Sarah.

She put her handkerchief aside, held her right hand over the remains, closed her eyes, and exhaled audibly. Her breath formed a spectral cloud in the cold air and hung for a moment above the body. She took several slow, deep breaths, despite the stench. After a while, Sarah opened her eyes and withdrew her hand. She blew on it for warmth and rubbed it against the other. She shook her head and repeated the process without success.

"I'm sorry," she said, "I can't seem to get anything."

"Mr. Pickford?" asked Professor James, inviting him to try.

"No, thank you." Nigel grabbed a corner of the burlap shroud to throw over the remains, not wishing to look further. But the instant he touched the rough cloth, he jerked back as though stung. An intense vision struck him: He found himself running across a field, pursued by baying hounds and white-clad Klansmen on horseback. Thick leafy plants and uneven ground hindered him as he ran. Profuse sweat stung his eyes and caused his shirt to stick to his back. The Klan was gaining on him.

"Mr. Pickford?" repeated Professor James.

Before he could answer, Annabelle turned and said, "I'm about to be sick." She stepped away but lost her footing on the muddy floor. Nigel broke free of his fugue state and tried to steady her, but she collapsed onto him in a faint. The unexpected weight caused him to stagger back.

Nigel reached out behind him and caught the edge of the coffin, tipping it over. He and Annabelle fell to the muddy hay-strewn ground as the pine box and the doctor's putrefying remains landed on top of them.

At the touch of the human carrion, Nigel's mind again reeled away to the night of the murder. Once more, he was the doctor, this time on his back—with the snarling visage of a giant wolf, inches above his face. He held a pistol and shoved it beneath the creature's jaw. Nigel repeatedly fired, to no effect. The creature's hot foul-smelling breath washed over him. Its gaping maw revealed the points of canine teeth glistening in the moonlight.

The beast lunged, twisting its head, and clamped its jaws onto either side of his face. Pain, like multiple bolts of lightning, seared through his skull. Unbearable pressure.

Nigel screamed.

The beast whipped Nigel back and forth as its jaws crushed his head.

Darkness.

Chapter Three

Stripped to his undergarments, Nigel awoke in an unfamiliar room. He ran his hands through his hair and winced at the touch of a large bump on his head. Nigel threw back a light blanket, moved his bare legs off the side of the bed, and sat. In addition to his sore head, his thoughts seemed fuzzy, as though cotton filled his brain. He looked around the room to orient himself.

A kerosene lamp burned on the bureau, and in its light, he could see himself in an oval gilt-framed mirror, sitting on the bed staring. It still came as a surprise to see himself in his new incarnation. A couple of weeks ago, he had been a bearded derelict, covered in filthy rags. This remarkable transformation came at a price—flashes of the vision he'd had in the icehouse returned. He repressed the images with every ounce of psychic will.

The effort left him sweaty and a little nauseous. Nigel stood on unsteady legs and staggered to the bureau. He grasped it with both hands to steady himself and looked again at his reflection. Recalling his recent experience passing through a mirror into a nightmarish world beyond, Nigel moved the mirror from where it hung on the wall with his left hand to see what lay behind. Only wallpaper.

On the bureau stood several daguerreotype and tintype photos in small frames of a colored couple and, judging by the similarity, their relations. One showed a black man wearing a surgeon's white apron over a Union uniform. He stood in front of a hospital tent with a look of determination and pride on his countenance. In the war, Nigel had been a Confederate lieutenant, and the sight of a colored surgeon for the Union filled him with disgust.

He set the picture, face down, onto the bureau, then snatched the picture back again and stared intently. It showed the man in the vision, a colored man he had become. *I was him*. Nigel recalled his vision in more detail—including having his head crushed. He let go of the picture, which fell, knocking over several others. Reexperiencing the vision brought on a wave of nausea. The walls seemed to be closing in, and he felt compelled to escape.

Nigel lurched across the room to the door, exiting into a darkened hall. He threw open the first door he found.

Across the room, Annabelle in a white nightgown spun around, startled. Her long dark hair hung from her head, unbound, and she wore a guilty expression on her face. She held a blue medicine bottle and a tablespoon.

"Mr. Pickford! Have you no shame?" Annabelle set the bottle and spoon upon the chest of drawers and turned back to confront him. "Have you lost all sense of propriety?"

"Where am I?"

"It appears to be my room. And neither you nor I are fit for social discourse. Leave now!" She pushed him into the hall.

"But what are we doing here?"

Annabelle held the door cracked open a few inches

and spoke through the gap. "I am glad you have recovered. Go back to bed. We'll talk in the morning."

With that, the door shut, and Nigel could hear the key turning in the lock.

Stunned by what he'd just seen, Nigel stared at the closed door. Eventually, he turned and noticed faint light and muffled conversation emanating from the other end of the hall. Nigel stumbled in that direction and turned a corner. He stepped into a large room. Professor James and Sarah sat at a dining table at the far side, in an area that served as a kitchen. Closer to Nigel stood an unlit river stone fireplace bordered by two chairs. The clothes he and Annabelle had been wearing earlier hung over the backs of these chairs.

Seeking to retrieve his pants, he tripped over his feet, almost toppling onto the hearth. At the commotion, both Professor James and Sarah turned his way.

"Mr. Pickford!" said Professor James, springing from his seat. "Glad to see you up and about. Are you well? No ill effects?"

"Well enough. My head aches from a bump, but otherwise fine." Nigel grabbed his pants and felt their dampness. "It appears someone has laundered my clothes."

"Yes, you have Sarah to thank for that."

"What happened?"

"Here." Professor James approached and took his arm. "Let's get you seated." He led Nigel across the room to the dining table.

Once they all were seated, Sarah scrutinized him with such intensity, Nigel had to look away. He turned his gaze to Professor James. "You were about to tell me what happened…"

"The minister has billeted us in the home of Doctor Curtis. His wife and children have fled, and she left Reverend Green in charge of the place. Given that we are investigating the doctor's murder, he felt it apropos to have us stay here. Otherwise, we would be scattered among different homes in the colored community. I imagine you would not have been happy with those arrangements."

Nigel stopped himself from making an untoward racial remark. Instead, he said, "No. Here *is* better."

"We also needed to tend to both you and Annabelle after the unfortunate mishap in the icehouse. In this place, we can all meet tomorrow and determine the next steps in our investigation."

"What happened at the icehouse? I know I hit my head, but beyond that—"

"I think you know," said Sarah, cutting him off. "Why do you deny it?"

"If *you* know, why are you asking?" Nigel retorted. He looked at her and froze. Her stare became downright scary. She seemed to be looking into his soul and was unhappy with what she saw.

"You *know*," she said. "You *became* the doctor."

Nigel coughed and broke free of her stare. "That's ridiculous. You're hallucinating. Is Annabelle sharing her laudanum with you? Do we have a couple of opium-eaters in our midst?"

Professor James looked shocked. *"What?"*

Nigel, feeling self-righteous and glad of the change in topic, straightened his spine and looked at Professor James. "I saw her with the bottle just now when I walked into her room. Of course, I've known for several days. In many ways, I'd say it's an improvement. Taken the edge off. Still, if she's to be second in command, I felt compelled to say something."

Sarah slapped the flat of her hand upon the table and leaned forward. "Stop trying to distract! You saw something. Tell us now!"

Nigel sat back with a start and fell silent. He had never seen Sarah so forceful. "I want a drink," he whispered.

"Tell us!" Sarah demanded.

"All right."

Nigel swallowed hard and relayed both what happened when he touched the burlap shroud and the second vision, precipitated when the coffin upended, spilling its contents onto him and Annabelle. He described fleeing for his life across the tobacco field, being chased by the Klan, and the hellhound bounding from the trees and cutting off his escape. He repeatedly fired a pistol without effect before the creature lunged at him and crushed his head in the jagged vice of its jaws.

When he finished, Nigel shivered. "It's evil," he pronounced.

"The Klan *is* evil incarnate," said Edgar, who stood at the entrance to the room, his shirt draped around him untucked and his black braces hanging still lower on either side of his green plaid trousers. His hair on the left side was pressed flat from sleeping. "I heard the hubbub in the hallway," he said, "and thought I should investigate. 'Seems Nigel has a new appreciation for being colored. They say you can't know a man 'til you've walked a mile in his shoes—or run, as in this case."

"Hogwash!" Nigel struggled to stand. His legs turned to rubber. He gave up and plopped back onto the chair. He craned his sore neck around toward Edgar. "I saw what I saw."

"Sounds like you *became* a colored person, and that's stuck in your craw." Edgar wouldn't let it go.

"Enough!" said Professor James.

Edgar continued. "What we have here is a Klan murder, pure and simple. As terrible as that is, and believe me, I know, I fear we were drawn here under false pretenses."

"Go to hell, under any pretense you choose!" yelled Nigel

"Enough!" commanded Professor James. He took a deep breath to compose himself and then said to Nigel, "So it appears the Ku Klux Klan killed the doctor by setting their dogs upon him?"

After some consideration, Nigel nodded, though it hurt his head. "So it appears…"

Sarah shot a hand across the table and grasped Nigel's right wrist. Her touch made him flinch, but she held tight. It felt as though she had gone inside and clutched his soul. He couldn't breathe.

"No," she said.

He could feel her searching his mind. A presence within that wasn't himself. He felt violated.

Sarah removed her hand, freeing him from her brief but intense spell. He gulped and looked at the others, who seemed oblivious to what had just happened.

Sarah now shook her head. "There's something more."

Professor James narrowed his eyes at Sarah. "How can you say that? You told me you had limited abilities here. You had no insights at the icehouse."

Sarah sat back and massaged her temples. She groaned and pulled her hands away. "It's true. I am frustrated I haven't contributed in my usual way, but I am sensing much about what happened to Mr. Pickford in his vision. There's more to the murder than meets the eye. A demonic creature."

Nigel noted the formal way she now referred to him, after the disconcerting intimacy of her touch. "Don't you ever do that again," he told her, feeling his face flush with anger. The nob on his head throbbed. "Peer into someone else."

They seemed to be ignoring him.

"The reverend mentioned his suspicions of dark forces at work here," said Professor James. "I considered dismissing that, as the murder seemed straightforward. Now I'm not so sure. It appears we have two lines of inquiry: the temporal and the supernatural. In any case, we have a murder to solve.

"For now"—Professor James removed his pocket watch from his black vest and read it—"given it's after one a.m., I suggest we turn in and plan our next moves tomorrow."

Chapter Four

Responding to a knock, Professor James opened the front door to see Reverend Green, smiling as he stood on the doorstep. Behind him, the world looked awash with bright morning sunlight, sparkling on the remains of the previous night's dew.

"Here, as promised," said Reverend Green. "A man of the cloth and a man of my word."

"Morning, Reverend." Professor James shook the preacher's hand and stepped back to hold the door open. In doing so, he noticed the preacher brought an extra horse, its reins tied to the rear of the wagon.

Reverend Green removed his hat and entered a room redolent with the smells of bacon, eggs, toast, and coffee. Sarah and Edgar stood up from the table and said their hellos. (Annabelle and Nigel were still abed.) The reverend motioned for them to retake their seats.

"Would you have some breakfast with us, Reverend?" asked Professor James as he ushered him to the table.

"I've already eaten, thank you," said the minister, who remained standing. "I know we arranged for me to assist you today, but some other matters have come up. I've borrowed a horse, so you may use mine and my wagon while you are here. I've also brought you some additional food and sundries."

Professor James bowed his head. "Thank you for

your thoughtfulness."

"You folks are well set, provided the doctor's wife and children don't return and give you the boot."

"About that…" Professor James arched one eyebrow. "What else can you tell us about them?"

"Not much more to tell. As I said yesterday, Mrs. Curtis packed up her kids and lit out after her husband disappeared. He had been taken away by Tom Garraty at gunpoint and never returned. Before she left, she asked me to take care of the place. Said if she didn't come back by October, I'm to sell it and send the proceeds to her brother's address in Omaha."

"Running from the Klan?" asked Edgar.

"That's right." Reverend Green nodded. "Thomas Garraty's a Grand Wizard and pretty much runs things hereabouts. He pressed the doc into helping Garraty's pregnant wife with a difficult delivery. She died, and Garraty blamed Doc Curtis. It weren't fair—she'd even given birth before he'd arrived, but…" The reverend's voice trailed off, speaking volumes.

"Whoever said the Klan was fair?" asked Edgar, with rhetorical bitterness. Both Professor James and Sarah knew Edgar's parents and two younger brothers were killed when the Klan set fire to their home.

"True enough." Reverend Green shook his head.

"But your letter prompting our arrival had mentioned the devil having a hand in things." Professor James narrowed his eyes. "Did I misunderstand? Were you speaking metaphorically?"

"No," the minister said with some hesitation. "There have been many killings in the county, going back years—more, if you add in the neighboring counties. Most of the victims have been sharecroppers.

Some of these murders have been attributed to the Klan, others to a mysterious beast haunting the woods."

"Mysterious?" asked Professor James.

Both Edgar and Sarah pricked up their ears.

"All efforts to find this creature have proved fruitless. It seems to vanish into thin air. We're not even sure it exists."

"Occam's razor suggests that the Klan is the sole perpetrator," Edgar opined.

Sarah looked at him from across the table. "Occam's razor?"

Edgar set his cup on the saucer with a clink. "A principle in science stating the simplest hypothesis is the best," he said with a condescending smile.

" 'Plurality must never be posited without necessity,' " quoted Professor James. "From William of Ockham, a late Medieval scholar, friar, and theologian. The razor is the shaving away of other assumptions and weaker options until you have the simplest and most elegant, which is likely correct."

Reverend Green hesitated as he moved toward the door. "Well, whoever or whatever is behind these deaths, we appreciate your efforts to get to the bottom of it. We've all been praying for deliverance." The preacher removed a folded sheet of heavy paper from inside his hat. "I've drawn you a map to Garraty's place and to where the doctor's remains were found."

He handed the paper to Professor James, who nodded his thanks.

"Speaking of razors," said Reverend Green, "I've shaved off all the time I can spare you this morning. Perhaps you all could join us in a prayer meeting we're holding tomorrow night at my church? At which time, you might update us on what you've learned."

"Rest assured, we'll be there," said Professor James, who saw him to the door. As soon as the preacher left, Professor James turned to the others. "It appears we should pay a call on this Mr. Garraty. Please get your things."

"What about Annabelle and Nigel?" asked Sarah.

Professor James shook his head. "Given the issues that arose last night, I'd like to let sleeping dogs lie. It'll just be the three of us." He told them to disregard the dirty dishes for now and bring in the supplies from the wagon.

While Sarah and Edgar prepared for departure, Professor James found a piece of paper and an inkwell. He removed his prized pen from his breast pocket and used it to scratch out a note to the other two. The news of Annabelle's dependence on laudanum had prompted his decision to leave her behind, and he tried but failed to control his disappointment and ire as he wrote.

Chapter Five

When Nigel came into the main room later that morning, he saw Annabelle seated at the table, frowning over a piece of paper.

"They've gone and left us," she said in a morose voice. Annabelle tossed the paper aside. It landed on a plate of half-finished food.

"To hell with them," declared Nigel. He crossed the room and sat opposite her. He felt better this morning. The bump on his head had decreased in size, and sleep had restored a large measure of strength. He retrieved the letter, on which a grease stain occurred from a crust of buttered toast. Nigel grabbed the toast and munched it as he read. The butter caused the ink to run, but the note remained legible:

Dear Mr. Pickford and Miss Douglas,

We have gone to survey the spot where Doctor Curtis' remains were discovered and may also visit Mr. Garraty, a Klan member whose wife the doctor treated. Garraty blamed the doctor for her death. When we return, I need to discuss your future in our organization.

Very truly yours,

Professor William James

Nigel tossed the letter back onto the plate. He lifted the cup of cold coffee next to it and drained the contents. As he drank, he looked around the cup at

Annabelle.

"So?" she said.

Nigel lowered the cup and made what he had been told before his years of drunken dissapation was a charming smile. "I think it speaks for itself. We have the morning free. Whatever shall we do?" he asked, trying to convey sexual innuendo.

"It doesn't bother you?"

"No, indeed. I'd find it enjoyable. I venture to say you would too."

Annabelle slammed her fists on the table. Plates, cups, and saucers all jumped. "I mean the letter!"

"Yes."

Annabelle's face flushed with exasperation. "Yes, what?"

"Yes, it bothers me. It bothers me to be here. I've said as much before our departure. I'd just as soon leave, but I owe you folks, and I gave my word to be a participant in your endeavors."

"But our participation may be in jeopardy! What caused him to write that last line?"

"I think you know."

Annabelle blanched. "You didn't."

"Perhaps we're not so different, you and me. We both have our little weaknesses. Yours has been found out."

Annabelle stood. "You had no right."

Nigel made his charming smile again. The prospect of bedding Annabelle had evaporated. He made a shrug. It had been a long-shot but worth the attempt. His mind flashed on his recent intimacy with Lenore Hutchenson, which almost cost him his life. Nigel shuddered and sought to distract himself from these thoughts. He looked straight at Annabelle. "You're quite fetching when angry."

Her face became a livid red. She grabbed an empty cup and threw it at him. "You had no right!" she shrieked.

Nigel deflected the cup with his forearm. It bounced off and shattered on the floor.

"Ouch!" he hollered, rubbing his arm.

Annabelle lifted the folds of her dress and ran from the room, sobbing. A few seconds later, Nigel heard her door slam.

"I think she likes me," Nigel said under his breath. He stood up from the table, still rubbing the sore spot on his arm.

He walked over to the stove and felt the coffee pot. Still warm. He grabbed a mug from the drainboard and filled the cup. After a swallow of the bitter brew, he decided brandy would be a definite improvement. Still holding the cup, Nigel cast about for some or any other potent libation. He opened all the cupboards and looked behind the curtains hanging from the edge of the countertop. Nothing but cookware, cheap china, and foodstuffs. Not a drop of alcohol in the place.

"Teetotalers?" he wondered. Then it dawned on him that this might be his companions' doing. "The Devil take 'em all," he muttered and made for the door.

He threw it wide open and stepped onto the stoop, seeing the area for the first time.

Nigel became rigid, except for his right arm, which fell to his side. The coffee sloshed onto the stoop. Without noticing, the mug slipped from his fingers and fell, narrowly missing the stone steps.

His stunned voice uttered: "Oh, my God…"

****

"How dare he!" Annabelle slammed the bedroom door and paced her room, trying to calm herself. "Damn him!" She cursed aloud and added, "If I had a gun, I'd shoot him!" She struck her right fist into her left palm as she paced. After a few blows, she stopped. Her left hand hurt.

This dandified derelict had derailed her life, she realized. What could she say to Professor James to make amends? Remind him of her dedication to their cause? The sacrifices she made to remain in this group? None of her former friends wanted anything to do with her, given her preoccupation with the supernatural.

I could confess my feelings for him. No, that would make things worse—more so in light of what he's learned about me.

With sudden clarity, she hit on it: *I could attack Nigel's veracity. Who would take the word of this cleaned-up reprobate over me?*

Annabelle stopped short before the bureau. On top lay her handbag, containing the bottle of laudanum he'd seen her use, a much larger bottle than the one she purchased in Nantucket.

Filled with sudden resolve, Annabelle snatched the purse and marched to the kitchen sink. Nigel was elsewhere. She removed the blue bottle, uncorked it, and was about to dump the contents when she stayed her hand.

Would it be better to wean myself? she wondered. What if stopping suddenly causes ill effects?

She replaced the cork and slipped the laudanum bottle back into her bag, telling herself she'd use less today, and every day hence, until free of the craving.

She grasped the edge of the sink with both hands and took a deep breath. As she did so, she looked through the lace-framed window above the sink to the sunlit landscape beyond.

She saw Nigel stumbling across a field.

Anger rose again in Annabelle. *How dare he impugn my character and try to wreck my career!* What rhyme or reason had motivated him? And here he was, drunk again—despite their best efforts. No doubt he had squirreled away another bottle. But as she watched, Nigel collapsed to his knees. He looked at the heavens for a short time before he sank to the earth and curled into a ball.

What's going on?

"To hell with him," she muttered under her breath and turned from the sink. The front door stood wide open. She shut it and surveyed the remnants of the others' breakfast.

Well, if I'm going to put my life in order, I might as well start with this room. She spent the next twenty minutes redding up the table and washing the dishes. As she placed the last cup on the drainboard, she allowed herself another look through the window. Nigel hadn't moved.

If I am made of better stuff than he, shouldn't I check on him? She dried her hands and returned the apron to where she'd found it on a nearby peg.

Outside, the late morning air swam with the buzz of insects. A crow's caw came from a distant stand of trees. Annabelle shaded her eyes from the bright sunshine and spotted Nigel's white shirt in the distance. A split rail fence cut the landscape in two, and beyond the fence, several dozen brown cows cropped grass.

She lifted the hem of her dress and stepped from the stoop. As she did so, she spotted the ceramic mug in the dirt. Annabelle fetched it and saw a brown rivulet run from the cup. Nigel must have dropped it, she realized. She sniffed the mug, expecting the scent of alcohol.

It just smelled of coffee.

She placed the cup on the stoop, turned, and made her way across the field. As she walked, she wondered if one added alcohol to coffee, would the latter cover the former's scent?

Beneath the blanket of green grass, the ground was rutted in unexpected ways, and occasional holes filled with water and weeds dotted the landscape. Annabelle realized someone watching her stumble along might think her drunk.

When she reached Nigel, he looked folded in upon himself, a pose that reminded her of Muslims at prayer. His arms, however, were not held before him in supplication. He hugged himself and rocked back and forth.

"Mr. Pickford, are you quite all right?" she asked, half-heartedly.

Nigel raised his face and stared at her. Tracks of tears ran from his eyes. "This is where they died."

"Who?" Annabelle looked around at the bucolic scene of cows grazing in the sun. A grassy slope led to cultivated land below and the foundation to an old house no longer there. It seemed hard to believe anyone had died here.

"My men in the war. All but me." He swallowed hard and looked at her with tear-filled eyes, his lower lip trembling, more vulnerable than she'd ever seen him. In a low voice he said, "I've been haunted by them ever since."

Chapter Six

Edgar drove the wagon while Sarah and Professor James tried to decipher Reverend Green's map. At last, Edgar gave voice to the ruminations troubling him since they left the house.

"Do you think it wise, Professor, to have left the other two? They may feel slighted." Edgar stared ahead and grasped the reins tightly in his fists—even though the horse plodded along. He held Professor James in high regard and rarely challenged him. However, once they left Nigel and Annabelle behind, the situation gnawed at his conscience like a tick. And just as a tick swells as it gorges on blood, the injustice in abandoning them loomed increasingly larger in his mind. In his peripheral vision, he saw Professor James hand the map to Sarah and shift around on the seat, turning toward him. An atypical frown darkened Professor James's face.

"Mr. Pickford needs to recover from the trauma to his head, and I am concerned about certain decisions Miss Douglas has been making."

"Forgive me for being frank," said Edgar, trying to focus his eyes on the road and the horse's rump before him, "but it seems unwise to exclude Mr. Pickford when his membership in our group is still tenuous. He's also the only one having visions at the present." Edgar risked a glance at both Professor James and Sarah.

Sarah lowered her head. He wondered if she felt slighted by this remark. He turned back to the road and the horse's rump. "As for Miss Douglas, she has proven herself an able leader in your absence, and, if you recall, her quick reflexes saved you from injury when we met that nasty poltergeist last March."

"I share Edgar's concerns," echoed Sarah.

Professor James sat back with a defensive "Harrumph." He remained quiet for quite some time. At last, he looked at Edgar and at Sarah and sighed. "You're right, of course. I have let anger and disappointment get the best of me. We shall endeavor to get her free of this dependence. The fact that I had no knowledge of it until Mr. Pickford's revelation indicates it has not compromised her noticeably. But I have seen too many people descend to depravity once this substance sinks its claws into them. I do not wish this to happen to our compatriot. How long have you known of this, Sarah?"

Sarah hung her head still further. "Since Nantucket."

"I would like us all to commit to being forthright henceforth. Secrets can destroy the esprit de corps we need to be successful. Moreover, we are sometimes dealing with dangerous forces, and we need to have our faculties clear."

Edgar coughed. "As Mr. Pickford demonstrates daily."

Professor James made a rueful smile. "Mr. Pickford has his own demons, yet he saved your life. Despite the many difficulties he presents, he brings more to the table than he takes. I shall make amends to both when we return."

Edgar relaxed his grip on the reins. He had braced himself for an argument with Professor James, but things seemed back on an even keel. Professor James impressed him with his self-control and his ability to acknowledge a mistake, things Edgar knew he could improve in himself.

At times Edgar knew white-hot anger. He often fought with himself to keep from flying off the handle. The fact he succeeded much of the time testified to his strength of will, but his will was not without limits. Edgar often reminded himself that circumspection was a virtue, yet he also knew some occasions called for quick action. He suspected this investigation might call for both.

Professor James decided they should first visit the site where the doctor's remains were discovered by a young woman who worked in Garraty's kitchen.

Garraty again, thought Edgar. This did not seem like a coincidence.

Edgar steered the wagon along a field of large leafy plants he identified for the other two as tobacco. A colored family tended the plants. A man and an older boy hoed between the rows while a woman culled withered leaves. Younger children scampered among the bushes, chasing each other with yellowed leaves waving in their hands.

Edgar found a shady spot and tied off the reins of the horse. They entered the woods, searching for the place indicated on the map.

Though morning, it was already hot and humid. Edgar had his collar unbuttoned before long and was mopping the perspiration from his face with a handkerchief. The others were doing the same. At least the trees offered some shade.

Edgar thought of the man and his family working in the field. That could've been me, he realized. The boy hoeing *was* me before I went away to school. Edgar felt grateful for the set of circumstances that brought him to university and eventually into Professor James's orbit—none of which he could have anticipated as a child of sharecroppers.

He recalled breathing in the scent of his mother when she hugged him after he got stung by a bee. She smelled of sweat, chicory, and rosewater. A combination he'd never forget. Another memory arose, this one of his daddy talking to him as they sat on the steps to their home. His father saying that Edgar *had* to go to Howard University. It wasn't a matter of choice. Edgar was having second thoughts about the offer of admission and a scholarship. He felt guilty about abandoning the family. His two younger brothers wouldn't be much help on the farm, so leaving would be a burden.

"We'll get along just fine," his father said, smiling and giving him a sideways hug. "You are doing us proud. Get yourself an education. Make somethin' of yourself."

So he left, but they had not gotten on just fine. Six months later, they were all dead, and the house torched. Seems the Klan objected to the fundraising campaign his father started to buy new books for the local colored school.

That the Klan might be behind the deaths in Petersburg made Edgar's blood boil and filled him with righteous anger he knew he needed to keep in check. He was on their turf—Klan Country—and needed to watch his step. Circumspection is a virtue, he told himself for the umpteenth time.

The group continued until they came to a small clearing.

"I believe this is the place," said Professor James. "The minister said it would be marked as such." He indicated a red bandana tied to a pine branch. He looked at Sarah. "I want to see if you might sense something here to corroborate Nigel's vision."

Sarah walked throughout the clearing with her arms held wide. Near the center, she stopped and closed her eyes. "Yes. At last, I sense something…" She became quiet for a period, and her eyes turned upward, the irises rising into her skull. An instant later, she screamed and teetered, about to collapse.

Edgar sprang forward, caught her by one arm, and held her up. Sarah's irises descended and returned to normal. The quaking thanks she offered Edgar for his help betrayed something of her experience. Edgar hesitated before he nodded and let go.

She turned to face both men. "I can corroborate Nigel." Her voice remained shaky. "I had a similar vision. I have no idea why my powers deserted me earlier. I hope it doesn't happen again. What I saw, however—"

Sarah stopped and coughed. She regained control of her breathing and resumed speaking. "What I saw confused me. The Klan *is* involved. They chased the doctor across the tobacco field we saw. Then he was attacked and killed, his body dragged here."

"Indeed." Professor James nodded. "So they set their dogs upon him?"

"I'm not sure. The band of Klansmen had hounds,

but another beast leapt from these woods and attacked the doctor first. The darkness kept me from seeing much, but I remember its teeth and its eyes." Sarah shuddered and wobbled, almost falling over. Edgar held her arm again to steady her.

A shotgun blasted behind them.

Edgar and Sarah flinched and crouched without thinking. Edgar still had hold of Sarah's arm and wrapped his other arm around her for protection.

"You take your hands off that white woman," came a harsh voice, "or people will find parts of your head in the next county."

Edgar stood and turned to see a muscular white man, in filthy but expensive-looking clothes, lowering a shotgun and training it on him.

Edgar backed away several steps, raising his hands. Fresh perspiration sprang from his forehead and ran into his eyes, causing them to sting and tear. He lowered his gaze, as expected of him when confronted by whites, but he still glanced up through his tears to appraise the situation.

Sarah's eyes had become white orbs again. She fell to her knees. Her disquieting face rose, and she pointed at the intruder. In a flat voice she said, "I smell death on you."

The man with the gun took a step toward her. "You all right, ma'am? He do anything to you? I heard screaming."

Sarah's head dropped, and she shook it clear. When she looked at him again, her face had returned to normal. "No." She swallowed and continued. "These are my friends. We were conducting an experiment."

Professor James said, "Lower your firearm, sir, that

we may speak amicably."

The man kept his gun trained on Edgar. "Amicability is not something I extend to trespassers," he said in a hard and ominous voice. He looked tall and strong—evidenced by the large biceps below his rolled-up shirt sleeves. He wore dark brown leather riding boots that came halfway up his shins and worsted gray breaches. His stained and wrinkled white shirt and gray unbuttoned vest appeared to have not been washed for many days. Thick blond stubble covered his chin. The beard was a little shorter than the hair on his head. Dark circles under his eyes marred his otherwise tanned and handsome face. "State your business."

"My name is Professor William James. This is Miss Sarah Bradbury and Doctor Edgar Gilpin. We are investigating the murder of Doctor Joseph Curtis," said Professor James. "We understand his remains were found here."

"News to me." He moved the end of the shotgun up and down, still pointing at Edgar. "Another coon doctor? You replacing the one that's passed?"

"Doctor of physics," Professor James corrected. "I believe the colored community hereabouts is still without a physician."

"Breaks my heart." The man swept his gun over all three of them and inclined his head in the direction of the trail. "Now, get off my land."

Edgar lifted his head and spoke for the first time. "You Mr. Garraty?"

The man brought his gun to bear on Edgar once more. "You're an uppity boy. Despite all your learnin', it appears you need to be shown a lesson."

Professor James raised his hands and walked

between Edgar and the gun. The barrel was now pointed at his chest. "Mr. Garraty, if that is indeed who you are, I assure you we meant no disrespect. Our coming here is purely in the name of science—"

"—and justice—" Edgar chimed in, undaunted.

Professor James looked back over his shoulder at Edgar with an expression of desperation. He shook his head before turning back to Garraty. "Reverend Green from Blandford Baptist brought us here from Boston, suspecting supernatural forces were at work."

Garraty laughed. "Darkie superstition. If that's why you're here, you Yankees made a long trip for nothin'. We got ourselves a nice quiet community where everyone knows their place. If they forget, we teach them how to remember. You get on now, all of you, before I lose my patience."

The three retraced their steps with Garraty bringing up the rear—to make sure, as he said, none of them got lost.

When they emerged from the woods, the family of sharecroppers stood huddled together, across the tobacco field, looking at them. Edgar realized it must have been one of them who alerted Garraty. He sighed and shook his head. "There but by the grace of God…" he said under his breath.

They boarded the wagon, and Edgar got it turned around and headed away from Garraty. They did not look back.

Sarah, who now sat in the center, looked back and forth between Professor James and Edgar. "You were both very brave. I must confess, my heart leapt halfway up my throat."

"Thank you, Professor," said Edgar, "for

interceding on my behalf. I'm sometimes foolish and hot-headed. You are the brave one, stepping between his gun and me."

"I'd hoped we could appeal to his reason," Professor James said, and grinned with apparent relief, "but I confess I had my doubts."

Edgar shook the reins to make the horse move a bit faster, without success. "The Klan in bedsheets are the only ghosts I find truly scary," he admitted.

No one spoke for some time. After a while, Professor James broke the silence. "Let's head into town. I want to report his threats to the authorities. The sheriff may also be able to help us in our investigation."

"Good luck with that," Edgar muttered loud enough for them all to hear.

The horse snorted, seeming to agree with Edgar's assessment.

Once in town, Edgar stopped the wagon before the impressive portico to the courthouse. The brick building had six stone columns at its entrance, above which stood a double-tiered clock and bell tower.

"We may have to wait to see the sheriff," said Professor James looking at Edgar. "Would you mind letting us off here? We'll go in and make arrangements to speak to him. You can join us after parking the wagon."

Edgar agreed. He drove the wagon around the building to a water trough on a shady side and let the horse drink its fill. As Edgar tied the reins to a post, he noticed an attractive young colored woman a short distance away carrying a basket of herbs and flowers. His heart skipped a beat.

The lithe woman appeared to be around twenty,

with thick black hair pulled back with a red ribbon from her unblemished mahogany-colored face. Her brown eyes shone bright with intelligence and humor. When she smiled, he noticed her brilliant white teeth.

A dark-skinned colored man in a faded red shirt blocked her way. The man's interest in her appeared one-sided. Each time he took a step toward her, she demurred and backed away. The young woman rolled her eyes in apparent frustration and caught sight of Edgar grinning at her predicament.

The woman made a feint to one side and stepped around the man. She headed toward Edgar. Edgar made to tip his hat but realized he'd taken it off on the ride into town. He hurriedly reached back into the wagon and found his hat and topcoat beneath the buckboard. Edgar threw the coat on the seat and placed the hat on his head just in time to tip it in her direction.

"Hello there," he said.

She smiled and stopped. "You were laughin' at me."

"No, I'd say enchanted. And impressed by your footwork, eluding the unwanted attentions of that gentleman."

"Him? He's no gentleman."

Edgar took a step closer and made a deep bow. This time he swept his hat from his head in a wide arc, so it came within an inch of the ground. "Doctor Edgar Gilpin, at your service."

"You the new doctor?"

Edgar shook his head. "Doctor of physics."

The woman squinted one eye and said, "Don't know what that is."

"I'd love to explain it to you."

"You ain't from around here."

Nonplussed, Edgar put his hat on his head and looked at her with surprise. "And how did you surmise that?"

"Your fancy clothes, the fact you speak like a white man who's had a lot of schoolin', and I would of noticed you before if you hailed from these parts."

"Well, you are astute as well as being a charming young woman."

"Saphne Taylor," she said, presenting her hand.

Edgar took it, removed his hat, and bowed once more. "Very pleased to meet you." Down the walk, Edgar could see the jilted man, staring daggers at them.

"Well, since you're willin' to be helpful, you headin' toward the Garraty estate? I'm one of the cooks there. We ran out of some seasoning for tonight's meal, so they sent me into town."

"Does everybody work for Garraty?" Edgar asked, surprised.

"No. But as the biggest landholder hereabouts, he has his finger in a lot of pies and a lot of folks under his thumb."

"Is he every bit the monster he appears to be?"

"I don't see him much. He got drunk and made eyes at me last Christmas, but his wife gave him what for. Now she's gone, I try to stay out of his way."

"Seems wise. Wiser still, would be to find some other employment," said Edgar.

"Momma's sick and has two young'uns at home. Dad died last year. I'ze got to pay for things and keep a roof over our heads. The wages is good. Better'n pickin' tobaccy or cotton."

"What happened to your father, if I may be so

bold?"

"Don't know." She looked at the brick walkway. "I don't talk about it much." She heaved a sigh. "He got strung up like the Klan would do, but all torn apart like the bogeywolf got to him."

"The bogeywolf?" asked Edgar.

"The thing has folks in these parts jumpin' at every shadow. And after finding Doc Curtis all torn to pieces a couple of weeks ago, I'm jumpin' with 'em."

"You found the doctor's remains?"

"Uh-huh. Poor man." Her eyes rose to meet his. "You goin' toward Garraty's, or what?"

Edgar weighed this information. "Well, we are headed in that general direction, but given he just ran us off his property at gunpoint, I don't imagine we could take you all the way. We also have some business here at the courthouse. If you're willing to wait, we can surely take you part of the way."

She considered this and shook her head. "Naw, but thanks. I'll just walk. There's a shortcut I take. Gets me there in less than an hour, and I can drop these flowers off at home." She stepped onto the street and called back, "Nice to meet ya!"

"You as well," said Edgar, smiling. He put his hat back on at a jaunty angle and grabbed his coat. As he turned from the wagon, he came face to face with the red-shirted man glowering at him.

"We don't cotton to your kind 'round here," he growled.

Edgar smiled and put on his coat. "I don't have anything to do with cotton, friend. Nor want anything to do with you."

"Well, you're gonna get to meet my fist if you

don't steer clear of Saphne."

Edgar made to go, but the jilted man put a hand on Edgar's chest to stay him. Edgar batted the hand away with one of his own and grabbed the jilted man's shirtfront. He jerked the man close. "I say we let the object of our attention decide for herself with whom she wishes to associate. But if you have a mind for fisticuffs, sir, I need warn you I am your better." Edgar let go, and the other man stepped away. *He's slow but strong*, Edgar thought, having taken his measure. *Be sure not to let him land a full blow*.

"For now," said Edgar, "no harm done. I have business inside. Good day, sir." He turned and proceeded around the building to its main entrance, mindful of being followed.

Edgar wondered what possessed him to almost come to blows over a woman he just met. He never gave much credence to the romantics' notion of love at first sight, but now he was not so sure. *Could I be so easily smitten? Will I ever see her again?*

Edgar found the sheriff's office inside and asked the secretary, an obese white woman with heavy facial powder, if Sarah and Professor James had gone inside to meet with the sheriff. When she indicated they had, he asked to join them. She refused.

"Just sit yourself there on a bench." She sneered and pointed at the seat with a thick finger. "They'll be out by and by."

Instead, Edgar walked past her and entered the sheriff's office. The dumbfounded secretary blustered at his temerity and came in behind him. "I'm sorry, Sheriff Wilson. He just walked right in. I've never seen the likes. What nerve!"

Beyond Professor James and Sarah, a cadaverous sheriff sat behind his desk. He looked over at Edgar, and anger flashed across his long thin face. He had sunken eyes, and a thick gray growth covered his pointy chin and hollow cheeks, which seemed to be the fashion for white men around here. The sheriff pursed his stubbled lips together and spat at a spittoon. The long string of brown spittle hit the mark, but stains on the wooden floor all around the cuspidor showed where he had missed. He glared at Edgar and stood waving an arm at him. "Boy, get on outta here, before I throw your black ass in a cell."

Professor James shifted to one side, blocking the sheriff's view of Edgar—interceding, as before, by stepping between Edgar and trouble. "Doctor Gilpin is part of our group. I told him to please join us as soon as possible. As I mentioned, Mr. Garraty threatened Doctor Gilpin's life."

The sheriff narrowed his eyes and eased himself onto his chair. He snatched the plug of tobacco from where it sat on the blotter, bit off a corner, and chewed. He leaned back, and the chair groaned. "And as *I said*," countered the sheriff, "it sounds like you were trespassing. Having this colored along, no wonder he run you off. I'd have done the same."

The sheriff put his hands behind his head and smiled.

Professor James fiddled with the hat he held in his hands by sliding the brim between his fingers. He nodded at the sheriff. "I understand. A troubling situation, but one, it appears, you will do nothing about."

An uncomfortable period of silence hung in the air.

Edgar knew Professor James wanted to enlist the sheriff's help in investigating the murders, but this appeared to be a fool's errand. *It wouldn't surprise me if the sheriff did the murders himself.*

"Regarding the other matter," Professor James continued at last, "can you give us any insight into the string of deaths happening in this county and the next?"

"What of it?"

"We've been asked to investigate them by Reverend Green."

"The black preacher? Well, it figures, since the deaths have all been among the colored. But what gives you the right to meddle where you don't belong?"

Professor James removed a card from his vest pocket and presented it to the sheriff.

"E-I-dola?" he read aloud.

"'Eye-dola' Project," corrected Professor James. "Eidola is a Greek word for ghosts."

The sheriff looked at the card again. "Paranormal Investigators?"

"That's right. As I said at the outset, I am Professor William James of Harvard University. Miss Bradbury and Doctor Gilpin are two of my associates. The reverend contacted us, worried supernatural forces may be at work, and asked us to bring our talents to bear."

The sheriff leaned to the side and spat. He straightened himself in the chair and made a toothy grin at Professor James. His teeth were brown. "Bull crap."

"I beg your pardon," said Professor James.

"You heard me," the sheriff said, as the smug tobacco-stained expression hung on his face.

"Well, what have your investigations brought to light?" asked Professor James.

"I ain't shining no light on this or any other darky matter. What's the point?" The sheriff inclined his head toward Edgar. "You folks breed like rabbits. So what if a few go missing? What's to concern me about this?"

Edgar, seething mad, could no longer hold his tongue. "These are human beings," he said through clenched teeth.

"Yeah? That's debatable." The sheriff stood. "I've listened to you crackpots long enough. Get on out, all of ya. I'll tell you what: You keep your investigating, or whatever you call it, confined to the colored. You come disturbing the peace in the white part of town, and I'll be running you all out on a rail."

Professor James ushered Sarah and Edgar from the room.

Edgar knew that leaving was the right thing to do—a minute or two more, and he would have lost control. At the doorway, he looked back and saw the sheriff lean over again and spit.

This time the sheriff missed.

Edgar smiled.

****

They rode the wagon in silence for several minutes until Professor James said, "Let's stop at the minister's place. He indicated he might be home at this hour, and I want to put some questions to him."

Edgar pulled on the reins and brought the horse to a stop. "You know the way?" he asked.

Professor James pointed at a faded lichen-covered signpost just ahead: Jerusalem Plank Road. Next to it, a new sign read Main Street. "I believe it's just a piece down the road, next to the colored cemetery."

As they proceeded, a white steepled church came

into view on their right. Next to it stood a small white house with a tidy yard, featuring blossoming hydrangea bushes. Gravesites filled the surrounding area, some marked with just a wooden plank—the cemetery Professor James had mentioned. Across the road rose the larger, older, and more impressive Blandford Episcopal Church, constructed of brick, with large stained-glass windows. Behind this church stretched a much larger cemetery filled with marble crosses and headstones—the white cemetery.

They arrived at the parsonage for the colored church, and the front door opened. Reverend Green emerged to greet them. "Well, there must be a divine hand in this," he said, "I've only just arrived. Come in, come in!" He gestured for them to enter his little house.

"I'll be along in a moment," said Edgar, wanting to attend to the horse.

When he entered, Sarah and Professor James sat at a table set for all of them. Reverend Green stood and smiled at Edgar. "Marie informed me dinner will be a few minutes yet. The others have agreed to stay and have expressed interest in seeing the church before we sup. Would you like to join us?"

Edgar became aware of his hunger. *If the price of eating means touring the church, I'll pay it.* "I would be honored."

"Splendid," said Reverend Green. "If you'll all follow me."

They left the small house and followed a gravel path to the church next door. The reverend opened the green double doors to the church and motioned them inside. Edgar wondered if the minister had the door painted to match his name.

Inside, it looked like any number of small churches, and Edgar decided this tour amounted to much ado about nothing. The place featured many rows of plain wooden pews on either side of a center aisle. In front stood a platform with a podium and behind it a wooden altar, on top of which sat a large open Bible, a bouquet of fresh flowers in a white vase, and a foot-high silver cross on a gray marble base. The raised clear-glass windows on either side of the room allowed a pleasant breeze to blow through.

"Very nice," commented Professor James. Edgar and Sarah nodded.

"We ain't as grand as the First Baptist or Gillfield, but we have an active congregation," said the reverend with evident pride. "Tomorrow night when you speak, the place will be packed with colored folks from all over looking for some answers and hoping to find 'em here."

"Might they return each week to find answers?" asked Edgar.

"Well, if the Lord leads them to my church on future Sundays, who am I—"

Edgar interrupted: "So is bringing us from Boston a publicity stunt to attract parishioners?"

"Edgar!" said Sarah in surprise.

Professor James looked at him with his mouth agape.

Ever since their arrival, Edgar had been mulling over the possibility they were brought to Petersburg under false pretenses but bit his tongue after raising it last night due to his respect for Professor James. The minister using this situation for self-promotion was the last straw.

"Isn't it obvious the Klan is the source of your troubles?" Edgar asked, continuing to confront the minister. "You lured us to Petersburg on a supernatural pretext when it's your white neighbors you need to fear."

Professor James found his voice. "Doctor Gilpin! You shall hold your tongue. We discussed this the other night, and Sarah's vision today proves—"

"It proves nothing more than the Klan set their hounds on that poor doctor."

"Gentlemen, please, and young lady." Reverend Green smiled at them and held up his hands. "There's no need for rancor here in God's house. Doctor Gilpin is a scientist and a Doubting Thomas. Well, if one of the Apostles could doubt, I believe Doctor Gilpin is in good company. Let us set all discussions on this aside for the present. I believe Marie has dinner waiting on us. Agreed?"

An awkward silence hung in the air until Professor James, Sarah, and Edgar nodded one by one.

They returned to the rectory. The scents of spices and frying meat now filled the minister's home. Several covered dishes already sat on the table. Reverend Green bade them sit, and he dished rice, beans, and cooked greens onto each plate. An old colored woman appeared from the kitchen, carrying a cast-iron pan. She wore a colorful mixture of fabric, a blue skirt, a yellow top, and a diaphanous pink shawl. A bright red cloth wrapped around the top of her head, hiding her hair. Large silver hoops hung from each ear and adorned her wrists, and she wore a thick band of silver around her neck. She placed a still-sizzling sausage on each plate.

"Merci, Marie!" said the reverend, smiling at the

cook. "*Très bon!*"

Reverend Green looked at the others. "Marie is a treasure I met in New Orleans after my work bringing Jesus to those in rural Louisiana, folks not often served by any church. She and I became fast friends, and she accompanied me when I came here three years ago to take this job. What she lacks in English, she more than makes up for in the kitchen."

Marie came by this praise honestly, as they soon discovered. The cook prepared everything with delightful Cajun spices.

"Tell us of your missionary work," prompted Sarah between mouthfuls.

Reverend Green smiled and agreed to indulge them. "I traveled the bayous and backcountry in a circuit. They welcomed me wherever I went, be they colored or white households—something I've not experienced in other areas of the South. After about a year of doing this, I became ill and came close to dying. Once the fever broke, I returned to New Orleans to convalesce. I hired Marie to nurse and tend to things. Months later, when I fully recovered, I received an offer for this position, and so came here to Petersburg."

"What caused your illness?" asked Sarah.

"Who knows? A miasma? A bite? It's ironic a place so Eden-like is rife with illnesses."

When they finished, Marie cleared the table and brought coffee. Professor James gave Edgar a long look that spoke volumes. He did not want Edgar to challenge their host. Edgar shrugged and nodded, agreeing to hold his tongue.

"Do you have an accounting of the deaths?" asked Professor James.

"Yes, I drew one up once you indicated your group would come. Should have given it to you right off. The list doesn't include two lynchings that clearly were the Klan's doing. Another death I put on the list, but I'm not sure it belongs. Ned Taylor was lynched and then savaged—possibly by this creature. Lord knows, we're used to crows and vermin going after the dead who are left hanging, but this was different."

Hearing the name, Edgar realized this was the father of the woman he met in town.

"Could they have set their dogs upon his body?" he asked.

Professor James gave him a sharp look at first, then relaxed and nodded.

"I don't see how," the reverend said, shaking his head. "His body, what little remained of it, hung well off the ground."

"Could the animals have attacked before they strung him up?"

The reverend paused on the way to his desk and scratched his chin. "Well, now, that's possible..." He rummaged around in his rolltop desktop and located a paper. Returning to the table, he presented it to Professor James, who gave it a quick look and handed it to Edgar.

Edgar saw numerous names, dates, and locales scrawled onto the paper in random order.

As Professor James continued to ask questions, Edgar studied the list. Thirty-seven names. He interrupted the questioning to ask for paper, pen, and ink. The reverend fetched the requested items.

First, Edgar sorted the fatalities by locale, which didn't provide any insights, then by date. It became apparent most of the deaths happened every twenty-eight days.

"The moon," he said aloud, interrupting the others.

"What's that?" asked Reverend Green. "The moon?"

"Most of the deaths follow the cycle of the moon," announced Edgar. "The full moon, if I am not mistaken."

"Is it lunacy then?" asked the minister.

Professor James shook his head. "Modern psychology does not give credence to Medieval concepts of lunacy; however, there are a few individuals who become obsessed with the moon and claim it compels them to act. It's rubbish, except their obsessions are focused on the moon. So a deranged individual could use it to justify his murders."

"A full moon is the easiest night to see one's way," said Sarah.

"True." Edgar said, "but that does not account for cloudy nights."

"May we take your list?" asked Professor James.

"By all means. You're not leaving so soon?"

Professor James nodded. "I'm afraid we must. It's getting late, and we are not familiar with the area's roads—full moon or not."

"To be precise," said Edgar, "the full moon is not until tomorrow night."

Outside, Reverend Green bid them goodbye and headed to the church, saying he needed to close the building for the evening. The group boarded the wagon, and Edgar was about to shake the reins when Marie came running from the house. She approached them, speaking spirited French, to which Professor James responded in kind. Edgar spoke the language as well, but they talked so fast he only caught a smattering. By and large, it sounded like pleasantries, compliments about the meal, and them discussing New Orleans.

Professor James motioned for her to join them on the wagon, but she shook her head. Her expression became serious. She studied the three. After doing so, she took three silver hoop bracelets off her right wrist and made a gift of them. She presented one to each with a nervous smile.

Marie moved to the front of the wagon and stood facing them, several feet in front of the horse. "*Prenez garde! L'heure entre chien et loup,*" she said in parting. Marie turned and walked away.

Edgar, Sarah, and Professor James all stared at each other.

"My French is a little rusty," said Edgar.

Professor James studied the unremarkable silver hoop he held in his fingers. "She said the reverend is a good man but does not understand the forces at work here. She said we don't either."

"I caught her saying something like 'beware the dog'?" Edgar prompted.

"Beware the time between dog and wolf."

"What did she mean?" asked Sarah.

"I wish I knew." Professor James raised his head and stared down the road. Edgar and Sarah did the same.

Marie had disappeared.

Chapter Seven

After the visit by the northern troublemakers, Sheriff Clifford Wilson decided to see Garraty. Abraham, the old house slave who stayed on after the war, greeted him at the door.

Now there's a boy who knows his place, mused the sheriff as Abraham led him to the library. What he saw shocked him. Garraty, the pillar of the community and bastion of white supremacy, lay flat on his back, stretched out on the floor with dried vomit on his unshaven face and filthy shirtfront. A near-empty bottle of bourbon lay on the floor beside him. The sheriff turned to Abraham, who shook his head at the figure of dissipation.

"What's the meaning of this?" demanded the sheriff.

"He refused to let us move 'im. Would start to hittin' and screamin' whenever we tried to help."

"Why didn't you send for someone?"

"Doctor been here twice this month for the same thing. Mister Garraty would straighten up for a few days, then sink back down the hole. Looks like he's fixin' to join the missus on the other side."

"Bull crap," pronounced the sheriff. "Get some help in here. Have them fetch some soup and bread, plus a bucket of clean water and a washcloth. Fetch clean clothes too."

"Yes, sir." Abraham left the room and returned with two black women and another old black man, but with none of the items the sheriff ordered. He repeated his demands, this time peppered with a prodigious amount of profanity, and everyone scurried off.

A while later, Garraty—now awake and considerably cleaner—partook of the soup and bread. The sheriff pressed the food on him, and Garraty's compliance surprised him. After having his fill, Garraty looked at the sheriff and frowned. "So what brings you here, Cliff? You doin' good to make up for all your sins?"

"How'd you know about those?"

"They're the stuff of legend 'round here. I figure those stories helped get you elected. That, and my endorsement."

"And the free booze."

"That too."

"For all of which, I am forever beholden to you. Had me a social call from a group of Yankees complaining about you threatening them at gunpoint this morning before you took your little nap."

"I should have shot them right off," said Garraty. "Damned trespassers."

"The colored preacher out on Jerusalem Plank Road brought 'em here to help go after that creature in the woods—the one that's got the darkies in a snit."

"So," Garraty said, "seems they're having trouble realizing there's danger from all sides."

The sheriff nodded. "I thought we might put it to them in another way. I can round up some boys, and I got myself a cross all set for the festivities."

Garraty considered for half an instant and nodded.

"I like it. Gives me a reason to greet the day. Go fetch the boys." He ran a hand over the stubble on his chin. "I'll engage in ablution and will meet you out front with the others."

Chapter Eight

Near dark, Professor James saw Annabelle limping along the road from the farmhouse. He pointed to her, and the wagon slowed to a stop.

"What happened?" called Sarah.

"Please come and quick." Annabelle's voice broke. "Mr. Pickford is in a bad way."

Edgar and Professor James helped her onto the bed of the wagon. Edgar got the wagon moving while the professor assessed her leg, and Sarah held Annabelle's hand in sympathy. The wagon's jostling made her bark in pain now and then; otherwise, Annabelle seemed to be putting on a brave face.

"Mr. Pickford collapsed in the pasture near the farmhouse," Annabelle told them. "He muttered some things about the war and passed out. He's remained unconscious all day, so I tended to him, awaiting your return. A short while ago, a fit overtook him, and he struggled to breathe. I could bear it no longer and ran to find help. I twisted my ankle on the uneven ground and limped down the road until you found me."

Professor James wrapped a large handkerchief around her shoe's sole and brought it around her ankle before tying it off. "You'll have to go easy on this for a few days, my dear," said Professor James.

"What more could I do to ruin my position in this organization?" sobbed Annabelle, the pretense of a brave face now gone.

Professor James smiled to reassure her. He patted her shoulder. "Let that be for now. You have nothing to fear."

Edgar brought the wagon onto the twilight-lit field, and it bumped and pitched along until it reached an odd tent erected above Nigel. The man lay on his side in the flattened grass, curled into a fetal position.

Annabelle sat so she could see from the back of the wagon while the others approached Nigel. "He's catatonic, and I couldn't move him, so I erected this tent with some sticks and a tablecloth to provide protection from the sun. I brought a basin of water, and I've been placing wet compresses on his brow. I didn't know what else to do."

"He's been like this all day?" asked Professor James.

"Until the onset of the fit I mentioned. That's when I left to find help."

"Mr. Pickford," asked the professor, shaking Nigel's shoulder, "can you hear us?"

Nigel did not respond, his breathing shaky and labored, almost a death rattle. Professor James swept a finger through the man's open mouth, removing some mucus and half-digested bits of toast. Nigel's breathing improved. The professor had a degree in medicine, though he had never practiced; instead, he taught anatomy and physiology at Harvard before drifting toward philosophy and the nascent field of psychology. Still, when on investigations, the medical training came in handy.

"Did he suffer another injury?" Professor James realized this should have been asked straightaway.

Annabelle shook her head. "I don't believe so. He seemed fine this morning. We had a row, but that's not unusual. At any rate, he seemed fine until he walked out here on his own and just collapsed."

"This could be an aftereffect of the blow to his head or, given his comment about the war, soldier's heart—a trauma to the psyche."

"So long after the war?" asked Edgar.

"Some may have mental scars for the rest of their lives."

"We need to get him into the house," said Annabelle.

"Yes," agreed Professor James. "Doctor Gilpin, if you would lift him under the arms, I'll endeavor to do my part with his feet."

Edgar and the professor hauled Nigel onto the wagon next to Annabelle, and they brought the wagon back over the uneven ground to the house. Annabelle limped inside while Sarah lit lamps around the room. Professor James and Edgar set Nigel on the sofa and propped his head up with pillows. Annabelle eased herself onto one of the chairs near the hearth, and Sarah pushed an ottoman over so Annabelle could elevate her leg.

"Sarah," said Professor James, "would you please chip some ice and place it in a cloth for Annabelle's ankle?"

Sarah nodded and went to the icebox. She grabbed a pointed metal rod with a wooden handle and used it to chip away at the block of ice within. She gathered the ice chips in a dishtowel and brought it to Annabelle, who struggled to remove the laces on her shoe.

During this time, Professor James went to the sink

and worked the cast iron pump until cool water ran from the spigot. He captured some water in a bowl and returned to Nigel with the water and a napkin. He dipped a corner of the cloth in the bowl and used the moistened fabric to swab Nigel's mouth and wipe his dry lips.

"I'm worried about dehydration," said Professor James, "but we can't give him anything to drink at present. In this state, he could aspirate."

"Before he became unconscious," said Annabelle, "he told me he fought on that field during the war. All his men died."

"I have sensed this trauma from him several times, though I hadn't realized he fought right here," said Sarah. "It haunts him."

"He used those very words," said Annabelle. "Perhaps it is soldier's heart."

"There is more to this," said Sarah. "More, perhaps, than he even knows."

"What do you mean?" asked Edgar. The others also looked at Sarah, awaiting her explanation.

"I don't know," she admitted, "but I sense something ominous hanging over Mr. Pickford like a poisonous cloud."

"The death of all his men must have been devastating," said Annabelle. "I can't imagine the guilt and recrimination."

Sarah seemed to be growing frustrated. "Yes, yes. That's part of it. A big part. But there's more."

"You keep saying that, but how do you know?" asked Professor James.

"I don't, but I aim to find out." Sarah brought a chair over from the table and set it next to Nigel. She sat and smoothed the light blue pleats of her dress over her knees. Sarah swept back a few stray strands of her red hair hanging over her face and smiled at the others.

"Here goes." Sarah placed her right hand upon Nigel's forehead and performed the deep breathing regimen they had seen her use many times. Eventually, her irises rolled up into her head, showing only slivers of white between her lids.

Sarah's breath caught in her throat before she yelled, "Noooo!"

Chapter Nine

Nigel became conscious as Sarah hovered over him. She was crying and pushing aside the hands of Annabelle and Professor James as they tried to comfort her.

"You *know*?" Nigel asked Sarah in a croaky voice.

Sarah looked at him and nodded, still sobbing. Tears fell from her eyes and struck his face. "How can you live with it?" she asked.

"I'm not sure I am." Nigel struggled to sit.

Sarah stood and pushed her chair back several feet, causing the chair legs to screech against the wooden floor. She collapsed back onto the chair, and her crying slowed to a few snuffles. She withdrew a small handkerchief from her sleeve, wiped her eyes, and blew her nose.

Nigel threw his legs off the sofa and pushed himself into a sitting position. He rested his head, face down on his hands, before he looked at the others. When he focused on Sarah, he felt self-conscious. The connection had been even more intense than when she probed his mind the previous night. They shared a brief period of intimacy, closer than any sexual act, and she had been repulsed. When he spoke, he stuttered. "Y-you went inside me?"

"Just for a moment," said Sarah. "The intensity became too much."

"Fires, murders, drownings, and more?"

Sarah nodded.

"And the War?"

"A brief flash before I broke it off. That poor man with half his face gone… I had only the vaguest idea of the mayhem you have seen."

Annabelle clutched a handkerchief to her mouth. Edgar and Professor James stood as still as stone as they listened.

"I am cursed," said Nigel. "When I foresee things, I can't prevent them."

"Like Cassandra," said Professor James.

Sarah looked perplexed.

"From Greek mythology," said Annabelle. "Apollo gave her the gift of prophecy, but when she refused to lie with him, he cursed her so that no one would believe her predictions."

"She foresaw the fall of Troy," added Professor James.

"But you saved Sarah and Edgar in Nantucket," Annabelle reminded Nigel, "the rest of us as well. You prevented that."

"Just barely."

"Just barely trumps the alternative," said Edgar.

"Perhaps something has changed," Sarah offered.

"I don't know what to think," said Nigel.

Professor James paced the room. After some consideration, he spun around to face Nigel. "Annabelle and Sarah are right—your ability to take action in Nantucket proves you *can* act against these calamities. Perhaps you can't prevent them all. That power is reserved for God."

Nigel shook his head. "I had my misgivings about

coming to Petersburg, and they have been born out. I can't stay here."

Nigel stood, pushed past the others, and left the room.

The rest looked at each other, stunned. At last, Edgar turned to go. "I'll speak to him."

"No," said Sarah, drying her eyes.

Edgar paused.

Sarah stood and faced him. "No, let me. I have an idea."

Edgar turned to Professor James, who gave a slight nod. Edgar looked at Sarah. "All right."

Sarah went after Nigel. She rapped on his shut door and waited for a response. And waited. At last, she heard, "Enter," and did so.

She saw Nigel lifting a water pitcher and drinking from it. He set it in the washbasin on top of the bureau and, with the back of one hand, wiped away the rivulets of water clinging to his chin. Sarah noticed Nigel had placed some folded clothes into a carpetbag sitting on the bed. He did not acknowledge her entrance. Instead, he took a brush, comb, straight razor, and a shaving mug—all items the group had purchased for him—off the bureau and placed them into a leather valise, snapped it and the carpetbag closed and lifted the luggage off the bed.

He turned and stopped short. Sarah blocked his way.

"Please put your bags down, Mr. Pickford."

Instead, Nigel attempted to move around her. Sarah cut him off. Although her height only came to his chest, she had a presence about her belying her slight physique and relative youth. Besides, he felt reluctant to bowl over a lady.

"Please step aside, Miss Bradbury."

"No, sir. We need you to stay."

"There's no need for me with you in the group. Besides, Professor James's letter indicated he is ready to let me go."

"He has already taken back those words. He told us this morning they were ill-considered. He just hasn't had the chance to tell you himself."

Nigel still wasn't convinced. "And what about my being superfluous?"

"We both have talents, but their character is different. I rarely glimpse the future, and I have no precognitive abilities regarding myself. I am perhaps better in contacting spirits."

"There's no consistency to my visions," groaned Nigel. "And I'm impotent in the face of any predictions. Fate, it seems, cannot be denied."

"Is it fate you should leave?" she asked. Sarah reached over to take his bags. When her hands touched his, he flinched and let go of the carpetbag and valise. They thumped to the floor. Sarah retrieved them and set them on the bed. "A common vision brought us together—you saving me from drowning in a sea of blood. I think that symbolized both the mirror world and all the deaths in Nantucket. You risked your life for me, saving me when I became trapped. And, as Annabelle just said, you saved Edgar's life and probably all our lives. We owe you. We *need* you."

Nigel sat next to his baggage. He looked at her, feeling defenseless. "And my curse?"

"You keep using that word. Does it have special meaning?"

"What else would you call it?"

"When did your abilities first appear?"

"I don't know," Nigel said, suddenly testy. He rose, went to the bureau, and drank more water straight from the pitcher. He set it back in the basin and turned to face her. "I've always been able to anticipate things." He made a rueful smile. "Came in handy as a child, avoiding being caught when misbehaving. In school, I knew what would be on tests. In the War, I could anticipate the enemy. My men picked up on this. They thought I could keep them safe. I nearly did." Nigel made a remorseful grunt and lowered his head. I had my comeuppance out there on that field—at their expense." He returned to the bed and sat.

He raised his head but did not meet her eyes. "Just before the Battle of Fort Stedman, I foresaw my men mutilated and dying. You caught a glimpse of it just now—Corporal Archibald Smith, with his skull half-gone. Perhaps you also saw Tim Hayton, just seventeen, sitting on the ground with his guts spilling out and looking at me in shock. The same with all the others. I knew that to proceed meant doing so at the expense of our lives. The vision ended when General Evans arrived. He ordered me to advance at gunpoint when I refused. He could be very persuasive. The men rallied in my support, and the general lowered his weapon. We proceeded to our doom."

Nigel buried his head in his hands. "They trusted me, just as you trust me to do some good," he said in a muffled voice. "You saw all the good it did them…"

Nigel remained quiet for some time before he looked at Sarah and said, "After that, whenever I foresaw some disaster, I could do nothing to prevent it.

I tried but always failed. It drove me mad, so I retreated into the bottle."

"So the character of your abilities changed just before this battle?" she asked.

"Why do you keep harping on that?"

"Because I think it's key."

Nigel shook his head. "I need to leave." He stood, retrieved his bags, and strode out of the room despite Sarah's protestations.

Downcast, Sarah followed Nigel into the main room. Both Edgar and Annabelle rose from their chairs—the latter with evident discomfort. "Don't go," said Annabelle.

Professor James stood as well and held up a hand. "Please, Mr. Pickford. You've become a valued member of the group. I apologize for being intemperate in my note this morning. Stay with us."

"I owe you my life," said Edgar.

Nigel appeared on the verge of tears. He shook his head and went to the door, stuck the valise under his right arm, and turned the knob with his freed left hand.

Opening the door wide, he froze. The others came up behind him.

A tall fiery cross burned on the lawn before the house, its flames dancing high into the night.

Chapter Ten

They all stared at the burning symbol of hate. There came a horse's whinny, and several white-robed horsemen rode by just beyond the fiery cross. Edgar turned and ran back through the house. He returned, holding a derringer. He pushed past Annabelle and the rest to stand on the stoop.

Nigel dropped his bags in the house and stood next to Edgar. "I'll not leave you in the lurch," he said.

Edgar turned on him in a fury. "Why don't you join them? I'll fetch you a sheet!"

"Edgar!" Annabelle shouted, trying to intervene.

Sarah shook her head as she grabbed Annabelle's arm. "Leave them be," she said. "They both have wounds to sort through."

Annabelle took a deep breath to calm herself. Her lungs filled with the smoke of burning kerosene-soaked rags and wood from the cross. A fit of coughing ensued.

After the Klansmen departed, Edgar stuffed the derringer in his pants pocket and ran into the yard. He threw fistfuls of dirt onto the flames, to little effect. Nigel joined him. The others watched in silence as the two attempted to put out the fire. Eventually, Professor James, Sarah, and Annabelle retreated into the house.

Sometime later, Annabelle saw Nigel and Edgar come in, covered with dirt and soot. They wordlessly went to the sink. Nigel stepped back and allowed Edgar to wash first. When he had cleaned his hands and face, Nigel reclaimed his bags and returned them to his room. When he came back, he said, "Well, it seems as though Doctor Gilpin is right. This all appears to be the handiwork of the Klan. As such, why are we here?"

Professor James stood up from his books and looked at them all with tired eyes. A bedraggled lot, to be sure, thought Annabelle.

"We've been asked to put a stop to a spate of murders," said the professor. "Isn't that reason enough?"

Annabelle watched as he ran a hand back through his receding black hair. He lifted a book to his chest and cast his eyes around to each of them.

"I've been thinking about everything we've learned and seen. It's clear the Klan *has* a hand in things, but I don't think they account for all. The visions of Nigel and Sarah, the nature of the deaths, and the timing of the killings to match the full moon lead me to suspect we might also be facing a creature I have just now been studying: *lupus versi pellis*, a lycanthrope, also known as a werewolf—or someone who believes himself to be such."

Edgar shook his head. "Most of the deaths occurred on a full moon, but not all. Several recent killings did not follow this pattern."

Professor James shifted the book over to his left hand and patted it with his right. "It troubled me as well until I came across a statement in Friar Anton Liguerre's *The Devil's Legions*, which I have been rereading since its contents proved so helpful in Nantucket. Liguerre notes as a werewolf matures, he grows stronger and can transmogrify with increasing frequency without the benefit of a full moon. Of course, if this is a product of mental illness, the person may discard the moon pretext at any time.

"There have been numerous accounts of werewolves from all over the world, going back to ancient times. Ovid, in *Metamorphosis,* has an account of Zeus turning King Lycaeon into a wolf as punishment for the king serving up his son cooked in a dish for the god as a test of the god's power. Two famous cases exist, a German, Peter Stumpp, and a Frenchman, Gilles Garnier. Both were accused of cannibalism and werewolfery."

Edgar shook his head again. "But they may simply have been insane."

"I'm not discounting insanity here," said Professor James, "though I don't like to use the word. It's an imprecise legal term and applied erratically in the courts. In any case, we have a killer in our midst and need to keep a top eye open."

"So," Annabelle asked, "how do we proceed?"

Professor James looked at them all and said, "Trying to get some rest right now makes the most sense."

Edgar grabbed two chairs from the table and carried them to the door. He braced one chair against the doorknob, since the bolt on the door was broken, and sat in the other. "I'm staying right here." He pulled the small gun from his pocket and rested it on one knee. "If they try to set fire to the place, I'll be ready for them."

"Do you want me to spell you later?" Nigel asked.

"No," said Edgar, "I'll be fine. Professor, do you want my bed tonight?"

"Thank you, but no. I have some more reading to do, and then I'll stretch out on the sofa."

Sarah, Nigel, and Annabelle wished everyone well and went off to their respective rooms.

****

When Annabelle shut her bedroom door, she leaned back against it and heaved a sigh. It had been quite a day: The angry letter from Professor James—regarding which she felt sure there would be more to come. The row with Nigel, him becoming unconscious, and her tending to him so he wouldn't die from sunstroke. Twisting her ankle when she ran for help. The revelations once Sarah revived Nigel. The terrible flaming cross on their doorstep. Finally, Professor James's conclusion that they were up against both the Klan and a deranged person or some mythical beast.

She joined Professor James's investigations of the supernatural two years ago, exploring purported hauntings, mediums, and clairvoyants. The others, Nigel most recently, joined in due course. Despite all she encountered in these endeavors, she would have discounted any explanation that involved a monster before two weeks ago. Nantucket proved that thinking wrong. Her head swam with all these happenings and their ramifications. They were more than she could hope to come to terms with any time soon. How would she manage any sleep? She felt exhausted but keyed up at the same time, and her ankle throbbed.

Annabelle limped over to the bed and fetched her handbag. Annabelle sloshed some water from a pitcher into a glass, removed the blue bottle from the purse, and uncorked it.

Just a little tonight, she told herself. So I can sleep.

My ankle hurts. I have given my all today—possibly saving Mr. Pickford. I deserve to sleep.

Annabelle picked up the spoon and poured herself a full measure.

Oops.

Oh, well, just this night.

With the greatest of care, Annabelle brought the spoon to the glass, poured in the contents, and stirred.

Chapter Eleven

Tom Garraty took a long pull from his flask and watched the sheriff take off his white robe and hood. The near-full moon illuminated all five of the men where they gathered on the banks of the town's reservoir. Garraty still wore his outfit but with his hood thrown back. Elizabeth had sewn the hood to the rear of his robe, allowing him to do so. He heaved his shoulders and shook his head to exorcise thoughts of Elizabeth crowding into his mind. Thinking of her still made him choke up. That wouldn't do in front of these men.

Garraty held his flask toward the sheriff. "Here you go, Cliff," he said with a gruff voice conveying power and commanding respect. "You deserve it. Perhaps the finest cross burnin' I've seen."

The sheriff wadded his bedsheets into a ball and stuffed them between him and the saddle horn. He took the proffered flask, spat out his chaw, and drank. Once he handed off the flask, Garraty pulled his robe over his head and leaned back to put the outfit into one of his saddlebags. Behind them, Mitch Condrey, a butcher, Roy Amblin, the owner of the largest mercantile, and Steven Snyder, editor of the *Petersburg Gazette*, passed around a bottle of something and laughed.

"So what if they don't get the message, Tom?" asked Condrey, his grin visible in the moonlight.

"Have us a lynchin' party?" suggested Amblin, laughing.

"There are white folks." Snyder, now serious, stated the obvious.

Garraty winced at the stupidity of Snyder's remark. Despite being the most educated among them, Snyder's intelligence didn't impress him.

"Some of them women." Another statement of the obvious from Snyder.

"Them fuckin' carpetbaggers can get the same as their colored friend." This from the sheriff.

While often crude, the sheriff's comments always served the desired end. "You heard the sheriff," said Garraty. He turned the horse to face them all. "Let's hope they get the message. If they don't, Steven, you may want to take a pass. We got plenty of others who will ride with us."

The editor blustered an excuse. "Now, now, that's not what I intended. I just meant to suggest—"

Garraty raised his hand, and Steven stopped mid-sentence. "No, need to fudge, Snyder. You've ridden with us many a night, but if your constitution can't handle the hard stuff—well, I understand."

"I'll be there, should it come to it," he said in a quiet voice.

"Fine. Now we best be on our way," Garraty said, dismissing them. "Condrey's young bride is pining for him. Kiss her once for me."

They all laughed. Amblin swatted Condrey with the back of his hand. "Let me put in for something more!" he shouted before Condrey galloped away.

Everyone but Garraty scattered, and he watched as they disappeared into the night.

I don't have anyone to go home to, Garraty told himself. *I should do something about that.* He'd spent most of the past month drunk. *Time I sobered up.*

Garraty gazed at the large moon above and scratched his stubbly chin, the growth since this afternoon's shave. He cast his mind over the help for prospects. That young cook, he recalled. *What was her name?*

Then it came to him: Saphne.

****

Basking in the glow of both moonlight and a job well done, the sheriff let his horse set the pace. He reflected on the day's events. No sense in rushing home. He had told his wife, Regina, he'd be late.

He appreciated Garraty approving his plan to send them Northerners a message. It had done Garraty a world of good too. *Nothin' like a little night ride to lift the spirits.* He chuckled at his pun, knowing Klan robes evoked ghosts to frighten the coloreds.

The sheriff thought about those Yankees visiting his office today, and it made his blood boil. He hoped they stuck around. He'd love to have at 'em. He wanted to give that uppity black man *what for,* to see him dance, kicking his legs in a futile attempt to free himself, as he dangled at the end of a rope. Even more irritating was that pompous professor. He wanted to see him try to lecture with his nose broken and a couple of front teeth missing, maybe an eye.

And the red-headed girl with them could use a lesson too. The sheriff's mind played with several prurient scenarios. He smiled and shook his head. He needed to go home to Regina. But she'd be asleep right now. *How would being an hour later matter?*

He decided to stop first at the Happy Palace, a parlor house on the edge of the darky part of town catering to a salt and pepper clientele. Whites had the exclusive use of the front door. He had taken a shine to one employee, a dusky little gal named Dinah.

The sheriff did not mention his extracurricular activities to any of his associates. For that matter, he'd seen a fair number of them in the place. When that happened, custom had it just to nod and go about one's business, without exchanging words (then or later) about being there.

His reverie shattered when an enormous wolf bounded from the woods. It landed on the road and blocked the way.

The wolf made a guttural sound, mouth wide and fangs bared. The creature's eyes glowed red, and it snarled again.

The sheriff's horse reared back, throwing him from the saddle. The jolting impact of his rump hitting the road knocked the wind from him. As his lungs fought for a breath, he stared ahead, helpless to stop the attack. The horse screamed and drove its hooves in the air, trying to keep the predator back. It worked momentarily. The wolf crouched low to the ground and withdrew a pace, then lunged forward and sprang, sinking its teeth into the horse's neck.

The horse screeched with pain and fear. It backed up, nearly crushing the sheriff, who still could not move. The horse swung this way and that, trying to free itself, keening all the while. But the wolf held on, jaws locked on the horse's throat. Blood splattered onto the sheriff as the animals swung past him in a macabre dance.

At last, the sheriff took in a desperate breath. He reached for his pistol. Gone. Nowhere to be seen. His rifle remained with the horse, in his saddle holster. His horse wouldn't last much longer. Then what? Would the creature turn on him?

The sheriff scrabbled away across the road and into brambles, but they offered no protection. The reservoir, it dawned on him, could be his best chance. The sheriff forced his way through the thorny bushes. The spikey plants tore at the bare flesh on his hands and face, shredded his clothing, and scratched him beneath, but he kept going. Scratches would heal, he told himself, if he managed to escape.

Just as he broke free of the brambles, he heard a final ear-piercing scream from the horse. Silence. Would that satisfy the wolf? No time to find out. He ran through the woods, swinging his arms before him to keep from running headlong into a tree trunk. The canopy above obscured the moonlight, so it was much harder to see.

He heard the wolf howl behind him.

The reservoir lay just ahead if he could make it. Perhaps it feared water. If worse came to worst, he could dive beneath the surface and thereby protect himself. He had been a strong swimmer as a boy.

The ground sloped down, and he could see a silvery light in the distance. It had to be the moon reflecting on the water.

The wolf howled again—this time closer. *Good God, it's the biggest wolf I've ever seen.* As a boy, he remembered seeing Hank Farrow, a local sharecropper puffed with pride, displaying the carcasses of a she-wolf he'd shot along with her two pups. The man had laid their bodies out on the boardwalk in front of the Blandford Drygoods Store. The she-wolf seemed massive to a boy of eight. Thereafter, no one sighted any wolves in the county.

Judging from the skins of wolves he'd seen as an adult, he figured this wolf to be more than twice the usual size. How could that be? The coloreds were spooked by some critter going after their people for the past couple of years. Since there hadn't been any white victims, he'd not paid it any mind—until now.

The ground fell away beneath his feet, and the sheriff stumbled down a muddy embankment and onto the shore. The silvery surface of the reservoir stretched before him. He'd made it!

The sheriff charged forward into the shallows before being knocked face-first into the water. Teeth sank into the back of his neck, and the sheriff roared with pain beneath the surface. A rush of bubbles erupted from his mouth. The wolf hauled him partway from the water, only to whip his head back and forth, snapping the sheriff's neck.

Before being thrust into oblivion, the sheriff became cognizant of someone screaming. It's me, he realized.

So close! he thought, despite the pain. *It wasn't fair...*

Blackness.

Chapter Twelve

After breakfast, the group decided to go into Petersburg. They needed to get a pair of crutches for Annabelle, investigate the other deaths the minister had cataloged, and report the cross-burning to the authorities. Edgar stated the latter amounted to spitting into the wind, but Professor James remained adamant. "Having a record of being harassed may prove useful, especially if we have to defend ourselves."

The drugstore, where they bought the crutches, buzzed with news of the sheriff's death. A cluster of five women swarmed around the druggist, all sharing what they had heard. After Annabelle purchased her crutches, she and Professor James returned to the wagon. They reported the gist of what they heard to the others: The mutilated remains of the sheriff and his horse were found this morning near the town's reservoir.

"I don't wish that upon anyone," said Edgar, "but he's the kind of law I grew up with. I'm not going to mourn his passing. I wouldn't be surprised if he had on a white sheet with those other Klan folks last night."

"He did," said Sarah. They all looked at her in surprise, and she shrugged. "I'm not sure how I know, but I do."

"Your abilities seem to wax and wane unaccountably on this trip," said Professor James.

Sarah folded her hands in her lap and took a deep breath. "I've been trying to understand why. I believe I've hit upon the reason. After what happened in Nantucket, I've been loath to make myself vulnerable in areas where there is a huge spiritual vortex—such as where many people have died or where spirits have congregated. Battles occurred in the area of the icehouse and the place where we're staying. The minister's home, near two cemeteries, is too much for me to bear at present. Likewise, getting a sense of what lurks within our friend, Mr. Pickford, overwhelmed me." Sarah made a nervous smile at Nigel. "My frustration with all of this has caused me to withdraw. But now, understanding what has been happening, I feel I can work to overcome this roadblock and become a more active participant in the investigation."

Annabelle shuffled close to the wagon, extended an arm, and squeezed Sarah's hand. "You do yourself wrong," she said. "You have been and remain a valuable member of this group." As soon as she said these words, Annabelle realized their irony, given her status.

Nevertheless, Sarah looked at the others and saw them nod in agreement. She exhaled and let her shoulders relax. "Thank you."

****

The group drove across town to the courthouse. Annabelle couldn't navigate the many steps in the building, so she and Nigel remained outside with the wagon while the others went inside to make the report. Nigel spread a blanket on the ground and helped Annabelle from the wagon. He produced her crutches, and she hobbled onto the courthouse lawn and sat on the blanket. Nigel sat next to her.

"We have some time to ourselves. Whatever shall we do?" he asked lasciviously. "My offer yesterday still stands."

Annabelle could not help but guffaw. "Here in front of God and country?"

Nigel gestured at the people moving along the street. "I don't think they'd mind."

"Not on your life."

Nigel looked hopeful. "So when we're not in front of God and country?"

"God is omnipresent. That doesn't afford you an opportunity."

Nigel shrugged as though giving up. He opened the cork on a water bottle, poured some into a tin cup, and offered her the drink. Annabelle drained the cup and returned it.

Nigel poured some for himself. "It's strong, but I'm starting to develop a taste for it."

They sat in companionable silence for a few minutes, watching the bustling town from their vantage on the lawn. At length, Nigel broke the silence between them but still looked off into the distance.

"I need to thank you for tending to me yesterday when I became senseless."

Annabelle looked at him for the first time with a sense of warmth. Learning about his inner demons made him somehow more human, more approachable. "Sarah's attempt to help you last night at least brought you around. I understand her reluctance to delve deeper, but I've been thinking…there is another way."

Nigel looked at her, and Annabelle lowered her gaze.

"What do you mean?" he asked.

"There's another way to get at this. Hypnosis. It could help you recall things and may bring to light why you have this gift."

"You mean curse."

"All the more reason to consider it," she said.

"I thought mesmerism is the stuff of carnivals."

"This is not the 'animal magnetism' of the mesmerists nor the stage hypnosis of the so-called mentalists. It's hypnotherapy and has been used to great effect in Europe, helping those with mental afflictions. Professor James or I could employ this technique. He trained me."

"You want to peer into my soul?"

"In a manner of speaking."

"Not on your life."

The others exited the building and approached them, so Annabelle dropped the matter.

"Well, you two look very comfortable," said Professor James. "We should have brought a picnic. In fact, what shall we do for a meal?"

"If you mean to eat in the white part of town," said Edgar, "I'll need to eat elsewhere."

"May we all eat together in a colored restaurant?" asked Annabelle.

"It'll raise a few eyebrows, but we won't be turned away."

"That settles it," said Professor James.

Across the street stood a portly dark-skinned man in a business suit hailing a carriage. Edgar ran over and spoke to him before the man boarded the vehicle and rode away. Edgar returned and reported that the public house on the corner of Sycamore and Wythe had excellent fare.

The place was a large clean room with white tablecloths and crowded with diners. Edgar's prediction of them causing a stir by being a mixed-race party proved true. When they entered the place, the entire restaurant fell silent. After a bit, conversations resumed in more hushed tones. Several groups of people settled their bills and departed, freeing a table for them.

Lunch consisted of pepper pot soup and cornbread followed by a main dish of fish for Annabelle, Sarah, and Professor James, boiled mutton and stewed livers for Edgar, and frizzled beef for Nigel. Each main dish had a side of succotash. Dessert was a lemon custard. The recommendation seemed deserved.

"Well," said Nigel in a voice loud enough for everyone in the place to hear, "we sure don't need to teach the coloreds how to cook."

Annabelle almost choked on a spoonful of custard. Folks at several nearby tables stopped their conversations again and held their utensils midway to their mouths. They looked askance at Nigel, who seemed oblivious.

Sarah placed a hand on Edgar's arm, but he shook his head, and she withdrew it. "No indeed," said Edgar, "but that didn't stop house slaves from spitting into their master's food now and then."

Nigel surveyed the remains of his meal on the plate.

Most of the people in the place burst out laughing.

Nigel looked at Edgar and smirked. "I suppose I deserved that."

"Glad you enjoyed your meal, Mr. Pickford," said Edgar.

Professor James paid the bill and indicated their next stop would be one of the newspaper offices in town. He wanted them to comb back issues to compile information on the various deaths. Edgar convinced them they should visit the Negro paper in town, as they would be much more apt to cover the deaths in the colored community than would the white newspapers. Edgar asked the people seated at a nearby table. He learned the paper was called *The Virginia Lancet* and got directions.

When they walked into the *Lancet*'s building, the same silence greeted them as when they entered the restaurant. The initial buzz of conversations between the half-dozen workers behind the low oak partition fell away, as did the clatter of typewriters. A woman toward the back of the room rose from a desk and went through a door marked "Editor." A short while later, an ebony-colored man with a bald pate and gray hair around the base of his head emerged, followed by the woman. The man had on a white shirt with rolled-up sleeves and gray suit pants with red suspenders. "Can I help you folks?" he asked.

Professor James and Edgar approached the partition.

"Good day to you, sir," said Professor James. "My name is Doctor William James of Harvard University, and this is my colleague, Doctor Edgar Gilpin. Reverend Green asked our group to investigate the attacks on members of your community over the past few years."

The editor cast a wary eye at them for a point in time, before stepping to the partition and offering his hand, first to Professor James and then to Edgar.

"Wendel Washington," he said and nodded to Nigel, Sarah, and Annabelle. He swung the gate in the partition open. "Why don't you step into my office so the rest of these folks—" He sent a look around the room and smiled. "—can get back to work." He had his secretary fetch two more chairs into his office.

A utilitarian room, the office featured a bank of windows behind the desk facing the bustling street. The desk held a green blotter, an inkwell, a couple of pens, and a photo of a handsome woman holding a baby in her arms. A set of bookshelves ran along one wall, with leather-bound volumes and gold-leaf lettering. Before the bookshelves sat a low table with a near-empty crystal decanter and a couple of glasses.

"I hope you will forgive me for not offering any refreshment," said the editor. "I have a little port, but not enough for everyone. It would be unfair to offer it to some and not to all." The secretary brought in two more wooden chairs to supplement the three already near the desk. She made a small curtsy and left the room. The editor indicated the group should be seated. "So what can I do for you?"

Professor James scooted forward on his chair. "We'd like to go through your back issues for any details you may have concerning all the deaths Reverend Green has listed here." Professor James removed the paper from inside his jacket, unfolded it, and handed it to the editor.

The newspaperman studied the list for some time and handed it back. "Looks like a full accounting, except, of course, the sheriff."

"What are your thoughts on that?" asked Edgar.

The editor leaned back in his chair. "Good for

nothin' as far as our community was concerned. Worse. Had he acted to protect us from this menace years ago, it may not have got him last night. In a way, it seems only right. There's that issue of fairness again." He stood. "Let me show you folks to the stacks."

The editor escorted them from his office and into an adjoining room, shared by typesetters working next to the windows. Rows and rows of wooden shelves filled the rest of the room, piled with yellowing newspapers, some bound, others in loose piles.

"Be careful when taking lamps up and down these stacks. We don't want to have a conflagration. When you find an issue, you may use that table over there." The editor indicated an empty table next to a window. "I hope you find what you're looking for."

"Between our efforts," said Professor James, "and the law finally getting involved, perhaps this menace will be eliminated."

"Nothing would make me happier." The editor began to leave, stopped, and turned back to face the group. "You see, my wife was attacked and killed last year. Her name is on your list."

Chapter Thirteen

After a couple of hours, they compiled all the available information reported by the paper over the last few years. As they exited, they stopped before the secretary. Professor James removed his hat and bowed.

"Would you please ask Mr. Washington to step out so we may thank him?"

The secretary shook her head. "No." She busied herself with a stack of paperwork and averted her gaze. After an awkward period of silence, she added, "Mr. Washington has gone home for the day." She grasped a handful of papers and pounded one edge of the stack on the desk to straighten them. She grabbed another stack and proceeded to do the same. After this, she looked at Professor James with an icy expression. "He seemed rather upset after meeting with you."

Professor James nodded. "I understand. We are investigating the mysterious spate of deaths in Petersburg over the last few years, and I understand his wife numbers among the victims. We shall trouble you no further." He put his tall silk hat upon his head and turned to go.

"Wait!" The secretary said, now insistent.

The professor turned back.

"Are you the group speaking at Blandford Baptist tonight?"

"We are."

The secretary's features softened. "Then I wish you Godspeed. I apologize for being short. I feel bad about Mr. Washington's loss and thought you folks brought it all up again for no good reason. Here you're trying to stop it from happening further, and I treat you like dirt."

"No offense taken," said Professor James. He turned and motioned for the rest to follow.

"I'll see you tonight," called the secretary.

Professor James turned his head and spoke over his shoulder as he went through the low swinging gate. "Very good," he nodded. "I'll look forward to seeing you there."

Outside, the group gathered around the professor on the wooden sidewalk, typical in this part of town.

"Let's recap where things stand," said Professor James. "This creature, or a deranged man or woman, has been terrorizing the area for several years. It struck only on the full moon until the last few months but now attacks on other nights. The colored community has been its primary target. Last night's attack indicates whites may be victims too. We can conclude from reading the news articles, it often first goes for the throat and, if undisturbed, will consume much of its victim. Most of the dead have been from this county, but there are also victims in neighboring counties.

"My research leads me to believe the perpetrator may be a werewolf. Edgar has devised a simple test to prove if this is the case, which he shall soon perform. In the midst of all this, we have the Ku Klux Klan, who themselves are murderers and have threatened us. Have I forgotten anything?"

They each looked from one to the other and shook their heads.

"Well then"—he gestured for them to board the wagon—"we should determine what we're up against before tonight's meeting so we may chart our course of action."

Professor James drove the wagon this time. The group made their way once again to the icehouse.

"Does coming full circle mean we're going nowhere?" quipped Nigel.

"I anticipate arriving at a conclusion, at least as to what we are facing," said Professor James. He hopped off the wagon, came around, and helped Annabelle down. The rest got off the wagon as well.

"Do we know if the remains are still here?" asked Annabelle.

"We don't," answered Professor James. "Let's find out."

They entered the small door and lit the lantern. Professor James led the way with the light, and the rest followed. As before, water dripped from melting ice in the loft above and splattered upon their hair and clothes.

After a bit, Sarah announced their arrival at the bay that held the coffin.

Professor James, who had been leading them further into the room, stopped and doubled back. He held the lantern aloft. The mound looked as they had left it. "It appears we are in luck," he said.

Edgar came forward and swept the straw from the oiled canvas beneath, which he pulled back to reveal the coffin. Nigel made a couple of involuntary steps backward, recalling what happened the last time. He joined the shadowy form of Annabelle, also keeping her distance.

"I guess neither of us is looking to reprise our

performance," he whispered to her.

"God, no." Annabelle shivered. Nigel assumed this had as much to do with what happened last time as with the building's temperature.

Professor James passed the lamp to Sarah, and he and Edgar removed the coffin's lid. The contents had the same rank smell Nigel recalled from before, though the cold made it tolerable—just.

Professor James moved back. "If you would be so kind, Doctor Gilpin."

Edgar approached the coffin and removed a silver dollar from his vest pocket. He set it upon the cadaver's ruined chest, where the rib bones had been pulled back.

A sudden sizzling sound occurred, accompanied by the smell of burning flesh.

Chapter Fourteen

The Blandford Baptist Church, crowded to capacity and then some, looked ready to burst. People wedged themselves into the pews, and latecomers either stood in the aisles or waited outside the double doors, hoping to catch some of the proceedings. The place throbbed with the din of numerous conversations fueled by nervous anticipation. And the hot air swam with a pungent mix of body odor and perfume—the latter from those women who could afford it.

Edgar and the rest of the Eidola Project sat on the dais. He spotted the druggist, the newspaper editor, and the editor's secretary in the sea of faces. Many looked familiar from studying passers-by during their trips through town. His eyes settled on Saphne, at the end of the second row back on the right. Next to her sat the red-shirted frustrated paramour who glowered at Edgar. To indicate she was his girl, the red-shirted guy squeezed closer to Saphne, who frowned until her eyes met Edgar's. She flashed him a smile and lowered her gaze.

"'Never thought I'd be at a coon convention," Nigel muttered.

Edgar bounded to his feet, prepared to give Nigel a piece of his mind and his fist for dessert, but he saw Annabelle elbow Nigel hard in the ribs and heard the man yelp with pain. Sarah touched Edgar's arm and shook her head. Edgar exhaled in exasperation and sat. He tried to focus his attention on Saphne.

Reverend Green approached the podium and greeted those who managed to crowd into the building. "Welcome, folks. If those of you in the pews would be so kind as to squeeze into the center, we may be able to seat a few more people."

At this, Saphne shoved hard against the red-shirted guy and bought herself some breathing room.

The rest of those in the pews shuffled their derrieres over, but just one pew yielded enough room for another body—a big-busted woman, with an enormous hat, which she removed upon being seated. Some space existed on either side of a thin man in raggedy clothing, but no one seemed inclined to fill it.

"Thank you all for coming," Reverend Green said. "Before we proceed any further, I'd like us to give thanks to the Creator, in whose home we have assembled:

"Thank you, Lord, for providing us with the comfort of community this evening and for our friends who have arrived here in our hour of need.

"Please, Lord, lend your strength to this undertaking and assist us in removing the scourge that has afflicted us for years.

"Take up your flaming sword of righteousness and smite this demon so it may no longer terrorize this community and take our loved ones from us.

"We ask you this in Jesus' name.

"Amen."

The room echoed a chorus of amens. Reverend Green nodded in approval. "Now," he continued, "I'd like you to welcome Doctor William James of

Harvard." The minister gestured to Professor James, and polite applause occurred. "And with him are the other members of his team, in particular, Doctor Edgar Gilpin, who is a graduate of Howard University and earned a Ph.D. in physics from Yale, one of a very few colored folks to have achieved this distinction. Please stand, Doctor Gilpin."

Edgar stood to rousing applause. Those seated in the church rose to their feet.

Reverend Green stepped back, and Professor James approached the podium. The applause died away, and people retook their seats.

Professor James thanked the reverend and the people of Petersburg. He launched into reviewing the situation, as he did earlier, outside the offices of the Virginia Lancet. However, when he stated the perpetrator was a werewolf, pandemonium broke out.

Folks shouted their incredulity and swore—despite the setting. A few even attempted to leave but were trapped by the crowd. Leaving had to wait until they could do so as a herd. Clearly, not everyone subscribed to the notion of a bogeywolf. Through it all, Professor James just stood at the podium and let the nay-sayers have their due. After several minutes of this, Professor James motioned with his arms for people to be seated and quiet. It took another few minutes, but the derisive comments and shouts died away until the big-busted woman with the enormous hat jumped to her feet and shouted, "Why should we stay here and listen to this folderol?"

Shouts of "Amen," "Uh-huh," and "That's right!" arose in support of her comment.

Professor James waited again for the commotion to

die.

At last, he continued. "I understand your skepticism and encourage it. Nevertheless, I ask you to indulge me as I perform a demonstration. It will prove the veracity of my assertion. Reverend Green, would you please step forward?"

The reverend, who had taken a seat next to Edgar, stood and approached the professor.

Professor James took a wooden box from the floor and set it on the podium.

"With your permission, Reverend?"

The reverend nodded, and Professor James removed the lid and pushed aside the ice and straw within until he withdrew an object that appeared to be about two feet long, wrapped in burlap. The professor replaced the lid on the box and set the wrapped object on top. He tore off the rough brown cloth and revealed the gnawed naked remains of a human calf attached to a foot, still in a brown leather shoe.

Several women screamed, and pandemonium again took hold.

Some shouts rose above the rest: "My God!" "It's a sin!" "Reverend, how can you allow this?"

This time, Reverend Green raised his hands and motioned for them to be seated and quiet their protests.

"My friends," the minister said, once the volume dropped, "I ask you to trust me in this. I invited Professor James and his associates to our town because we have been living in terror for years, and our attempts to hunt this killer have failed. The professor tells me he needs to demonstrate what we are up against, so there can be no doubt, and so we may devise a way to destroy it. Again, I ask you to trust in him. Please grant your attention without further interruptions."

The room quieted, so the reverend gestured to the professor.

"Ladies and gentlemen," Professor James continued, "I understand your feelings, but we face a creature far more powerful than you may have imagined. One whom ordinary bullets cannot harm. A werewolf—and one who is becoming stronger with each passing day. But this creature does have a weakness. For some reason, his kind is repulsed by silver.

"To prove both the nature of our adversary and its weakness, I needed to disturb the remains of Doctor Curtis, who fell victim to this creature, and whose body has been stored in your town's ice house, awaiting burial. Following our test, I promise the remains of the good doctor will be gathered together and afforded a proper burial in hallowed ground, with the blessings of this church."

Professor James stopped and assessed the impact of his words. Appearing satisfied, he continued.

"Little is left of the doctor, but the surviving pieces still bear the savagery of the beast. Its saliva remains on the flesh and is susceptible to the same inability to tolerate silver."

Professor James lifted the leg, nestled in the burlap, and showed it to those in attendance. He turned toward the minister. "Reverend?"

Reverend Green took a few steps back, turned, and reached between Edgar and Sarah. In doing so, the reverend's open suit jacket flapped in Edgar's face. The proximity also revealed that flakes of dandruff speckled the minister's black attire. Reverend Green straightened, apologized, and returned to Professor James holding the silver cross from the altar.

"Now, if you would, reverend," said Professor James, loud enough for all to hear, "please place the silver cross on the stump, where the teeth of the creature tore it from the unfortunate doctor."

Reverend Green set the cross down as directed. The flesh beneath it sizzled, and a small plume of smoke arose. The leg burst into flames.

Professor James dropped the bundle to the floor and stomped out the fire. The fetid flesh lay on the platform, still smoldering.

The room filled with half-whispered comments and prayers. The loud murmuring continued until a scream came from the rear-most pew. Marie, Reverend Green's cook and housekeeper, stood, waved her arms, and screamed again. Everyone stared, and she stared back, wild-eyed, as though possessed. "*Attention, attention!*" she shouted, saying the words with a French pronunciation. "*Écoute-moi! La bête est ici!*"

People asked those around them what she meant. Edgar translated for Sarah and Nigel, "She's saying, 'the beast is here!' " Edgar scanned the crowd looking for a threat. Were they all in danger? Nothing appeared out of the ordinary aside from the smoldering appendage.

Marie alternated between screaming and laughing with demented abandon. She fought off people trying to assist her until someone leaned over the back of the pew and grabbed her in a bear hug. Those nearby helped her over the rear of the pew. They removed her from the church as she continued to scream and laugh.

It took some time for the room to settle after this.

Both Professor James and Reverend Green motioned with their hands for people to be seated.

The reverend stepped to the front of the dais and spoke as soon as folks quieted. "I don't know what has come over Marie. I know her to be a kind and generous soul. I will pray she regains her faculties as soon as possible. This whole thing has all of us on pins and needles. But Professor James's demonstration has proved something evil is afoot, and we must press on. Professor, would you please continue?" The minister stepped back and gestured to Professor James, who nodded in return.

"Ladies and gentlemen"—Professor James scanned the room—"we are facing a werewolf and must use silver to destroy it."

This time the parishioners and guests remained quiet. The portly businessman who directed them to the restaurant earlier rose to his feet. "Should we test everyone in the community? Have them handle a silver dollar?"

Professor James shook his head. "I wish it were that easy. The sources I have consulted indicate this phenomenon only occurs when the man or woman has transformed into the beast, or some vestige of that state remains, such as saliva, scat, or blood."

An unfamiliar woman in a prim black dress rose to her feet from the fourth row back. "You really think a woman could be behind these killings?"

Shouts supporting her remark arose from the other women and a few men.

Professor James nodded. "I have no doubt it could be either a man or a woman. In its transmogrified state, the creature assumes supernatural size and strength."

"So what are we supposed to do?" asked the tall man in raggedy clothing. "Throw coins at it?"

Some nervous laughter occurred until people saw the professor nodding his head.

"In a manner of speaking, yes," said Professor James.

"This man be as crazy as the woman they hauled outta here!" shouted a shriveled gray-haired lady with her front teeth missing.

Again, the professor weathered the storm of derision until people were willing to listen.

"What I'm proposing," resumed Professor James when the commotion died away, "is that we cast silver bullets. We could use money or any other silver objects, such as jewelry. The purer, the better. We then arm a party of men with these bullets to hunt down and destroy the werewolf. The hunt needs to commence as soon as possible. The werewolf can appear at any time. All of you are in danger, even those of you who dwell in town, as it could well start to prowl the streets."

"Some of us don't have money to spare," said the raggedy man. "How's 'bout we start with that silver cross?"

Several shouts endorsed the idea.

Reverend Green again stepped forward. "I'd like to preserve that symbol of Jesus's sacrifice, so I am prepared to donate a month's salary toward purchasing the needed silver. If we all chip in, whatever we can, we should have plenty. We have a plan, and with a small sacrifice from each of us, we can rid the community of this spawn of Satan."

Donation baskets circulated the room. Eventually, they were set before the podium, full of silver coins, paper money, and some silver jewelry. The professor added to the collection the three silver bracelets Marie had given them and all the silver coins the group possessed. Professor James looked up and gave Edgar, Annabelle, Sarah, and Nigel a nod of appreciation.

"Those wishing to join the hunt, meet here tomorrow night at eight-thirty!" shouted Reverend Green. "Bring your guns."

Amidst loud conversations, discussing everything that happened, the crowd began to disperse.

Edgar mopped his brow. He turned his attention from Professor James to the people preparing to leave. He noticed Saphne looking at him and smiling.

Seeing Edgar approach, the red-shirt guy grabbed Saphne by the upper arm and tried to pull her toward the exit. Saphne was having none of that and shook her arm free.

"This man bothering you?" Edgar asked.

Saphne sent a sideways glance at Red Shirt and rolled her eyes. "Naw. It's just that Cicero doesn't know the meaning of no."

"Cicero?" asked Edgar with surprise.

"What of it?" challenged Cicero.

"You're the very likeness of the famous Roman orator."

"Huh?" said Cicero.

Edgar looked at Saphne with a wry smile. Saphne smiled back.

"His owners were puttin' on airs when they named him," she said.

Disgusted, Cicero turned, pushed his way through the crowd, and left the church.

"'Can't handle the truth none either," said Saphne.

"You mind my askin' what you see in me?"

Her directness caught Edgar off guard. He fumbled for the words. "I—I see a beautiful young woman, who hasn't had the chance for schooling, but who seems as bright as any fellow I met at university."

"I bet you say that to every gal you take a shine to."

"No, I do not," Edgar said, looking hurt. "I have never felt this way about anyone. The fact is, I would very much like to get to know you better. Forgive me if I seem forward, but I'm not sure how long we'll be in Petersburg. If there is something worth building, I'd like to know as soon as possible."

"Well, I'm feeling honored." Her smile became even brighter, and she lowered her gaze with unexpected shyness. She looked up at him and batted her pretty eyes. "But I got to go to work tonight. Garraty just promoted me to head morning cook. Made a couple of hens in the house a mite jealous, but I'm not going to turn down the extra pay and responsibility. No sir. But the point is, I got to head there now. I'll be working nights from now on, so that may derail your express train."

Edgar's jaw dropped. "You're heading there *now?*" he asked in disbelief. "After coming across the doctor's remains, and after what you heard and saw at this meeting?"

"I'm not going to let a bogeywolf thingamajig keep me from getting this promotion. But truth be told, I may end up heading there before dark from now on."

"I'll escort you there this evening," said Edgar without a second thought. He asked her to wait while he made his way back to Professor James.

Before Edgar could get to him, two strong-looking men approached Professor James and Reverend Green.

"Excuse me, Reverend," interrupted the one in stained overalls. "Professor," he gestured to the other man, "this here's Moses. I'm Tobias. We're both gunsmiths. We compete for business, but after what we've seen and heard tonight, we're offering to get together and help you cast your silver bullets."

"Hold on there," said the raggedy man who came up behind the gunsmiths. The grubby and odiferous fellow accounted for much of the body odor Edgar had smelled. "That's a lot of silver," he patted one of the baskets full of money and jewelry. "What's to stop these fellows from pocketing some of this, 'stead of doing what they promised?"

"I can vouch for their character," said the reverend. "They'll not cheat—"

"Beggin' your pardon, Reverend," the raggedy man broke in and shook his head, "I've been living hereabouts a good deal longer than you. Tobias, he's all right, but I wouldn't trust Moses as far as I can spit."

"And just how much did *you* put in the baskets, Leroy?" asked Moses, rising to the challenge.

"The point is, how do we keep you honest?" the raggedy man shouted back. Some of the attendees from the meeting gathered around, attracted by the argument, and shouted their own opinions.

Reverend Green raised his hands and waved them down. "Let's stop slinging mud when we have a crisis in our community. Gentlemen," he turned to Moses and Tobias, "would you agree to let Leroy, here," he indicated the raggedy man, "observe your work, thereby putting his fears to rest?"

The gunsmiths looked at each other and then simultaneously said, "No."

"Leroy got himself arrested last March," noted Tobias. "'Stealing from the Mercantile. What's to stop *him* from pocketing some of the silver and accusing us?"

Professor James spoke. "Nevertheless, I appreciate the concerns." He gestured to Leroy and the others who had gathered. "Were something to happen to this silver, it would no doubt be a tremendous hardship for your community." He turned to the gunsmiths. "Would it be acceptable if members of my team and I observed the casting to put everyone's mind at ease?"

The gunsmiths looked at each other again, but this time shrugged and nodded.

Professor James smiled and bowed to the tradesmen. "Thank you, gentlemen, for accommodating us." He looked over at Edgar. "Well, Doctor Gilpin, I know you have some interest in metallurgy. Would you like to take the first shift?"

Edgar shook his head. "I've already committed to seeing a young woman," he pointed at Saphne, "to her place of employment. I could spell you in a couple of hours."

Professor James's smile disappeared. He took Edgar's elbow and steered him a few steps away from the others. "Do you think this wise, in the face of everything that has happened?" he whispered.

"I shan't break my promise to her."

Professor James narrowed his eyes and cast a glance over at Saphne, who smiled her radiant smile at him. "I see," he muttered, turning back to Edgar. "Be on your guard. Have you your pistol? Though its lead bullets will not help against the beast, there are other threats, as you well know."

Edgar patted the right-side pocket on his suit jacket. "I have resolved to carry it from now on."

Professor James stepped back and put his hands on Edgar's shoulders. "Again, be careful."

"I am a paragon of caution," Edgar told him.

The professor glanced back and forth at Saphne and Edgar. He released his grip. "I wonder…"

"*Don't,*" Edgar said as he moved away. He noticed the reverend, the two gunsmiths, and the raggedy man all grinning at him. Edgar turned and focused on Saphne and her captivating smile. "Let's go," he said to her, gesturing toward the exit.

The two descended the steps onto the gravel drive outside the church. The busty woman with the large hat stepped before Edgar, cutting him off from Saphne. "Doctor Gilpin, I'm so delighted to make your acquaintance!" she gushed, holding a gloved hand before her.

Edgar decided to be polite. He took her fingers in his right hand and inclined his head in a small bow. "Charmed. Now, I must be going."

The woman bowed her head in turn, and the stiff rim of her hat smacked Edgar on the nose. Eyes watering, he stepped back and held up his left hand to ward off further blows and to keep her from conversing further. She would not be put off.

"I'm most anxious for a man of your stature to meet Hubert, my son," she continued, undaunted. "He is very bright and has expressed an interest in science. Would it be possible to come to supper tomorrow?"

Edgar suppressed his irritation at the woman's

audacity. He forced a smile toward the hat, unwilling to meet the woman's eyes. "No, I'm afraid we've other commitments." He sidestepped her and managed to escape. "Perhaps some other time," he added, moving away.

He stopped in his tracks. An encouraging word would have made all the difference to him before he headed off to university, to a young man about to face all the obstacles and prejudice he encountered on the road to becoming one of the first Negro scientists in America. He turned back to the woman, "Perhaps I could carve out some time in the next few days. Is he attending Howard University in the fall?"

"Oh, no, he's just five years old," she said, beaming.

Flabbergasted, Edgar stared at her in disbelief. Without another word, he turned, marched over to Saphne, and led her away from the crowd.

The full moon lit their way, bathing the road and the nearby cemetery in its silvery light. They walked in silence for a spell. Now and then, they had to step off the road when a carriage or wagon went by. This happened less and less until they were alone—except for a chorus of crickets and bullfrogs serenading them. Edgar's hand bumped Saphne's several times before Saphne took Edgar's hand in her own. He looked over at her and could see her smiling at him in the moonlight.

"Am I too forward?" she asked.

"I like forward girls." Edgar realized this sounded wrong and tripped over his words, trying to take them back.

Saphne laughed and gave his hand a squeeze.

"You've had a lot of girls?"

Edgar studied the road as they walked. His mind flashed back to Eusapia Palladino, who had mounted him in Professor James's study one night when he had been sleeping on the couch. His first and only sexual experience, Eusapia had been the instigator, and it only lasted one night. Instead of putting him at ease around ladies, he felt even more unsure of himself, not wanting to cross the line of propriety, but knowing where things might lead. While certainly pleasurable, having no emotional bond with Eusapia left him feeling disquieted and unsatisfied. He wondered what the act would be like with a woman he loved—even at first sight.

Embarrassed by his carnal thoughts, Edgar said, "No. Just one, and she wasn't my gal. May we discuss something else?"

"Like what?"

"Oh, the weather?"

"It's a mighty fine night." She swung his arm back and forth.

"That it is."

They fell silent for a moment before they both laughed.

"You done gabbing about the weather?" she asked.

"Yes. I'd much rather hear about you," he admitted.

"'Don't know that I'm all that fascinating, compared with the famous Doctor Gilpin."

"I am bewitched by you."

"Go on," she laughed, "I'm sure you say that to all the gals."

"As I said, I have little experience with the fairer sex."

"So, I'm fair, am I?" She raised a bare arm in the moonlight and regarded it. "A mite dark to be fair. Could be the light."

"I think you're beautiful. I've never said that to anyone before."

"You lookin' to steal a kiss?"

"If I have to steal it, I shall, but I hope it will be given."

Saphne stopped, grabbed his head, and pulled it toward her, so his lips met hers. Her kiss felt moist, sweet, and intoxicating—nothing like Eusapia's. Saphne's tongue found its way into his mouth and played with his. He breathed in her scent—rosewater and sweat. It, too, made him heady with desire. Edgar ran his hands along her back and pulled her to him. Saphne gasped and kissed him with even more passion. Before things could proceed any further, her hands worked their way between them, and she pushed him gently away. "I'ze gotta get to work," she said, breathing hard. "You want any more, you better get me there in good time."

Edgar stepped back and composed himself, grateful the darkness hid his excitement.

"There's a path around the bend we need to follow through the woods," Saphne said, retaking his hand and pulling him on.

"I wonder if keeping to the road would be any safer," Edgar speculated, trying to tame his raging desire.

"Don't think it matters. Some folks have been attacked on the roads, some even in their homes. I ain't worried with you here protectin' me."

Edgar shrank at the thought. "I would like to think

you have nothing to fear with me by your side, but I suspect it isn't so."

"Here," she said, leading him off the road. A footpath cut through a field and disappeared into the darkness beyond. Wisps of fog hung over the grass on either side.

Edgar looked all around, worried about what he might find. Nothing. They appeared to be alone, except for the crickets.

As they crossed the field, Saphne waved her free hand off to the left. "Over there a piece occurred some nasty fighting during the war. At one point, the Yanks dug a tunnel under the Rebs and filled it with explosives. They blew a huge hole in the Rebel lines, and the Yanks, many of 'em colored, were ordered to rush through. Trouble was, the dynamite blew a giant hole in the ground as well, and the Yanks didn't have ladders. The Rebs just gathered 'round and had themselves a turkey shoot. Later, they threw dirt on top of the mound of bodies and just left 'em. This bogeywolf you folks are after ain't got nothin' on what people can do to each other all on their own."

Edgar had heard of the Battle of the Crater but hadn't realized it happened right here. On the scale of human suffering, the relative carnage of war created more deaths than this beast. Still, the bogeywolf, as the locals called it, presented an immediate threat and hence the one to worry about.

They entered the woods, and the light all but disappeared. Nonetheless, Saphne knew the way and pulled him after her with confidence. Chivalry demanded he lead the way, but he couldn't do anything but follow, so he swallowed his pride.

She asked him about his family as they walked, what going to university had been like, and the history that had brought him to Petersburg. Edgar detailed his life. Never had he shared so much with another. Saphne seemed interested and asked many questions to clarify things. As they tramped through the forest, a half-hour flew by. He realized he had been doing most of the talking. "Tell me about yourself," he said, but a few seconds later, Saphne halted, and Edgar bumped into her.

"My apologies."

Ahead lay a large field of leafy plants.

Saphne turned and grabbed his head again and kissed him. She broke off the kiss and said, "Garraty's place is just across that field of tobaccy. We made it. Safe and sound." She kissed him again with passion, and Edgar gave free rein to his desire. He pulled her to him, and she gasped as before, but this time she pressed herself still closer. Edgar's hands ran over her backside and down her thighs. Without thinking, his hands grabbed her and pulled her up onto him. She wrapped her legs around his midsection, kissing him all the while.

"Should I stop?" he asked, breaking off the kiss.

"Don't you dare!"

Edgar kissed Saphne again and pressed her up against the mossy side of a tree. His hands lifted the bottom of her dress, but at the sound of a wolf's howl, he froze.

Chapter Fifteen

Leroy opened a fifth of whiskey and took a long pull from the bottle. He belched and looked at the label, visible in the moonlight. Old Crow, his favorite. But it didn't taste right. Leroy had palmed two silver dollars from the basket full of donations when he made a stink about things back at the church, so he could afford this bottle and then some. But something tasted off with the liquor. It dawned on him—guilt.

While sitting on a wooden crate behind a warehouse on Bollingbrook Street, he thought about what he had done. He called out the two gunsmiths as cheats when he did the very thing he accused them of doing. He hit on this technique as a boy and employed it many times over the years, but this time felt different. Lives were at stake, and he'd stolen in a church.

Leroy watched with the others in horrified awe when the remains of Doc Curtis's leg caught fire. The white professor seemed to know all about this. What did he call it? A *where wolf*? Strange name. Bogeywolf sounded better. But whatever you called it, the creature killed folks.

He'd known two of the victims, Doc Curtis—everyone knew Doc—and Tom Taylor. Doc had been good to him. Gave him medicine several times and even took off two toes he said were infected by *gang green*. Had said that gang was gonna kill him if them toes weren't removed. He never had to pay the Doc a dime. The man just did it out of the goodness in his heart.

Leroy took another drink. It still didn't wash away the guilt. That professor showed them all what they were up against and how to defeat it, yet Leroy had stolen some of what they needed to do the job. He knew he looked bad and smelled bad, but he had never thought of himself as *being bad*. He felt bad now.

Tobias's and Moses's gun shops were nearby. They'd be making the bullets there. Perhaps he could help. Make amends. He didn't know how to make bullets, but he could learn. A teacher—what was her name?—Miss White, once said he was smart as a whip. He felt sure he could contribute in some way.

Leroy stood on rubbery legs and took another drink to fortify his resolve, the first swallow from this bottle that tasted good. He staggered off to offer his help.

Chapter Sixteen

The casting shed behind Tobias's gun store stank. The rank odor arose from the pot of molten silver on a coal-fired stove. The miasma caused Sarah to pull a lace handkerchief from her handbag and cover her nose and mouth. The smell still found its way through, and she coughed. The doctor's body in the icehouse seemed sweet by comparison.

One entire wall of the tin-roofed shed lay open to the night air. For this, Sarah was grateful; otherwise, she didn't think she could tolerate the stink. She looked over and saw Professor James in the lamplight. He had a white handkerchief over his nose and mouth.

Tobias looked at the two of them, smiled, and shook his head. "It don't smell too nice, that's for sure, but you get used to it. Fact is, this smells a whole lot nicer than some of the lead I get."

A church bell tolled, and Sarah counted twelve. Midnight. Tobias said he and Moses—who had gone back to his shop for supplies—planned to work through the night and through as much of the next day as might be necessary. They wanted to have as many bullets as possible for tomorrow night's search for the bogeywolf.

"Let's put an end to it," proclaimed Tobias.

All through the night? thought Sarah. Could she stay awake? She didn't see any place where she or the professor could take turns sleeping. Edgar had said that he'd take over at some point. She decided to worry about all that later. For the present, she didn't feel sleepy.

Sarah watched as the gunsmith put some pieces of wax into the pot.

Tobias must have seen the curious look in her eyes. He smiled and said, "It's for fluxing."

Sarah shook her head and made a shrug.

Tobias pointed to a pan where he had deposited some material he removed from the top of the pot of melted silver a minute ago. The stuff already hardened into black and lumpy shapes. "Getting the crud out I couldn't skim off. What we don't want will collect around the bits of melted wax and make it easier to remove."

Moses arrived, pushing a wheelbarrow full of supplies. He nodded at everyone, "What's cookin'?" he said with a grin.

"Howdy, Moses," said Tobias. "Just set your stuff next to mine on the table."

Sarah offered to help, but Moses thanked her and said no. "I want to keep track of my molds."

"That's cause his equipment is inferior," Tobias joked. "He'd be embarrassed to end up with some quality stuff like mine."

"My daddy gave me some of these twenty years ago when I first opened my shop on Wythe Street," said Moses.

"That's cause he didn't want em no more!" Tobias continued to poke fun.

Moses set his molds on the worktable. He pulled from the wheelbarrow a leather apron and large elbow-length work gloves. Moses donned them and looked much like Tobias. "You done fluxing?" he asked.

"Just about," said Tobias, skimming material off the molten metal, as one might skim excess fat off soup.

"Which size are you planning to do first?" asked Professor James.

"Good question," said Moses.

"Well," said Tobias, "Between us, we know what many folks have, and it's a mishmash of different guns. We asked folks after the meeting, and they confirmed our concerns. We'll need to make various sizes, starting with the most common, and go from there. Most folks still have pieces they got during or right after the war. So, we'll start with .58 caliber Minie' balls for the 1861 Springfield. There's a few Sharps and Winchesters, so we'll fill some casings for those and do the same for different revolvers. We're going to forget about shotguns." He looked over at Sarah. "This make any sense to you, young lady?"

Sarah coughed and shook her head. "Gracious, no. You are the experts."

"That's me!" Moses grinned. "Not so sure about Tobias." He grabbed two wooden handles on one of the devices he brought and pulled them apart. This separated the iron molds' halves on the other end, which swung open on a hinge. After lubricating the molds' interior, he closed them and held them next to the fire to warm.

Tobias lifted an iron ladle full of molten silver and poured it into the molds Moses now held over the pot. When the molds became full, Moses waited a few seconds before closing a latch, trimming off the excess metal. He turned and opened the mold above a wooden tub full of water. The bullets splashed down with a hiss.

The two gunsmiths repeated the process.

Sarah removed the handkerchief from her face and sniffed the air. Still foul, she determined, but better than earlier. Sarah turned to Professor James, who followed her lead and lowered his handkerchief. "May I speak to you outside for a moment, Professor?" she asked.

Professor James nodded, and the two stepped into the yard, illuminated with moonlight.

"Why are we still here?" Sarah asked. "These gentlemen seem competent and trustworthy. Do we really need to stay further?"

Professor James frowned at her. "We made a promise to Reverend Green and concerned parishioners to provide a full accounting of the silver."

"I know, but that seemed more of a pretext to diffuse the fight happening with the other man, the tramp."

"A promise is a promise," said Professor James. He glanced back at the shed before raising his eyes to stare at the night sky. He then leveled his eyes at her. "If you're tired, I'm sure Tobias has a chair in his store where you can repose. Perhaps even a cot."

Sarah sighed in resignation. Professor James's rigidity became trying at times. Still, he had the best of intentions. She nodded at him. "I'll inquire when they take a break."

She and Professor James made their way back to the shed just as Moses opened the mold. More bullets dropped into the tub of water.

"Perhaps we shoulda got a priest to bless the water," said Moses with a grin. "It coulda gave the bullets an extra kick."

"This'll give 'em an extra kick," came a drunken

voice. They all turned to see the raggedy man from the church meeting, the tramp to whom Sarah had just referred. He held a bottle of whiskey aloft and pushed past Sarah and Professor James.

"Leroy," yelled Moses, "stay the hell away! You'll get yourself hurt."

"I'm just trying to do my part." Leroy poured some of the alcohol into the water.

Tobias made a grab for the bottle, and Leroy jerked it away. The bottle slipped from his fingers and flew toward the stove.

"No!" shouted Moses, diving for the ground.

Tobias dove at Professor James and Sarah, knocking them over and causing them all to go tumbling from the shed.

Leroy still stood when the half-full bottle hit the rim of the pot. The bottle shattered. When the glass and liquid hit the melted silver, steam, glass, and molten metal exploded outward.

The blast hit Leroy full-on—splattering him with melted silver and impaling him with shards of broken glass. From where she lay on the ground, Sarah saw that Leroy appeared to be covered in silvery boils.

Leroy screamed and fell to his knees, holding his ruined arms halfway to his equally ruined face. His skin sizzled.

Moses sprang from the dirt floor and grabbed the tub of water, upending it over Leroy's head. Water and a dozen bullets rained down upon Leroy, who collapsed to the ground in a silent heap.

Sarah and Professor James got up and stared, stunned by what happened.

Tobias ran back into the shed. He took Leroy in his

arms. "I'll lay Leroy inside and run for Doc Curtis," he said to Moses. "See what you can salvage here." Tobias carried Leroy toward his store.

"Doc Curtis is dead," Moses shouted after him.

Tobias stopped in his tracks. "That's right. What am I gonna do?"

"Professor James is a doctor!" said Sarah, her voice shaking with emotion as tears ran from her eyes.

They all looked at Professor James, who seemed rattled. He stood, wobbly, staring at the silvery mess on the ground. Even in the lamplight, his face looked ashen.

"P-professor?" Sarah asked in a quavery voice. She touched his arm. He flinched and took a step back, blinking his eyes several times.

"Forgive me," he said. "Everything happened so fast." The color crept back into his face. He turned to the gunsmiths. "I graduated from Harvard Medical School but chose not to practice. I will help to the best of my abilities." As though a lever had been pulled, Professor James regained his usual demeanor. He straightened his shoulders and strode past Tobias, who still had Leroy in his arms. Professor James opened the rear door to Tobias' store. "Let's get the unfortunate man inside."

Sarah stood still, recalling Leroy as he screamed in agony. She wondered if she would ever be able to scrub the image from her mind.

Professor James came back toward her and took one of the lanterns from the shed. "Come, Sarah. I'll need your help if this man is to stand a chance of making it until morning."

Sarah wiped her tears away with the back of her

shaking hand and followed the men into the rear of the building. Tobias's store was also his home, and it contained a full kitchen in the rear. Tobias laid the unconscious man on a table and lit several lamps.

Sarah felt sick, but she knew, to be of any use to the professor and Leroy, she needed to numb herself, to wall-away her emotions until some other time.

She and Tobias watched while Professor James assessed Leroy's injuries. Leroy's face and arms appeared covered in silver carbuncles. Splashes of metal covered both his eyes, and Sarah wondered if he would ever be able to see again, should he survive. Numerous glass fragments protruded from his flesh, some surrounded by silver. The glass and silver also struck the man's tattered clothes, piercing or burning their way to the skin.

After a quick assessment, Professor James said, "I'll need water and a clean sponge, a bedsheet, a strong pair of shears, some gauze, tweezers to remove the glass and a container to put it in."

Sarah went to the sink and filled a pot with water, while Tobias ran around collecting the other items. When Tobias returned, Professor James removed the man's clothes without the use of shears. In most places, the clothes tore free like tissue paper. Professor James wet the sponge and squeezed it out all over the man's body. Bloody water ran off onto the wooden floor, but no one paid it any heed. He covered the injured man up to his neck with the sheet.

Is that for my sake? Sarah wondered as she refilled the pot with water. Modesty could not matter to Leroy at this point.

The professor worked on Leroy's face, squeezing

water over an area and removing pieces of glass. Each piece made a clink as it landed in the white enameled pot Tobias provided.

"It's amazing he's still breathing," Professor James said of Leroy. "If he regains consciousness, he may be in excruciating pain. Do you know someone who uses chloroform?"

Tobias shook his head.

"Morphine? Laudanum? Ether?"

Tobias shrugged.

"Go, wake the neighbors," said Professor James. "Ask about. Someone's bound to have something. We've some laudanum back where we're staying, but it would take a while to retrieve. See what's available in the neighborhood. Perhaps a druggist or dentist lives above his shop. Leroy may not be able to take anything orally, so if you locate morphine or laudanum, see if you can also find a hypodermic needle. There must be other doctors in town."

"No other colored doctors," said Tobias. "We got midwives, dentists, and barbers, but no other doctors. Folks do a lot on their own."

"Well, he needs more help. What about white doctors?"

"Sure, but they won't come."

Professor James weighed the implication of this and said, "I'm sorry. You'd better go."

The professor continued to wash and treat the injured man's face by teasing out pieces of glass but let the pustules of silver remain. Sarah asked him about this.

"They've seared into the skin and won't come off. The cool water may help in the meantime. The burns

127

must have cauterized the wounds. He's not bleeding much."

As Professor James worked, Leroy's breathing became labored. The professor stopped and turned to her. "We need to prop him up. Ask Moses for help. Hurry!"

Sarah ran outside and enlisted Moses' help. Together they found a board and a box of lead and used these to create an angled surface to raise Leroy's head and torso.

"Holy Mother," said Moses, appraising Leroy's injuries. "Lord, help him."

"I don't think he's going to make it," Professor James said in a quiet voice.

Leroy's breathing came in jerky, phlegm-choked spasms. Finally, he took in a single deep breath that rattled into his lungs. It seemed to catch. He never exhaled.

The three stood in silence for some time. At last, Moses asked, "Now what?"

Professor James walked over to the sink and washed his hands and face. Not seeing any towels nearby, he ran his hands over his face a few times to wipe off the excess water and ran his damp hands back through his hair. When he looked at them, a drop of water still hung from his nose. "How much silver could you salvage outside?" asked the professor.

"Whatever I could find, but it's filthy—dirt and twigs all mixed in. It'll take a lot of fluxing to clean, plus I'll need to cook it over a low heat first to get rid of any moisture." Moses pointed to the deceased. "We lost a fair bit to what landed on poor Leroy."

Professor James cast his eyes about the kitchen

before locating a sharp knife.

"What are you fixin' to do?" This from Tobias, who returned with a medicine bottle and a hypodermic needle.

Moses pointed to Leroy. "Dead." Then Moses jerked his thumb at the professor. "The man wants to cut off all the silver that landed on Leroy."

"I'll not let you defile his body," said Tobias.

"It's not right," echoed Moses.

"Gentlemen," Professor James spoke as he gestured at Leroy, "need I remind you he *is* dead. He's beyond pain, and we need the silver."

"But it's not right," repeated Moses, stepping closer to the body and balling his fists.

"We'll not let you." Tobias set the items on the table, next to Leroy's disfigured face. He came around to the other side of Leroy's body as if to protect him from both sides.

"Let's ask him," said Sarah.

The three men turned to look at Sarah.

"Ask who, little missy?" said Moses.

Sarah inclined her head toward Leroy. "Let's ask him," she repeated.

Moses grinned and shook his head in disbelief.

"Young lady," said Tobias, "you're crazy."

"I assure you she's not. Our Miss Bradbury is a noted medium, but I sense some hesitancy on her part. Perhaps because this man experienced so much trauma and only just passed?"

Sarah nodded, amazed, as she had been many times before, by Professor James's powers of deduction.

"He may not be able to speak if he is still too traumatized," said Sarah, "but it is worth a try."

Professor James looked back and forth at the two gunsmiths. "Miss Bradbury is offering to feel and be Leroy for a period time. This can cause her considerable distress, but she is willing to subject herself to it so that we may complete our mission and cast the necessary bullets."

"How do we know this ain't some sort of trick?" asked Tobias.

"Perhaps the deceased will convince you himself," said Professor James. "Do you agree?"

The two gunsmiths looked at each other, then at Sarah. They nodded.

Sarah fetched a plain wooden chair from where it had been shoved out of the way. She brought it next to the body and sat. She closed her eyes and performed her ritual breathing, as she worked to clear her mind of all thoughts except making a connection with Leroy's spirit—which she felt still dwelt in the room.

Her head inclined, and she breathed in a ragged manner. Without warning, Sarah fell forward onto her knees and held her hands halfway to her face. She screamed, replicating Leroy after being hit by the explosion.

Professor James ran to Sarah and tried to help her stand, but Sarah batted his hands away. "No, don't touch me!" she said in Leroy's voice. "Oh, God, I can't see!" Sarah stumbled around on all fours. She raised herself by grabbing the side of the table and stopped moving. "Wait, I can—I can see, but it's different." Sarah studied the body before her. "It's me...I'm dead, ain't I?"

"Yes," said Professor James.

"Oh, Lord," Leroy said through Sarah, "what a

wasted life." Sarah turned to Professor James. "You tried to help me, and I thank ye." She looked over at Moses and Tobias, "You too. Not sure I deserved your help, the way I've acted."

"No hard feelings, Leroy," said Moses. "It is Leroy, ain't it?"

"Who the hell do you think it is?" Sarah snapped with Leroy's old piss and vinegar.

"I don't buy it," said Tobias. "This is some sort of trick."

"You want some proof?" Sarah, as Leroy, took a step toward Tobias and grinned. "You want some proof, Tobias? I can see things different now. Know things I didn't when alive."

"For instance?" challenged Tobias.

"For instance, I know in your nightstand beside your bed you got a deck of special playin' cards you took in trade from a salesman who came through town. They's got pictures of French women on them. White women without clothes!"

"That's enough!" yelled Tobias, looking shaken. "I believe you."

"Fine." Sarah swung back toward Professor James. "So you want to know if it's okay to cut the silver off my body? Hmm… Well, I really did want to help, just didn't know what I could do. Now I've gone and messed up your work and got myself killed in the process."

After a long pause, Leroy's voice announced, "I say yes. Cut the stuff off. It's the least I can do to put things right."

Sarah started to wobble.

"One more thing," said Professor James in a rush

of words. "Do you know who the werewolf is?"

Sarah collapsed onto the wet kitchen floor.

In her half-conscious state, she noticed Professor James rush to scoop her into his arms. "Is there someplace I can put her until she recovers?" he asked.

Tobias nodded and moved to the doorway. "Follow me. She can rest on my bed upstairs. I just want to remove something from the nightstand."

Chapter Seventeen

Before leaving with the gunsmiths and Sarah, Professor James told Annabelle and Nigel to return to the doctor's house. Reverend Green would take them. As a result, Annabelle and Nigel had to wait for the reverend and several parishioners to put the chapel in order after the meeting.

The loquacious reverend talked nonstop as he drove the wagon to the farmhouse. Nigel didn't trust himself to say anything civil to a colored man, minister or no, so he let him talk. Nigel realized Edgar had become an exception to this, though not a consistent one.

Reverend Green managed to hold his interest for a while when he spoke about Marie's odd behavior at the meeting and how she had been acting peculiar of late. Perhaps the stress of the attacks brought on her lunacy, the minister speculated. He pledged to make her the focus of his prayers. Next, he waxed on and on in his praise of the Eidola Project for coming in the town's time of need. Nigel's interest evaporated when Reverend Green segued into discussing, ad nauseam, individual members of the congregation, people who Nigel did not know nor had any interest in knowing.

Annabelle lay on the bed of the wagon with her injured leg propped up on some gunny sacks. The reverend pitched a few questions her way, but she couldn't hear him over the sound of the wagon. Nigel wished he were back there with her. He sat as far away from the reverend as he could on the plank seat. After what seemed an eternity of hearing the reverend prattle, Nigel's posterior became as sore as his patience. He wanted to tell the minister to shut the hell up, but out of deference to Annabelle, who might hear him, he held his tongue. He hoped she appreciated his self-control.

Reverend Green pulled the wagon to a stop before the late doctor's house. Before it entirely came to a halt, Nigel hopped to the ground and breathed a sigh of relief. He went into the dark house to find a lamp. Returning with the light aglow, Nigel saw Reverend Green assisting Annabelle down from the wagon's rear. Nigel realized he missed a chance to be gallant. Trying to salvage something from the situation, he used the lamp to locate Annabelle's crutches. But the minister preempted him again by taking the crutches from his hands and presenting them to Annabelle himself.

"Thank you, gentlemen," said Annabelle, looking from one to the other. "You're most gracious."

"We appreciate you sayin' so," said Reverend Green, sweeping the hat from his head and making a deep bow. In doing this, his arm bumped into Nigel, who recoiled and shouted:

"Don't touch me!"

"Nigel!" Annabelle responded in just as harsh a voice.

Nigel heaved over and retched.

"Oh my," she said. She hobbled over to Nigel and put a comforting hand on his back. She turned to the minister. "No doubt this accounts for his rudeness. He must have been fighting back nausea. Look at us, a couple of invalids!"

"What can I do to help?" asked Reverend Green.

Annabelle shook her head. "You've done plenty. As soon as he's recovered his composure, we'll go inside and recuperate. I appreciate you bringing us here."

"Very well," said Reverend Green. "I hope you're feelin' better soon, Mr. Pickford."

The minister climbed aboard and steered the wagon back toward town, where Professor James and the others would retrieve it the next day.

Nigel's retching subsided. He spat his mouth clean and stood.

"What's come over you?" asked Annabelle.

"That man," said Nigel in a croaky whisper, "the reverend. Just got a flash. Something bad is going to happen to him."

"One of your visions? Will he be attacked? Is there some way we can warn him?"

Nigel shrugged.

Annabelle shouted at the reverend to stop. She ran in his direction, forgetting her crutches, but her sprained ankle went out from under her, and she collapsed to the ground. Reverend Green hadn't heard her. He and the wagon disappeared as the road led into a wooded area.

Nigel helped Annabelle stand and retrieved her crutches.

"You must run after and stop him."

"No. Won't matter in any case."

"Then what shall we do?"

"I don't know," Nigel shook his head in disgust, in part because of how the minister's touch made him feel, and in part because of his impotence in the face of his visions. "I can't figure out what will befall him. It may not even occur for some time. I just had a feeling of dread that made me ill. Whatever it is, if it gets him to shut up, perhaps it won't be so bad."

Annabelle socked him in the arm so hard he yelped. He looked at her and saw no humor on her face.

"Hey, have some pity for the sick."

"You'll get none from me." Annabelle hobbled into the farmhouse.

Nigel followed with the lamp. He shut the door, and they both sat at the table, Annabelle taking the seat opposite Nigel. She leaned her crutches against the tabletop.

"Do you often get sick after premonitions?" she asked.

"Sometimes, but nothing like that." Nigel took off his hat and set it on the table. He raked his fingers through his dark hair.

Annabelle pressed him for more: "Your premonition lacks specificity. Does this happen often?"

"No. I'll think on it more when I'm up to it." Nigel pressed his palms over his eyelids. "I can't right now. In any case, there's nothing to be done. It's what drove me to drink—seeing disasters one after another and never being able to stop them." Nigel shook his head and made a face. "My throat is sore, and I've got a nasty taste in my mouth."

"I'll fix us some tea." Annabelle made an awkward attempt to stand, but Nigel rose and motioned for her to sit.

"Don't trouble yourself." Nigel rekindled the smoldering fire in the stove and brought the water in the kettle to a boil. He threw some leaves into a pot and added the boiling water. After a minute of steeping, Nigel judged it done. He poured the tea into two mugs and set them on the table.

Once seated, Nigel lifted his mug in a toast and took a swallow. It scalded his tongue, and he spat the hot liquid back into his cup. He set the mug on the table with a thud. Tea splashed onto the table close to a stack of Professor James's books. "Blast it all," he swore. Nigel swiped the surface dry with his sleeve.

He blew on his tea to cool it. After a while, he looked at Annabelle. "I've decided to accept your offer," he said.

Annabelle looked at him, askance, from over her cup of tea. "Not this again," she sighed in frustration, "I've not offered you any favors, nor shall I."

"For once, I'm not trying to proposition you— though please consider that a standing invitation. What I mean to say is, I'm prepared to take you up on hypnotizing me." Nigel sipped the still hot tea, but this time swallowed. He decided the burning sensation felt good. Cleansing. "You say it may help me put an end to the visions?"

Annabelle set her cup on the table and leaned forward. She cocked her head to one side as she regarded him and qualified the statement she had made on the courthouse lawn. "Perhaps," she said. "I think it's worth a try."

Nigel liked the way Annabelle looked as she regarded him. Her wide dark eyes. The way her naturally red lips pursed. He wanted to kiss those lips. *This process may have a benefit one way or another.*

"At the very least, it should provide you with some answers," she continued. "Perhaps help us chart a way forward so, in the end, you may be able to control your abilities, rather than letting them control you."

"That's quite a promise."

Annabelle shook her head. "That's not a promise. It's a goal. And to reach any goal, one must begin with the first step. I need you to trust me. Furthermore, I give you permission to break off and return to the here and now, should anything become too much to bear. Understood?"

Nigel gulped in spite of himself. "I understand. I have faith in you, Annie."

Annabelle slid the lamp over next to Nigel. "I want you to look into my eyes," she told him.

Nigel's heart gave a skip. *Damn, this could be the first step toward those favors after all.* He straightened his spine, took a deep breath, and met her gaze. Her large brown eyes had flecks of gold and green. The fact he never noticed this before surprised him. He gave her his best smile.

Unflappable, Annabelle continued her stare and said. "Please concentrate and take slow, deep breaths. Continue this as you listen to my voice and know you are safe. When you wish, you may close your eyes."

Her voice droned on like this for some time.

****

Annabelle noted his eyelids appeared to be getting heavy and suggested he close them. Nigel did so. He continued his deep breathing. Annabelle's voice continued in soft, reassuring tones.

After a while, she grew quiet, then said, "I'm going to ask you a series of questions. I want honest answers. Answer yes if you understand."

"Yes," Nigel said in a clear but soft voice. His eyes

remained closed.

"What is your full name?

"Nigel Edmund Pickford."

"Is that your true name?"

Nigel's head gave a slight nod. "Yes."

"What is your occupation?"

"A drunkard." This he said in the same low voice, untethered from any humor or self-derision. Then Nigel added, "Perhaps I'm becoming something more."

Annabelle's sprained ankle began to throb, so she raised it onto a neighboring chair and continued. "Why have you been a drunkard?" she asked.

"To forget my curse and to dull its effects."

"Tell me about this. When did it begin?"

"During the war."

"Tell me about the first occurrence."

"It afflicted me just before the Battle of Fort Stedman, on the fields outside this house. The Yanks had been pushing toward Richmond but couldn't get past us. It remained so for months, but that night we planned to break the stalemate.

"The main battle focused on Fort Stedman in the center of a line of Yankee forts. My soldiers and I were to move against Fort Haskell, a mile south.

"We waited in the dark. In the distance, someone set a house ablaze, and in its light, I could make out my men, formed along either side of me. I raised my arm to signal our attack, then stopped. My men—all of whom had been fine—were now disfigured.

"Tim Hayton had a gash across his belly and guts spilled from his abdomen. He whimpered, 'Why'd you let us die, Lieutenant?'

"Corporal Archibald Smith stepped forward from

the shadows. Half his skull was gone. His brain shone in the flickering light. "It's a trap, sir," he said."

"What did you do?" whispered Annabelle.

"I refused to advance."

"So you saved those men?"

"No. General Evans rode up, fit to be tied because we hadn't moved. His arrival broke the spell—all my men returned to normal. The general's men waited to follow us into battle. I told him a trap awaited us. He drew his sidearm and threatened to shoot me if I didn't advance.

"My men gathered 'round. They said I had just given the order, and they weren't afraid. The general lowered his revolver, and we moved ahead into the slaughter I foresaw."

"Before this battle, did you have similar premonitions?" asked Annabelle.

"Not like this. I've always had the sight, but different. Before, I could see what *might* happen— where the Yanks would be, from what direction, and when they would come. It gave us an edge. Kept my men safe. But from then on, my premonitions preceded only tragedy and death I couldn't prevent. I turned to drink. Alcohol dulled the visions."

"And thus we found you, several weeks ago, living as a derelict."

"Just so," Nigel agreed.

"What caused the change in your visions?"

The calm of Nigel's trance shattered. "No!" he shouted. *"No!"* Vacant eyes flew open and stared around.

She never encountered someone becoming so agitated during hypnosis. "Nigel," she said, *"Nigel, listen to me.* You are back in the present. The hypnosis is over."

Nigel seemed to ignore her. He sprang to his feet, shoving the table to the side. This knocked over the chair on which Annabelle's injured leg had been resting. Both chair and leg thudded to the floor.

"Ow! Damn it!" Annabelle swore as her eyes welled with tears.

"*No!*" Nigel repeated, oblivious to Annabelle's pain. In a low stunned voice, he uttered, "It can't be!" He stumbled around the room and then made for the door. He fumbled with the knob. "Let me out!" At last, he threw the door wide, but instead of leaving, he stopped on the threshold, facing the moonlit landscape beyond. His manner and voice changed, resuming the trance-like affect he exhibited earlier.

"He's in danger," Nigel said.

"*Who?*" Annabelle's voice was sharp, preoccupied as she was with pain as she reset her foot on the righted chair.

Nigel's voice seemed far away. "Edgar." He walked through the doorway and into the night.

"*No!* Stop!" Annabelle struggled to her feet. She tried to retrieve her crutches, which had fallen to the floor during Nigel's hullabaloo. She nearly fell herself and decided to abandon them. Annabelle hopped to the door. The bright moonlight made everything visible in shades of black and white. She could see Nigel running from the house.

"Nigel, stop!"

He halted and turned to face her. "I have to go." He sounded clear-headed, resolute.

"Don't leave me alone! You said you can't stop

your visions from becoming true."

He took a step toward her, then stopped and shook his head. "I have to try. I don't think I could live with myself without making an effort."

"But you'll be in danger! *So will I!*"

"Bar the door. You'll be safe."

"Don't go!"

Despite her protests, Nigel turned and resumed running. A few seconds later, he disappeared from view.

Annabelle shut the door and tried to bolt it, but she realized the bolt was broken. She dragged a chair across the floor and braced it against the doorknob, as she had seen Edgar do the night before. Having done this, Annabelle limped back to the table and sat in a chair. She put her face in her hands and wet them with tears.

Chapter Eighteen

Edgar's heart pounded in his chest as he and Saphne made it to a drying shed at the edge of the field. He looked back across the tobacco field. *Did they have a chance?* He expected to see the demon creature hurtling toward them.

The moonlight shimmered on the expanse of dew-soaked broad-leafed plants and the wisps of fog forming across the field. *No sign of the wolf.* Edgar studied the building and realized the shed offered no protection—being open on all four sides. They needed to get to Garraty's house.

The wolf's howl sounded again. Nearer, but from which direction? From Garraty's place? Between here and there? Did they have any other option? Edgar's mind raced with the possibilities until he realized they had to act. Any action was better than inaction.

"Come on!" He took Saphne's hand, and they ran onto the road leading to the mansion.

"What if Garraty sees you!" cried Saphne, panting for breath.

"No choice," Edgar answered, pulling her forward.

The two rounded the bend, and the mansion came into view. From here, they could see the side of the impressive white-washed building. Most of the windows shone bright with light. "At least they are up and about," Edgar said. He had imagined them being attacked on the front porch while the household lay abed.

Edgar and Saphne called for help as they cut across the lawn and came around to the front. Garraty stood alone on the porch waiting for them, holding a shotgun propped up on one hip. The servants peered through the windows behind him.

"Thank God!" shouted Saphne. "Save us, Mr. Garraty."

Garraty lowered his shotgun so it pointed at them. "Hold up, you two!"

Edgar came to a sudden halt, but Saphne slipped as she tried to stop on the dew-slick grass. She landed hard on her backside, still holding onto one of Edgar's hands. Edgar got her to her feet, and they headed for the porch.

"Not another step!" Garraty snarled as he stared down at them, still pointing the shotgun.

"You heard the wolf?" asked Edgar.

"I heard it."

Edgar tried to reason. "You can't just leave us out here to fend for ourselves."

"I can do anything I goddamn well please. This here's my place, and you're trespassing."

"But Mr. Garraty, sir!" Saphne wailed, tears springing to her eyes.

"*You* can stay," Garraty said, "but not him."

"What?" Saphne's voice caught in her throat, and she turned to face Edgar.

"Go inside," said Edgar. He put his hands on her cheeks and used his thumbs to wipe away her tears. "I want you safe."

Saphne shook her head. "I can't."

144

"Yes, you can." Edgar insisted, letting go and taking a step back.

Garraty descended the steps and grabbed Saphne's right wrist. He hauled her onto the porch, then put his arm around her waist and pulled her to him. "Don't you worry now," he said to Edgar, leering, "I'll take real good care of her. Now, git!" Garraty fired a shot into the air, then lowered the gun again and pointed it at Edgar. "Next one's for you! Get the hell outta here!"

Edgar turned and considered his options. Back the way he had come seemed the most dangerous, next to trying to take on Garraty. He still had the small pistol in his pocket but decided against using it. Saphne might be hit in an exchange of fire between him and Garraty. He would get even with Garraty some other time.

Straight ahead stood a copse of trees. To the left lay the tobacco field where they had come. To the right stretched a long barren field with a wooded area beyond. Were he to go that way, he could see anything approaching, but then what? He'd have no options, and the creature could run him down unless he could make it to the woods. Off to the right of the house stretched a huge field of what appeared to be cotton. No protection there. Edgar opted for the open field with the woods beyond. He began to sprint, accompanied by Garraty's jeers and Saphne's sobs.

As he ran, he became aware that the air around the mansion smelled of honeysuckle. *Odd a place so vile should smell so sweet.* Edgar tripped on a rut when crossing the road, recovered his balance, and struck out across the open field. The furrowed ground made it difficult to run, and he decided to try to stick to the low part of one row as he ran. Whatever had grown here had been harvested, and tops of rows now featured a low-cut stubble. He had to concentrate on where to place each foot, but worry for Saphne kept crowding his thoughts.

A wolf's loud howl shattered his concentration, and he fell. The stiff remains of stalks cut into his hands as he hit the ground. He sprang to his feet and resumed running, wiping his bleeding palms on his shirt.

Positive the howl came from the left, Edgar veered right, cutting across the rows, but still heading for the woods. He tried to put on more speed, running as fast as he could across the moonlit field, but the semi-darkness and rutted ground limited his pace.

He thought he heard a growl.

Edgar drove himself on. He made it through the field, crossed a weed-choked path, and dove into the woods. He put his arms before him, running near-blind under the canopy and through the underbrush. Low branches whipped his face and tore at his clothing. Several times he almost crashed into a tree.

Sometime later, he slowed, exhausted and his throat bone-dry. He needed to stop and take stock of the situation.

He broke out of the underbrush and into a small glade. Moonlight revealed a stream cutting through the clearing, and Edgar threw himself to the ground before it and drank its brackish water. He splashed his face, grateful for the respite.

A sudden painful kick to his side pitched him over onto his back. His head hung off the bank, just above the stream. A large dark figure loomed over him, growled, and then attacked, landing on his chest.

"You sonofabitch," Cicero swore as his hands took

hold of Edgar's throat and pushed his head back under the water. "I'll teach you to mess with my woman."

Edgar cursed and sputtered in the stream. He forced his head above the surface, but when he did so, the hands on his throat prevented him from breathing. He only had his right hand free, the other pinned beneath him. Edgar couldn't break Cicero's grip on his throat. In desperation, he clawed at his attacker's face. A finger dug into one of Cicero's eyes. The man released his grip and screamed. Edgar scrambled to the other side of the stream and stood.

He could see Cicero clutching his face. The man continued screaming in pain.

"Serves you right, you dumb yokel!" Edgar yelled. "Saphne can have anyone she damn well pleases." The fight brought forth the colorful vernacular of his youth. Edgar turned away. "You'd better hightail it outta here," he added as he headed for the woods, "I'm sure you heard the wolf."

"Stop, or I'll shoot!" Cicero sobbed.

Edgar froze.

"Turn around."

Edgar did so. Cicero had recovered enough to be pointing a pistol at Edgar. The gun's nickel plating shone in the light of the moon. As he held the gun on him, Cicero's left hand cupped his injured eye. "I wanted to take care of you with my bare hands, but if I have to shoot you, I will." He drew back the hammer with his thumb.

Edgar dove to one side, hit the ground, and rolled.

Cicero fired and missed.

"Where'd you go?"

Edgar raised his head. Cicero appeared blinded by

the flash of his gun. The man stumbled around, waving the pistol this way and that.

Before Edgar could take advantage of this opportunity, he saw a large beast with fiery red eyes attack Cicero from behind. The creature clamped its jaws on the back of Cicero's neck and shook the man like a rag doll. Cicero screamed even louder than before.

The wolf looked at least two or three times the size of wolves he'd seen in zoos. Its long and shaggy coat appeared black, as did its nose and muzzle. But its eyes burned red with a light of their own.

Cicero's voice ended in a choked gasp.

"My God," said Edgar as he forced himself to his feet. He ran as fast as he could for the trees. Through his mind ran the words, "What can I do? What can I do?" He broke into the brush, and the thought occurred to him—*a tree*.

Edgar jumped for a limb on the nearest large tree and hoisted himself off the ground. The process caused the ribs where Cicero kicked him to stab with pain, but he paid it no mind and climbed limb after limb, higher and higher.

The werewolf crashed through the brush next to the tree and snarled at him. It leapt for the lowest branch but could not gain purchase and the limb snapped. The beast yelped as it hit the ground. It sprang to its feet and ran at the trunk, scrabbling at the bark with its claws, snarling and snapping its jaws at him with bloodlust. Edgar stopped his ascent and pivoted around with his left hand clutching the branch above him. He drew the derringer and fired both shots point-blank into the maw of the werewolf's mouth. The beast gave a little cough and shook its head, then continued its attempt to get him.

Edgar scrambled still higher.

The eyes of the creature burned bright. Its jaws snapped at him with each attempt to scale the trunk. Each time it fell to the ground and howled in frustration. After several more tries, it gave up. The wolf circled the base of the tree a few times, emptied its bladder against the trunk, then slunk away.

From his view in the branches, Edgar could see the wolf lope across the glade and begin to feed on Cicero's body. Edgar shouted at it, trying to drive it away. This only caused the beast to stop feeding and turn toward him briefly before resuming its grizzly feast. At length, the creature appeared sated and left the remains. It made its way back in the direction of Garraty's house and disappeared into the woods.

Edgar did not descend from the tree until well after sunrise.

Chapter Nineteen

At the pounding on the door, Annabelle jerked upright from where she fell asleep at the table. She glanced around, wide-eyed with fear, and saw the window above the sink shining bright with light. It's OK, Annabelle told herself, it's morning. Then she wondered if daylight made a difference anymore. Professor James said the beast was evolving and becoming more powerful.

The pounding on the door resumed, and Annabelle stood, got her crutches, and tottered over. Who might it be? she wondered. Nigel? The beast? Professor James and Sarah? Could it possibly be Edgar? That seemed the most remote, given the inevitability of Nigel's visions. Might he be mistaken? Nigel had run off without the benefit of a silver weapon or a weapon of any sort. Could it be the Klan? The fear of the unknown caused her to freeze at the door.

"Who—who is it?" Annabelle asked. She could hear the fear in her words.

"Open the door, dammit!" came Nigel's muffled voice from outside.

Annabelle tried but failed to move the chair she braced against the doorknob. "I can't!" she yelled with frustration, then explained about the chair.

Nigel pulled the door back toward him. "Try it now!"

The chair slid free, and Nigel entered. He looked haggard, and his gray suit had several burs and twigs stuck to it; otherwise, he appeared fine except for his grim face. "I came across the body of a colored man in the woods, mauled beyond recognition. I arrived too late."

Annabelle gasped and put her hands to her mouth, causing the crutches to slam onto the wooden floor. She started to collapse as she sobbed, but Nigel snagged her and held her upright.

"Steady," he said.

"I can't help it," she wailed.

Nigel helped her to the table and then fetched her crutches, but instead of thanks, Annabelle gave him a critical look. Between sobs she said, "And you could have joined him! What were you thinking, running off?"

Nigel sat opposite her and said, "I can't claim to have been thinking much at all. My vision filled me with such dread, I felt compelled to do something. Had I stopped to think, I'd have realized I couldn't stop what happened. It's my curse."

"What would you have done had you encountered the werewolf? You had no means of defense."

"I don't know," he admitted.

"You left me to fend for myself— Oh, what a selfish fool am I to be thinking of me after what happened to Edgar." Annabelle's sobs returned in full force.

Nigel lowered his head with uncharacteristic remorse. "I should not have left you."

The door crashed open, and in staggered Edgar.

Annabelle screamed.

Edgar stopped short. "Perhaps I should leave."

Edgar appeared to have had a much harder night than Nigel. A scarecrow would have rejected his torn and filthy clothes. They hung from his body in shreds. Numerous scratches—some still bleeding—covered his face and arms.

Annabelle stretched her shaking hands before her, and Edgar crossed the room and took them in his own.

"We thought you were dead!" she said, smiling through her tears. Annabelle glanced over at Nigel, who stood with a shocked look on his face. She wondered for an instant if he objected to her holding hands with Edgar, then she saw the relief wash over Nigel's features.

"Nigel had a vision," Annabelle explained. "He went after you and found a dead man in the woods."

"I thought it killed you," said Nigel in a stunned voice.

"It very nearly did." Edgar let go of Annabelle's hands and looked back and forth between her and Nigel. "Another man, Cicero, was not so fortunate." Edgar exhaled a long slow breath and became quiet. He glanced from one to the other. "Let me wash and get some coffee in me, then I'll tell you about it."

"Of course," said Annabelle.

Edgar wearily shuffled off to his room.

Annabelle pulled a lace handkerchief from her sleeve and dabbed at her eyes, then wiped her nose. She patted her hair, checking to see that it remained in place. When ready, she looked at Nigel, who remained in a daze.

"I can't account for it," he said. "Perhaps I misinterpreted the vision."

"If so, we can be glad you did."

****

Annabelle began to prepare a breakfast of flapjacks and bacon. Nigel felt pity, given her sprained ankle, and offered his help. The two prepared the meal while Edgar washed himself and changed his clothes. During the repast, Edgar related the events. Following which, he shook his head in dismay. "Everyone and everything had it in for me. What did your vision show?"

Nigel set aside his coffee, raised his head, and looked at the ceiling—bare boards and crossbeams. An old water stain on the ceiling looked like the face of an angry old man with a beard. That you, God? Nigel wondered. He lowered his gaze to Edgar and shrugged. "I saw you being choked, the flash of gunfire, and the snarling face of a demonic wolf. It appears I had the abridged form of your festivities."

"You didn't actually see me die?" Edgar stared at him gravely. His eyebrows knit together.

"No," Nigel answered. "Only those images. I assumed the worst when I found the body. I came back and told Annie. I'm glad I was mistaken."

"So am I," said Edgar.

Annabelle put a hand on Edgar's arm. "When Nigel went off to look for you, I couldn't sleep for worry and prayed you both would be all right."

"I thank you for your prayers," said Edgar. "Perhaps they helped. Perhaps dumb luck. I'm not a religious man, but a phrase keeps going through my mind, 'There but by the grace of God.' Whatever the source of my good fortune, I am grateful to be here." Edgar yawned, and the other two echoed with those of their own. "Given that I spent a sleepless night in a tree,

I need to get some rest. I want to be a part of the hunt tonight. I've got payback in mind." He leaned across the table and regarded Nigel and Annabelle. "Looks like you two need shut-eye as well. Where's Professor James and Sarah?"

"Don't know," said Nigel. "I assume they're still casting bullets. They never returned last night."

"Casting metal can be tricky. I promised to spell them, but I'm just not up to it. I hope they'll understand."

Edgar groaned as he stood, holding his injured ribs, and slowly walked from the room.

Annabelle began gathering the plates and silverware together. Nigel put his hand over hers, and this time she did not jerk it away. "I'll clean," he said.

"Mr. Pickford, you are a gentleman and a scholar." She smiled, squeezed his hand, and rose with some awkwardness from the table. She then put a crutch beneath each arm and hobbled away.

Nigel looked at the dirty plates before him. "So much for gallantry," he mumbled.

****

Instead of washing the dishes, Nigel nodded off at the table for several hours. A thumping on the door awakened him.

"Professor, is it you?" Nigel called when he went to the door. He had braced the door again before falling asleep.

"Yes," came the muffled voice. "Please be good enough to open the door!"

Nigel removed the chair and held open the door.

Professor James stood on the stoop with Sarah in his arms. The late afternoon sun shone behind them.

Sarah appeared to be sleeping, and for his part, Professor James looked exhausted, with dark circles under his eyes.

"Sarah hasn't yet recovered from a trance last evening," Professor James said in a low voice.

Nigel nodded and assisted Professor James in getting Sarah into her room. They placed a quilted comforter over her and turned from the bed to see Edgar and Annabelle standing in the bedroom doorway. Professor James put a finger to his lips and then motioned for them to leave.

They all went into the living room.

As they entered, Professor James went to the table, lifted one of his books from where it lay on a corner, and then slammed it down. "Doctor Gilpin," he said, still looking at the book, "could you have forgotten your commitment to giving us some respite from the casting process, which only just finished?" He turned to confront Edgar and saw the man's face was bruised, swollen, and lacerated. "What the devil?" he exclaimed and then stepped over to Edgar and braced him by grabbing each shoulder. Professor James's face showed real concern. "My apologies. You are hurt."

Edgar shook his head. "My injuries are nothing. I feel fortunate to have escaped the werewolf with my life. I climbed a tree and was there all night."

Professor James looked shocked. "You escaped the beast? I need to know every detail. It appears neither of us has had an easy go of it." He indicated they all should sit. Edgar recounted his narrow escape, Cicero's death, and confirmed traditional bullets did not affect the creature. He described the werewolf's appearance, emphasizing its size and glowing red eyes. Professor

James bombarded him with questions. Those involving Saphne caused Edgar to mumble and look uncomfortable, more so than when he described his escape from the beast.

Nigel broke into a laugh, inferring what may have happened between Edgar and Saphne.

"I fail to see the humor in almost getting killed," Edgar responded.

"No," said Professor James, "nothing funny about that."

Professor James recounted his own experiences, including witnessing the horrible accident, Sarah's channeling the victim and getting his permission to recover the silver, and then the morbid task of cutting the silver from the unfortunate man's body. Before Nigel or Annabelle could share anything, Professor James yanked his watch from his vest, viewed the time, and snapped it closed. "It's after four, and I need to head back into town. There are things to do before the hunt. Given everyone's condition, it looks like I'll go alone."

Edgar, despite his infirmities, rose. "I'll not miss a chance to strike back at the creature."

Professor James scrutinized him for several seconds and then nodded. He turned to Nigel. "Are you, sir, willing to man the fort, so to speak?"

Nigel weighed the options. He considered insisting on going on the hunt too, not wishing to be upstaged by Edgar, then acquiesced. Tramping through the woods in the dark with a band of armed coloreds did not appeal to him. He stood, then nodded. "All right. Makes sense, should the Klan return, that a white man is here."

Edgar glared at Nigel and took a step in his

direction. "Hold on. You implying I can't stand up to a bunch of crackers in bedsheets?"

Nigel couldn't help himself and took the bait. "I am. They're less apt to cause a fuss if I meet them than you."

Edgar balled his fists and took another step toward Nigel. "Perhaps you can throw on a bedsheet so you can fit right in?"

Professor James stepped between the two with a hand held before each. "Gentlemen. Let's not give them the satisfaction of us tearing ourselves to pieces. You are both able and brave. Edgar, I've seen it numerous times over the past year, and you evidenced it just last night."

"He ran and then hid in a tree," said Nigel.

"Sensible," opined the professor. "Which is why he's here today." He turned to face Nigel. "Our acquaintance has been considerably shorter, but you showed your true colors in Nantucket. Please..." He took a breath and looked from one to the other. "Put down your dukes."

First, Edgar lowered his fists, then Nigel.

"Thank you, both." Professor James and Edgar went to the door.

"Should we be worried about Sarah?" asked Annabelle.

The professor turned back and shook his head. "I don't believe so. She seems to be resting. The channeling upset her, and she needs the rest. However, do check in on her."

Professor James and Edgar went outside, leaving the door open behind them. Less than a minute later, Nigel heard Professor James shout to the horse and

157

shake the reins. The wagon drove off.

"What was that all about with Edgar?" asked Annabelle as she tottered over to him.

Nigel grinned. "I touched a nerve."

"You alternate between coming to his defense and nearly coming to blows. You risked your life on his behalf last night, yet you try to humiliate him because he climbed a tree."

He dismissed her concerns with a wave of the hand, then shut the door. He turned to her and smiled lecherously. "Once again, Annie, we find ourselves in favorable circumstances."

"I agree."

Nigel did a double-take. *Could she be serious?* She had just been criticizing him. Had she been seduced by his clumsy attempts at charm and innuendo these past few weeks? There must be some mistake. Now he appeared to have her, but he wasn't sure what to do. He felt nervous. "I beg your pardon?"

"It's a favorable time to try hypnosis again." She beamed her beautiful smile, and his smile wilted. "We hit on something last night. It terrified you and made you want to escape. The fact you then had a vision of Edgar and the wolf made your desire to escape even more compelling and clouded my analysis," Annabelle continued. "We also saw the pernicious effects of all this when you collapsed in the field the other day. I'm convinced hypnosis is key to understanding your visions—why their character changed from helping you and benefiting others to seeing unavoidable tragedies."

Nigel sat at the table. He put his hands over his face, covering both eyes, and moaned. This wasn't about seduction. It concerned the albatross he had been carrying for a score of years. This group had lifted him from the gutter and offered him hope. How could he say no?

He sat in silence for some time. "All right," he muttered from behind his hands.

He kept his eyes covered, listening to Annabelle hobble over to the table and sit down opposite him. He heard her strike a lucifer on the wooden tabletop and could smell the sulfur from the match head. It made his nose twitch. He heard her lighting the lamp: lifting the globe from its stand, the squeak of the knob as she raised the wick, and the sound of her replacing the globe. *Why did she light a lamp in the late afternoon? It won't be dark for hours.*

As if she read his mind, Annabelle said, "The lamp will help focus your attention. Should it become dark before we're through, I won't need to interrupt our session to light it." She slid it over the tabletop next to Nigel, and he could see red slivers of light between his fingers. Then Annabelle gently pulled his hands from his face.

She looked at him with concern. "You are safe here. I will be with you the entire time. If anything becomes too much to bear, you may break off as before. Understood?"

Nigel looked her straight in her eyes and nodded. Sweat sprang from his pores. He loosened his tie until it came undone, unbuttoned the top two buttons of his shirt, and ran a hand through his hair.

"Stop fussing," Annabelle told him. She had him sit up and stare into her eyes, as before, while taking slow deep breaths. Her voice droned on, and she told him to close his eyes when he felt ready. At length, he did so.

Chapter Twenty

Nigel felt his mare shift beneath the saddle, anxious about the coming battle. He was anxious too. Nigel saw Corporal Archibald Smith approach, illuminated by both the moon and a burning farmhouse in the distance. The missing half of Corporal Smith's skull exposed a glistening brain. Nigel yanked the reins on his horse to move away, but Smith grabbed the horse's bridle. "It's a trap, sir," he said.

"No," came Annabelle's disembodied voice, "go back further. To before your abilities changed. *What caused the change?*"

"I can't," said Nigel.

"*Yes, you can.* Don't allow fear to hold you back. I shall be with you."

"I can't," he repeated, then added, "Wait, I—yes, I believe I might..."

"Go on," said Annabelle.

Images flooded Nigel's mind. He returned to the same battlefield, on the frosty morning before dawn, on March 25, 1865, but it was before the vision of his troops becoming mangled and eviscerated. He sat on horseback with his men on foot around him, poised, waiting for the signal to attack. Nigel breathed in the cold spring air scented with smoke. He could hear gunfire off in the distance, from the main thrust of the attack on Fort Stedman. Nigel felt more nervous about

161

this encounter—more so than any engagement he'd had in the war. No visions had preceded this day to guide his actions. For the first time, he and his men were fighting blind.

Nigel studied the burning farmhouse in the distance, wondering which side had set it alight. He stared into the flames, transfixed.

With abruptness, it became daytime. Nigel looked up but could not find the sun, only a gray overcast sky. He glanced around. His men had disappeared—all of them. In the distance, the farmhouse stood whole. *A vision?* he wondered.

"Not like any vision you've had, heretofore," said a melodious voice with a slight French accent. "It's my vision for you."

Nigel looked around again. A voluptuous blonde-haired woman stood before him, patting his horse's head. Her bright green eyes regarded him, and she gave him a full-lipped smile broad with good-humor. "Lieutenant Pickford," she said, "so good of you to come! I'm Monique Dubois."

"What's happening? Where are my men?"

"Not to worry. They will keep."

Nigel climbed off his horse, and the woman came around to meet him. He made a slight frown as he recalled her. "I've seen you before, but always in the distance, watching me."

She nodded. "When I've chosen to show myself."

"But when I've approached, you always disappeared."

The woman smiled and fluttered her eyelashes. "I'm a bit of a tease."

"What's happening?" Nigel asked, instinctively

taking a step back.

She stepped closer. "I've chosen you."

"For what?"

"Come." The woman took Nigel's hand.

The touch triggered a response like a bolt of lightning. Attraction to this woman seared through him, coursing through his blood from head to toe. Any misgivings evaporated. Never had he encountered a woman so alluring, so suited to him. His penis became swollen and hard. Nigel embraced her.

She pushed him back with a laugh. "Not just yet," she cooed. She broke free of his embrace, ran a few steps, then returned to take his hand and pull him in the direction of the farmhouse. "Come!"

Hand in hand, they ran to the two-story house with the gingerbread woodwork, laughing. Nigel gave a half-hearted glance back at his horse and saw it contentedly cropping at the hillside's green grass.

Monique threw open the door to the house and pulled him across the threshold, a tidy place with a cheery fire in the hearth. Comfortable furniture filled the room. Ahead, on the dining table, a feast awaited: Suckling pig, roast chicken, greens, butter, biscuits, fresh fruit, gravy, and several bottles of wine, all set by candlelight.

Monique bade him sit while she stood next to him and poured red wine into two crystal goblets. She gave one to Nigel and stroked his cheek. "To us," she said in a merry voice and clinked her glass to Nigel's. They drank. Nigel gulped his wine and set the goblet on the table before him.

He grabbed Monique and pulled her onto his lap. She laughed and managed to avoid spilling the rest of her wine. She set her glass next to his, turned back to him, and said, "Well, all right. We'll eat later." She kissed him, pressing her soft lips to his and then opening her mouth. He did the same, and her tongue darted between his teeth and withdrew, then again, toying with him. Her scent made him heady. She stroked his face, and then her hands found other areas. Nigel's passion grew.

He lifted her into his arms, and they made their way to the bedroom. He had never been with a woman, but Monique taught him what she wanted, and he brought her to a climax three times. His orgasm, far more exciting than anything accomplished on his own, happened early, but Monique didn't seem to mind since he was motivated to please.

As they lay exhausted on the sheets, Monique turned to him and stroked his face. "I have chosen well."

Nigel frowned. "What does that mean?"

"All in good time. First, it appears you've pitched another tent." She indicated where the sheet rose halfway down the bed. She hummed "Tenting Tonight" as she reached under the sheet and took hold of him.

****

Days passed in a haze of sex, food, wine, and walks through the fields in weather warm for March. Though the temperature remained pleasant as they walked hand in hand, the sun never appeared in the overcast sky. She put off his questions, always with the promise to reveal everything in good time. Finally, during one such walk, Nigel stopped and pulled Monique to him and said, "Enough of this."

Monique played coy. "Have you tired of me, Mr.

Pickford?"

Nigel smiled at her upturned face, taking in her striking green eyes, smooth soft skin, full lips, and perfect teeth. "I doubt I shall ever tire of you. But I'm tired of you dodging every question I pose. I want some answers. Now."

Monique stroked his cheek with her fingers, and Nigel was filled with the desire to kiss her—even to ravage her—right now, in the middle of this field. Instead, he pushed her away and shook his head.

"Enough!"

"All right."

Nigel looked at her with furrowed brows. "All right?"

"Yes. It's time. This has been a test. I have taken lovers before, many through the years, but they never broke the spell to confront me as an equal. As such, I tired of them. But you are a remarkable man, Nigel Pickford, one who could be my partner in all things. I have chosen well."

Nigel paced back and forth, flattening the grass underfoot, trying to take in what she said. *So, I'm not the first.* Well, he had figured. But many lovers? How could that be? She did not seem much older than his twenty years.

"Are you a prostitute?"

She laughed and shook her head. "I am a witch."

Nigel stopped his pacing and frowned. "Enough jokes."

Monique's face became serious. "I am a witch. Seventy-seven years old. You are indeed with an older woman."

Nigel shook his head. "I asked you to speak

straight."

"And I am doing so."

"What proof have you?"

"Look around. I created this for you—for us—so we might get to know one another. And, like I said, as a test."

"Have I passed?"

Monique nodded and took his hand. "Though it took a while, you broke free of my love spell. You are the first to question and confront me. That's why I have chosen you."

"Chosen me for what?"

"In good time. Haven't you learned enough for now?"

Nigel pulled on her hand and brought her to within a few inches. "All of it. I need to know all."

Monique smiled and kissed him. She seemed somehow pleased by this. She slipped from his grasp, then reached back and took his hand. "Let's return to the house. It's a long story, and I'd like to wet my whistle. I shall tell you all."

The two returned to the house. The dining table was once again resplendent with fresh food and drink. Nigel realized he had been in such a fog, he had not questioned how the food appeared. *Where were the cooks? The other help to tend to the house and the farm?*

Could her story be true?

The two sat next to each other at one end of the large table. Monique poured herself a glass of white wine and was about to fill Nigel's glass, but he put a hand over it and shook his head. "I'd like to keep my wits about me if you don't mind." Instead, he took a red apple from a bowl of fruit and bit into its crisp flesh. He spoke with his mouth full. "Please continue."

Monique finished her glass and refilled it. She leaned back in her chair and smiled.

"I came into this world on March 21, 1788, in New Orleans, while much of the city burned in the Great Fire. Our house, though bordering the fire on Place d' Armes, remained unscathed. I came to understand this was no accident.

"My father worked as a sugar and slave broker, and we lived well. My parents hired a nanny, a white woman—unusual for the time, but again, no accident—named Genevieve. Both my nanny and my mother—when I saw her—were kind and nurturing. My busy father, I rarely saw. At the age of six, another fire struck the city. I was terrified, but Genevieve told me to have no fear. She told me I was special, and fire could not harm me. I soon discovered her lie when I stuck my index finger into a candle's flame. What I didn't realize then was that Genevieve protected our house, as she protected me.

"The years passed. At seventeen, I attended the city's debutante ball. Many men asked me to dance. As the evening wore on, a charming young soldier, Corporal Andrew Melancamp, monopolized my attention. I didn't mind. As I said, he was charming. At the end of the evening, he kissed my hand and asked if he might call on me in the future. I told him I would enjoy that and looked forward to the next time we'd meet.

"At home, as I lay abed, reflecting on the evening and Corporal Melancamp, Genevieve entered my room without a knock. Startled, I sat up, clutching the bedclothes to my chin. We had kept Genevieve on, now as a chaperone, but not since I was very young had she come unbidden into my room.

" 'Relax, my sweet Monique,' she said as she fetched the night candle and a chair from the vanity across the room. She set the candle on the nightstand and settled in the chair next to the bed. 'We must discuss your future.'

" 'Why shouldn't this keep 'til morning?'

" 'We need privacy, and your young corporal will be calling on you tomorrow.'

"I'm sure I looked shocked. 'You know about him?' I asked.

" 'My dear,' she said, 'I've known everything about you since the day you were born. It is time for you to make a choice.'

" 'A choice?'

" 'You have reached the age of consent, and now must decide which path you shall tread. You may lead a normal life with a husband and children of your own if you wish. You may find happiness and grow old together.'

"I studied Genevieve's face as she said this and realized she had not changed—hadn't aged at all in the years I had known her.

" 'Or,' continued Genevieve, 'you may choose to follow the order—the Daughters of Cain—and assume your rightful place as one of the most powerful women in the world.'

"She had baited the hook and put it before me. To have such power intrigued me. She set the hook further.

"Genevieve described this group, an ancient association more commonly known as witches. She said only certain individuals possessed the gifts allowing them to become a witch, and even still, it would require many years of training.

"I made my choice and told her. The corporal, while handsome, had not yet captured my heart, and I was fascinated, as I hope you shall be, at the prospect of such power."

Nigel interrupted. "This order accepts men and women?"

Monique nodded. "Indeed, they do. Both sexes have been followers and leaders."

"And you see something in me?" he asked.

"Your visions marked you as a strong candidate. I have watched how you have used them to keep you and your men safe during the war. The fact you are handsome is a bonus I must say I've enjoyed."

"You were seventeen. I am twenty. Why was I not approached earlier?"

Monique smiled. "We, rather, I have been watching and waiting for the appropriate time."

"Huh." Nigel considered the implications of what she had been telling him. He gestured at the feast before him. "Is any of this real?"

"For our purposes, yes."

"Could we stay here forever?"

Monique laughed. "Why should we want to? Once you have learned to use your talents, you and I could rule the world." Her voice took on a hard edge. "Men, women, and nations will be our playthings."

"We could end this damn war?"

"If we chose."

"Such power exists?"

"I assure you it does. But what's important is I

need and want a partner. That you should be my lover makes you even more appealing."

"Then, I say yes."

Monique bolted upright in her chair. "Just like that?"

Nigel grinned. "Just like that."

Monique stroked his face, and Nigel took her hand, kissed it, and then stood.

"You don't need to work your magic," he said. "I want to be with you."

Ecstatic, Monique threw her arms around Nigel and kissed him with abandon. Her tongue entered his mouth and met his. She then sucked his tongue into her mouth. He loved her taste, her feel, her passion. Monique jumped up and wrapped her legs around his midsection. As she kissed and clung to him, Nigel steered them to the bedroom. His head swam with feelings of lust, love, and power.

****

"Good morning," said Monique when Nigel's eyes opened.

"Is it?"

Monique looked hurt. "Is it *good*?"

Nigel shook his head on the pillow. "Is it morning? I can't tell."

"Yes, but it can be any time you wish."

"Morning is good—especially with you," he added to make amends. Now he stroked her face, copying her love-spell gesture.

"Mmmm." Monique smiled. "Today, we begin your training." She followed her statement with a kiss.

"I thought you didn't age?"

"What!" Monique pushed him away with a look of

shock.

"Hold on," said Nigel trying to take her back into his arms. "It's just there are some crows' feet at the corner of your eyes when you smile. I haven't noticed them before, but they're quite fetching."

Monique rose, naked, from the bed and went to the mirror above the bureau. She examined her eyes, then cupped her hands beneath her sagging breasts.

"Monique?" inquired Nigel, worried.

An old woman turned from the mirror. Her hair grew gray as he watched. Wattles now hung from beneath each of her upper arms. Her shoulders and spine slumped in a stoop.

Monique waved a gnarled hand, and without warning, Nigel could no longer move. She came over to the bed, her face now wizened and worn. She raised the crooked fingers of her right hand, whose joints looked swollen with arthritis, and closed Nigel's eyes.

Blackness.

****

A child's shrieking caused Nigel to fight his way back to consciousness, though his mind remained clouded with Monique's spell. His jumbled thoughts refused to focus, and he slid back into the inky darkness several times, but each time the child's cries brought him around.

Nigel struggled to open his eyes and managed a crack. Through the slits of his eyelids, he saw daylight or some facsimile. He still lay on the bed with the door to the room shut.

It came again, faint but distinctive, the cry of a child in distress. A primal response drove him to investigate.

Nigel forced his legs over the side of the bed and used their weight to help him sit. He rubbed his eyes and shook his head to clear his vision and thoughts.

He rose on unsteady bare legs and became aware of his nakedness. Nevertheless, he stumbled to the door and tried the knob. Locked. Nigel swung around and nearly fell. He righted himself, staggered to the bed, and sprawled across the top. He fought the desire to succumb to sleep.

Instead, he climbed off the bed and went to the window, which stood open several inches. The screams became louder. They had to be from outside.

His lieutenant's uniform and boots lay scattered at the foot of the bed, and he donned them as quick as he could. The boots he'd inherited from Lieutenant Thaddeus Faringsworth when a cannonball had taken off the man's head at the Battle of Belle Grove. The soles had developed a hole Nigel patched each day with playing cards from an old deck he kept in his pocket. Today, he didn't take the time.

The child's voice became hoarse, but it continued to scream.

His mind became clearer, and he felt sturdier on his feet. He went to the window, shoved the curtains aside, and raised the sash. An empty farmyard stretched to the barn.

The barn!

Nigel worked his left leg through the open window. He followed with his head and torso and then his right leg. The ground lay farther away than anticipated, and Nigel tumbled to the earth in a heap. Righting himself, he ran around to the main door of the barn. As he did so, a sharp pebble jammed through the hole in his boot.

He winced, then swore as the rock bit into his foot but did not stop to remove it.

The child's cries rose in intensity, then abruptly ended. Fear gnawed at him as he limped as fast as he could the rest of the way. He drew to a stop a few feet inside the barn.

Monique and the child were within, but the sight caused him to recoil. He tripped and fell, then bent over double and vomited onto the fresh straw before him. Nigel continued to scramble back, crab-like, then stood and ran from the barn.

He fled across the field, ascending the hill. Monique appeared before him, naked and beautiful once more. "Darling, I did not want you to see that. You're not ready. Please come back to the house." She lifted her hand to stroke his cheek. Nigel shoved her aside and continued running up the hill toward his horse, unmindful of the pain in his foot.

When he got to the mare, Nigel struggled for breath, both from exertion and fighting back tears. The horse still wore the saddle and tack it had when they arrived, but it did not look in distress. Nigel put his foot in the stirrup and swung himself onto the saddle.

Once more, Monique appeared before him. "Darling, we belong—"

"*No!*" he yelled, cutting her off. "I want nothing more to do with you!"

"You can't leave." Not a plea, a threat. Her voice now hard, flinty.

Nigel could not be cowed. "I'll not be your partner in anything, should you force me to stay."

Monique's face turned blood red and twisted with rage. "All right, go," she hissed, "but you shall never really escape. You'll come back, begging for my good graces, like a sniveling dog. In the meantime—my parting gift—you shall be a modern Cassandra. Your visions will foresee tragedies, but you'll be incapable of preventing them." Monique's baleful laugh continued for several seconds after she disappeared until it too faded away along with the light.

In the sudden darkness around him, Nigel heard the murmur of many low voices and the metallic clinks of weapons being readied for action.

He blinked several times until his eyes became accustomed to the dark. He remained on the same hill, but now his troops stood around him, shortly before entering the battle. In the distance, fire consumed the farmhouse he had shared with Monique—For how long? he wondered. The fire's light and the moon provided a faint illumination of the men around him. He could hear the fighting a mile away at Fort Stedman in the center of an arc of forts and parapets. Time for Nigel's soldiers to move against a fort on the Union flank, Fort Haskell.

Nigel raised his arm to signal the attack but stopped short. In a panic, he glanced back and forth at his men—all of whom appeared disfigured.

Seventeen-year-old Tim Hayton whimpered as he tried to hold in guts spilling from his abdomen. He looked at Nigel in anguish. "Why'd you let us die, Lieutenant?"

Corporal Archibald Smith emerged from the shadows, the left half of his skull gone. Blood spilled from the cavity where his gray brain glistened and throbbed in the flickering light. "It's a trap, sir."

"Lieutenant Pickford!" General Evans spat fire as

he rode through Nigel's men, who had suddenly returned to normal. Following the general were two aides-de-camp. "Why the devil do you not advance as ordered? We are waiting to follow!"

Still stunned by his vision, Nigel echoed Corporal Smith, "It's a trap, sir."

"Speak up."

"It's a trap."

"I don't care if the gates of Hell await you. You were ordered to advance, and you'll damn well do so. Gordon has opened a hole in the Union line. We need to support his flank. Move out!"

"I can't do that, sir."

The general drew his revolver and leveled it at Nigel's skull. "You will proceed as ordered, or I'll find some other bastard who will."

An outcry sprang from among Nigel's men. "We ain't afraid, sir!" Corporal Smith told the general, "And neither is our lieutenant. He just gave us the signal to advance before you arrived." Everyone shouted in affirmation.

"Very well." The general lowered his pistol. "Proceed, Lieutenant."

The corporal grabbed the reins to Nigel's horse and led him forward into the valley of death. The rest of the men followed....

****

Nigel opened his eyes and shoved the lamp away. Across the table sat Annabelle, regarding him as though he were some sort of exotic bug, and she a naturalist. Will I be skewered with a pin and put on display? he wondered.

He took a deep breath and said, "My men died in

the manner I had foreseen. I could do nothing to save them. And Monique has cursed me to this day."

Nigel shoved the chair away from the table and stood. "Did you find what you were looking for? Was the experiment a success?" he asked, his voice testy.

"I'm trying to help you find some answers." Annabelle's voice remained neutral.

"The answer is I've been cursed."

"But you knew that. You described your abilities as such several times. You *had* blocked Monique from your memory. You've made a big step. But you left out a critical piece."

"Did my carnal story shock you? It's pure fiction." Nigel grinned at her. "I have a vivid imagination."

Annabelle continued to speak in a calm voice Nigel found infuriating. "You are lying now," she said. "When hypnotized, people tell the truth."

"What do you want from me?" screamed Nigel, surprising himself with the passion behind his words. He saw Sarah had awakened and stood at the edge of the room.

"I want you to discover the truth, all of it," Annabelle said in an even tone. "That is how we heal ourselves—by confronting our demons."

"The cure is worse than the disease."

"Is it?" Annabelle struggled to her feet. "You have been suffering under this spell for twenty years, and it destroyed your life. When we found you, you lived in the gutter."

"I have already expressed my gratitude," he said in a sullen voice.

"Another thing," she said, "your vision of Edgar did not prove accurate."

Nigel turned away and faced the door. Part of him wanted to escape, to run from this place and never come back. Instead, he mumbled, "I misinterpreted it."

"It seems the calamities of your visions may be avoided after all. Perhaps you are breaking free of the curse."

Nigel turned back to face her. "If only that were true."

"What did you see in the barn?"

"I can't remember." Nigel glanced up out of exasperation and again saw the image of an angry God in the watermarks on the ceiling. He looked away, feeling guilty.

"Search the recesses of your mind. If you wish, I can hypnotize you again."

Nigel came forward and gripped the edge of the table. "*I can't—*" he cried.

Annabelle mirrored Nigel by gripping the edge of the table before her. "*You can!*"

Nigel stared at the lamp before him so long it hurt his eyes. He then squeezed his eyelids shut as tears streamed from their corners. His voice sounded hushed, almost inaudible.

"When I entered the barn, I saw a child, a three or four-year-old, trussed up and hanging by her feet from a beam, like a deer being dressed. The old woman—Monique—had a knife in one hand, and she—she—"

Nigel collapsed to his knees, still holding the edge of the table, as his face shook in anguish. Annabelle worked her way around to him, knelt, and then cradled his head against her bosom, Madonna-like.

"Tell me what you saw," she said, her voice cracking, betraying the horror she knew would come.

Nigel threw his arms around Annabelle and sobbed into her chest, "Monique was showering in the child's blood!"

Chapter Twenty-One

"No, sir," said Edgar, shaking his head. He and Professor James had argued for several minutes while the draft horse drank its fill from the trough outside Petersburg's Courthouse.

Professor James persisted. "While you report Cicero's death, I'll go to the asylum to visit the reverend's cook. I want to see if something substantive lay behind her ravings at last night's meeting. I need to establish this before tonight's hunt, which will begin in just a few hours."

Edgar continued to object. "Cicero may have loved ones missing him, but I'm not willing to discuss his murder with anyone in the sheriff's office. They'd sooner lock me up and announce the case solved. Northern police might even do the same. It doesn't matter that I'm educated. Authorities often take pleasure in going after Negroes who have risen above their station. You're a white man of means. It's different when you're colored. Especially in the South."

Professor James considered this in silence. "Perhaps we could work through Reverend Green," he said. "The reverend might know his family. He could also find a way to report it to the authorities."

Edgar nodded. "That's more to my liking."

"Do you wish to accompany me to the asylum?"

"Why are you asking? I agreed to come to town

with you. I assumed we would stay together. Would you rather interview her alone?"

"I'd appreciate your company. Your impressions might prove helpful. On the other hand, illnesses of the mind can make many people uncomfortable. You've already been through a lot." Professor James pointed at Edgar's hands, which shook with a small tremor since his encounter with the werewolf.

"Lunacy will pale in comparison to last night," Edgar said, trying to sound strong. He removed his hat and turned his face into the evening sun with a wan smile. It's good to be alive, he told himself, trying to drive away the recurring thought of him firing his derringer into the snarling mouth of the werewolf. Edgar replaced his hat, then looked at his hands and clenched them tight, stilling the shakes.

Sniffing audibly, he looked up from his hands and saw Saphne approaching along the walkway where they first met. She carried the same basket, this time filled with a long loaf of bread, a catfish, and some vegetables. With her eyes downcast, she seemed almost in a trance.

Edgar turned from Professor James, jumped from the wagon, and ran to her. He doffed his hat.

"Saphne?"

Saphne seemed to snap into awareness and looked startled to see Edgar standing before her. She burst into tears. "You're alive!" Saphne sobbed. She dropped her basket, scattering its contents, and held both hands to her mouth. "I heard they found a body near Garraty's place and feared the worst."

She wiped her cheeks with the back of one hand and smiled despite the tears. For a moment, she appeared happy. Then she turned her head aside, but not before Edgar saw her bruised and swollen eye.

Edgar's heart dropped. "Saphne?" His mind raced with sympathy for her and self-recrimination. He reached toward her arm, but she jerked it away.

"Don't touch me."

Edgar's voice became harsh. "He did this to you?"

"What do you think?" she huffed. "That and a whole lot more."

"What do you mean?"

"You're the great man of learning," said Saphne, "figure it out."

Oh, God, thought Edgar. I saved her from one monster by delivering her into the hands of another. "I'm going to kill him," he growled.

Saphne turned to him and frowned. "No, you're not. I need this job." Then her expression softened some, but this emphasized the fact that one eye remained swollen shut. "I see you're hurt too. I'm glad you survived the bogeywolf."

Edgar reached for her again, and this time she let him touch her arm. "Come away with me," he said. "We'll go up north. It's not perfect, but a damn sight better. I don't care what has happened to you."

At this, she shook herself free and frowned once more. "You don't care what happened to me?"

"I didn't mean—" Edgar stammered. "I meant it doesn't change how I feel about you. I love you."

"Oh, Edgar." It sounded as though she pitied him. Saphne bent over and righted her basket. She raised her head and looked at him with the one good eye.

"Come away with me," he repeated.

"I ain't leavin' Petersburg. I got my momma and

two little brothers to look after." She stood and shook her head. "Momma is sick and can't travel. Why would you burden yourself with all that?"

Edgar took a deep breath and set his shoulders. "I could teach at Howard University. Come here on the weekends."

Saphne looked stunned. Slowly her lips parted in a beautiful smile. "You'd do that for me?"

"I said, I love you."

Saphne threw her arms around him. The pressure hurt his injured ribs, but he hugged her as well. A momentous decision that just struck him, but he'd do it. They could have a life together, and she could be free of Garraty. They kissed, and Edgar swelled with desire and pride.

Professor James drove the wagon alongside them and cleared his throat. They disengaged and turned to look.

"Sorry to intrude," said Professor James, "but time is of the essence." He drove the wagon ten feet up the road and waited.

Still holding her arms, Edgar stepped back and looked at her injured face. "I don't want you going there."

Saphne moved away and slipped from his arms. She patted her hair and straightened herself. "He's not going to be bothering me, looking as I do. I'm safe for a while."

"But why go there at all, risking yourself and knowing how I feel?"

"I heard what you said. It warmed my heart, but we hardly know each other, and men have a reputation of saying anything to get what they want."

"I'm not like that. I'm steadfast. What about last night—before things turned bad?"

"You sleep on it," said Saphne laying a hand on his chest. "Think on everything you're committin' to. If you feel the same tomorrow, meet me here at this time and let's talk." She touched his cheek with her free hand. "Till then, I gotta job to keep. Don't fret. Nothin's gonna happen tonight."

"I'm not so sure."

Saphne pulled her hand from Edgar's chest and held it before her as she stepped away, not wanting him to follow. "You ain't the only one who's steadfast. Good evening, Doctor Gilpin."

"Be safe."

"I intend to." Saphne recovered her basket and strode away.

He watched as she moved along the brick walkway that circled city hall, turned at the corner, and disappeared. He returned to the wagon, and Professor James shook the reins.

"I'm considering staying," Edgar announced a few minutes later.

Professor James continued looking at the road ahead. "I'll be sorry to lose you," he said, "but you have a powerful incentive to stay." He shook the reins again to move the horse along. "What did she say to this news?"

"Told me to sleep on it."

Professor James turned and smiled at Edgar, then returned his attention to what lay ahead. "Beauty and brains," he said. "Yes, that's a powerful incentive."

As they drove along, the air seemed to grow more humid. Edgar saw the sky above remained clear, but a bank of thunderheads lurked on the horizon.

On the outskirts of town, they came upon a long gravel drive with a brass sign on a post announcing the Central Lunatic Asylum for the Colored Insane. They turned up the drive and soon approached an impressive three-story red brick building with granite trim. The grounds showed evidence of construction: piles of debris, stacks of bricks, and churned earth. But elsewhere showed signs of recent landscaping, including new grass, small shrubbery, and flowers. A team of colored people raked one area of bare earth as Professor James and Edgar rode by. The workers regarded them with curiosity.

After parking the wagon and tending to the horse, Professor James and Edgar ascended the broad steps and entered the building's double doors. Inside, a marble foyer smelled of fresh paint. A few paint cans and a drop cloth sat in a corner. Across from the entrance, a colored woman waited behind an oak desk. She wore a dark blue uniform with a white pinafore. She peered up from a book and smiled in greeting, her mouth full of crooked teeth. In other respects, the woman looked quite attractive, with full lips and dark brown eyes.

"I'm Professor William James of Harvard, and this is my associate, Doctor Edgar Gilpin. We would like to speak to the director."

The receptionist gestured to a door to her right. "Director" was outlined on the frosted glass of the door, but only the D had been painted-in. Inside, they found another woman, this one white, of late middle-age and with her gray hair in a tight bun. She looked tired as she put a second arm through a light blue jacket and snatched a pair of white gloves and her handbag from the top of a desk.

Professor James made introductions and requested to meet with the director.

"Rather late to be dropping by. You don't have an appointment."

"No," said Professor James, "I beg your pardon, but we are pressed for time, and I must speak to him."

The woman gave Professor James a thin smile and put on her gloves. "I'm the secretary to Dr. Rouse. The director has left for the day. As I said, it's rather late. I need to get home to supper." She collected her handbag and took a step toward the door. She turned back and smiled again, without any warmth or humor.

Edgar could feel himself getting angry. Professor James, however, turned on the charm.

He bowed and gave her a disarming smile. "I wouldn't dream of detaining you longer than necessary. I'm afraid this is quite urgent. Is there someone who could take us to have a brief conversation with one of your patients?"

The secretary's eyebrows arched. "Who do you wish to see?"

"Marie Dubois, who you took on as a patient only today."

"Oh, her." The woman rolled her eyes. "You won't get anything from her. She just babbles on and on. Crazy as a loon."

"Please. It's of the utmost importance, or I wouldn't dream of imposing upon you."

The secretary relented and waved a white-gloved hand in the direction they had come. "You could see the Assistant Medical Director. His office is on the other side of the foyer."

"One last thing," said Professor James, "if you would indulge me. I'm curious about what you have on display here." On either side of the office stood long glass cases filled with dozens of musical instruments: violins, clarinets, trumpets, and many more. They all looked new.

The secretary beamed with pride. "Oh, those were gifts to the hospital by Dorothea Dix when she visited us in our old location. We are quite proud of them."

"Are they ever played?" asked Edgar.

The secretary pursed her lips and answered while looking at Professor James. "We tried. On the very first day, a patient broke a violin over the back of a chair. Those who are musical are allowed access to other instruments. Now, I must be going." She shooed them from the office, locked the door, and left the building without another word.

Edgar glanced at the receptionist, who stood at her desk, smiling her snaggle-toothed smile. "The Assistant Medical Director?" he asked.

The woman gestured at another door across the foyer. Edgar realized she had not spoken either time. A patient? he wondered.

He and Professor James entered through a door marked "Administration." The waiting area inside featured an empty secretarial desk in the center with four office doors on the wall behind. One of the doors stood open.

"Hello?" called Professor James.

"Yes, hello." A bald white man with a fringe of gray hair and rimless spectacles emerged from the room. He wore a white lab coat over a dark suit.

Professor James introduced them both, and the doctor seemed impressed. He came around the desk with his hand held out in greeting.

"Doctor Victor Potok," he said to Professor James, shaking his hand. "I'm honored to meet you." He gave a perfunctory nod to Edgar. The doctor spoke with a thick Alabaman accent. "If you are hoping for a tour of our new facility, I won't be able to help, and the rest of the administrative staff have gone home. I'm the Attending Physician tonight, so I can't be leading a tour. I could fetch one of our orderlies if you don't mind."

"We're not here for a tour. We would very much like to see a new patient, Marie Dubois, who arrived from the Petersburg jail today."

"Oh, yes, that can be arranged, but she was just given a hypnotic and is in one of our mechanical restraints, so I don't think an interview will be productive. Perhaps tomorrow?"

"I'm sorry, time is short," said Professor James. "Your help is much appreciated."

The doctor removed his spectacles and polished the lenses with his tie. "Very well." He went to the door and opened it. "Rose?" he called across the foyer. The receptionist looked up from her book. "Would you please fetch us an orderly?"

The woman nodded and left the room. The doctor closed the door.

"Excuse me, doctor," said Edgar, "I noticed that the young woman hasn't spoken. Is she a patient?"

The doctor turned to Professor James to answer. "Rose is one of our success stories. Before she came here, she would not stop screaming—not unlike the woman you wish to see. After several years, Rose is now a contributing member of our facility. We know she can speak because she did so when she first arrived. We're hoping this faculty will return."

There came a knock, and the doctor opened the door. In the foyer stood a colored man in a white shirt and black pants.

"Louis, please take these gentlemen to see our new patient, Marie Dubois. She's in isolation room number three."

"Yes, sir," said the orderly. "Y'all follow me."

Professor James and Edgar trailed the orderly as he crossed the foyer and unlocked a solid wooden door behind Rose's desk. They came into a large room with many empty chairs, a small stage, and a piano. Several xylophones leaned against a wall. Are they the extent of the music program? Edgar wondered. A sullen colored man wearing a nightshirt sat at a small table near the stage, smoking a cigarette. Across the room, double doors opened on a dining hall full of male patients. Edgar could hear the clatter of metal plates and spoons punctuated by shouts, screams, and unbalanced laughter. He glimpsed colored orderlies moving among the patients as they ate.

Louis guided them forward. "This here's the social hall and the dining hall beyond," he said. "The women have already eaten. Now it's the men's turn. We only mix 'em on special occasions. The women's wing is this-a-way."

He indicated to his right, and Professor James and Edgar followed him as he unlocked, and relocked behind them, two sets of double doors. The second set of doors opened into a long dormitory wing. The patients filled the room with a cacophony of voices. Two rows of cots stretched across the room with an aisle down the middle. A small dresser stood next to each bed. Colored women in white nightdresses milled about the room or sat atop their beds. Other colored women in the same uniform as Rose attended to them. Many patients talked to themselves, some shouted, a few huddled in small groups.

On entering the room, Edgar stopped. "Is it proper for us to be here?" he asked. "The women are dressed for bed."

The orderly looked back at both Edgar and Professor James, who also stopped. He shook his head and didn't seem troubled in the least. "It's how they're always dressed on this ward. Don't mind it at all. It's the only way to the patient Doc Potok okayed you to see. Them docs are always traipsin' through. You docs too?"

"Of a fashion," said Professor James. "Please lead on."

Louis cleared a path through the women, sometimes asking them to move, other times pushing someone aside.

One woman sat on a bed, pulling out her hair while reciting scripture. A colored nurse intervened, attempting to stop the hair-pulling. Edgar suspected the nurses were just townsfolk in uniform. He wondered if the staff received much training. The woman pulling her hair turned on the nurse and raked her fingernails across the nurse's cheek. She launched herself at the nurse and drove her to the ground, tore off the nurse's cap, and flung it away. Next, she grabbed two fistfuls of the nurse's hair. Louis rushed forward and put the attacker in a chokehold.

When the hair-puller became unconscious, Louis and the nurse lifted the patient back onto her bed.

"Thank you," said the injured nurse.

"'Glad I could help. You should get those scratches tended to."

The nurse touched her cheek, winced, and noticed her bloody fingertips. She nodded and went off in the direction of the entry door.

Louis rejoined Professor James and Edgar, but a coquettish woman stepped in front of them with a seductive smile.

"Step aside, Ginny."

"When am I going to see you again?" she pined.

"There ain't nothin' between us but air," said Louis as he waved a hand in front of him. "I told you, I'm happily married."

"Perhaps, the white gent?" Ginny asked. She shot her hand in the direction of Professor James's privates.

Louis responded with lightning reflexes. He grabbed her hand and held it aloft. Ginny spat profanity until a couple of nurses took her away.

As they approached the end of the ward, a woman standing next to a bed let out a horrific series of screams. Most of the patients ignored her, but two nurses attempted to calm the woman with little effect.

"You need some help?" Louis shouted to the nurses.

"No," one shouted back, "Dinah does this every night just before bedtime. She'll be all right in a minute."

At the end of the long room stood the charge nurse, a heavy white woman with a key ring. She unlocked another set of double doors so that they could exit. The doorway led to a stairwell ascending two more floors. Louis took them to the top, unlocked the door, and let them in. This floor contained numerous shut doors for rooms on either side of the hall. Muffled cries and shouts emanated from the rooms. Two nurses chatted and laughed at a desk halfway down the hall.

"Here to see the new woman," said Louis. The nurses nodded, waved them on, and continued their conversation.

Louis led them to the third door on the left, which he also unlocked. He stepped in first and turned up the lamp on the small table. White tile covered the walls of the room. Small square tiles, alternating pink and black, covered the floor except for a drain in the center. Above the drain, a long coffin-shaped device with bars on all six sides rested on several large sawhorses. Within the cage, leather straps stretched across the base to form a sort of bed for Marie, who lay trapped inside. The air smelled of feces.

"What the hell is that?" asked Edgar

"A Utica crib," said Professor James. "Sometimes used to contain violent patients."

"That's right," Louis nodded. "You know this gal? Arrived acting like a wild animal. The police brought her in, kicking, scratching, and screaming gibberish. She's been given something to calm her, but she's not asleep. I hear her muttering."

Edgar and Professor James stepped closer to the crib. Marie's appearance had so altered, Edgar could hardly recognize her. The woman's silver jewelry had been taken away, as had her headscarf—revealing her thick matted gray hair. Her half-open eyes didn't seem to be seeing anything as she mumbled a phrase in French almost like a chant: "*Prenez garde! L'heure entre chien et loup.*"

"What she sayin'?" asked Louis.

Edgar translated: "Beware the time between dog and wolf."

Edgar and Professor James looked at each other in puzzlement.

"Is she referring to the werewolf?" asked Edgar.

Professor James nodded. "Perhaps she has talents akin to Sarah's or Nigel's and has been trying to warn us."

The woman managed to work her hand up and held it against the top of the wooden cage.

"Please," she mumbled in French, her voice thick with narcotic, "get me out."

Professor James placed his right hand above hers on the outside of the bars. As he spoke to her in French, tears ran from the captive woman's eyes. "Madame Dubois, I am so sorry for your condition. I'll do my utmost to have you released from this device and treated with more kindness."

The woman's fingers worked their way through the bars and laced through the professor's.

"Be strong, Madame," Professor James counseled.

Madame Dubois sobbed and nodded her head inside of the contraption.

"Now," continued Professor James, "I need to inquire about the meeting last night. You became agitated when I revealed what we are up against—a *loup-garou*. Do you have knowledge of the beast? The werewolf?"

Without warning, the woman's eyes opened wide.

She screamed and sank her nails into Professor James's hand, pinning it against the crib. She continued screaming and banged her head against the bars. Several gashes opened on the woman's forehead. Blood ran into her wide eyes and down her cheeks. Over and over, as her head hit the bars, she yelled, "*Prenez garde! L'heure entre chien et loup!*"

Louis assisted Professor James by prying the woman's fingernails free. Professor James pulled away his hand, which had become streaked with blood—his own.

As they stepped back from the Utica crib, the madwoman fell silent and ceased beating her head. She turned her bloody gaze upon them, and in a guttural voice whispered in English, "Be careful."

Marie renewed her screams and headbanging.

Her actions—including the brief period of clarity—sent a shiver up Edgar's spine.

"You two need to go," Louis told them, pushing them out of the room.

In the hall, the two nurses were running to investigate. The other patients, hearing the screaming, raised a ruckus of their own. Muffled shouts and screams filled the hall. Above the din, Louis shouted for the nurses to fetch some ether.

Professor James put his uninjured hand on Edgar's shoulder, and the two turned from the bedlam. They attempted to exit the ward but discovered they needed assistance to unlock the door.

As they waited, Marie howled like a wolf. Edgar shivered once more, and the hairs on his neck stood on end. It sounded like the real thing.

The men retraced their steps and peered back into

the room.

The woman remained trapped in the cage. It was not some beast. She had stopped her headbanging and now stared at them, her bloody face split by a wide toothy grin.

Continuing to stare, Marie resumed howling.

Chapter Twenty-Two

When Louis unlocked the door to the foyer, Professor James marched straight to Doctor Potok's office with Edgar at his heels. The administrator sat at his desk holding a knife and fork, with a large white napkin tucked into his collar. A colored orderly was placing a chicken dinner and a glass of red wine before him. Both doctor and orderly looked surprised at the intrusion.

"I'm sorry to interrupt, Doctor Potok," said Professor James, "but I must speak to you."

Louis arrived at the office door. "You okay, Doc? These two busted in here before I knew what they were doing." The other orderly edged around the desk so he could act without hindrance should the situation call for it.

Doctor Potok cocked his head and placed his silverware on the desk with infinite care. He pulled his napkin off and set it next to his plate. The doctor looked at each of the orderlies. "I think things are fine." He stood and gestured for Professor James and Edgar to take a seat before his desk. "You'll have to excuse me, gentlemen. I had assumed you would be showing yourselves out. As you can see, it's my suppertime. May I offer you something? A meal? A glass of wine?"

Professor James shook his head. "Just a moment of your time, sir."

"As you wish." The doctor looked at the orderlies. "You may go." Both left, and Doctor Potok retook his seat. Professor James and Edgar remained standing. "Now, what can I do for you? Did you find the woman's condition troubling?"

"To say the least," Edgar blurted.

Professor James nodded. "Her treatment is nothing short of depraved."

Doctor Potok had been lifting his glass of wine. He set the glass back on the desk with such force a good deal of its contents sloshed onto the blotter and his dinner. Now he stood, blustering as he tried to mop the spill with his napkin. The white cloth became blotched with red.

The doctor stopped cleaning and met Professor James's gaze. "This is uncalled for," he said, finally putting words to his emotions. "We are known for our compassionate care of the Negro. You have no right to make allegations without understanding the case."

Professor James shook his head. "If your use of the Utica crib is intended to keep the woman from hurting herself, it is an utter failure. If it is to keep a disturbed woman caged so as to not trouble the staff, it is achieving its purpose."

The doctor threw down his napkin, braced his hands on the desktop, and leaned forward. "I welcomed you two into the facility unannounced. I now realize my mistake. I must insist you both leave. The orderlies are just beyond the open door and can show you out."

Edgar looked behind him. Indeed, the two men waited in the outer room. He saw Professor James glance back at them too. The professor turned around to face the doctor.

"We'll try your patience no longer," said Professor James. "But should you do nothing to alleviate poor Marie Dubois's situation, I will be doing my utmost to challenge the reputation this institution enjoys. I'm sure Dorothea Dix would appreciate hearing how you keep some of your unfortunates in a cage, just as her gift of musical instruments is kept away under lock and key."

****

"Do you think your words did much good?" Edgar asked Professor James as they drove the wagon away from the asylum.

The horse moved at a brisk canter, and the professor gave it full rein. The speed and growing darkness made Edgar uncomfortable. He gripped the bar on the side of the seat to steady himself. Perhaps the horse wants to get away from this place as much as I do, he speculated.

Professor James glanced at Edgar before returning his eyes to the winding gravel drive, which was hard to see in the gloom of twilight. The professor leaned forward, squinted, and said, "Let's be careful before we condemn them all outright. Doctor Potok may be a decent man. The asylum does have a reputation for compassion, perhaps ill-deserved, and the Utica crib is widely used. Nevertheless, that device is clearly not keeping that poor woman from harming herself."

Professor James pulled on the reins saying, "Whoa." The horse slowed to an easier gait, and he gave the reins more slack. Edgar sighed with relief. The professor shot him a grin, his white teeth visible despite the approaching darkness. "Forgive me. Her situation and the doctor's apparent lack of interest got under my skin."

"Well, I don't think you made any friends in there," Edgar observed.

"I appeared adamant, nothing more. There are many humane alternatives for Marie besides that cage."

"Threatening to report her treatment may have carried some weight," said Edgar, "but threatening to inform Dorothea Dix seemed the most telling."

Professor James shot him another grin. "Sometimes, one must fire the largest cannon in one's arsenal."

At the bottom of the hill, the road led through a stand of trees, making it darker still. To their good fortune, a lamp now hung from the signpost at the end of the drive, so the professor managed to steer the wagon onto the main road without mishap. After doing so, he announced, "Unless we can find someplace with food already prepared, we may have to forego supper. We need to be heading back to Reverend Green's church."

"Stop at a pub in the dark part of town. I'll get us something."

Once in Petersburg, they decided to try a place called The Cottonmouth. A sign above the door featured a large snake with a wad of cotton in its fangs. Professor James set the brake and prepared to jump off his side of the wagon.

"You'd better stay out here," said Edgar, exiting on the other side. "Better yet, drive around the block a few times until I return."

"Whatever for?"

"Mingling the races when alcohol is involved may be incendiary." Edgar didn't wait for a retort and went inside. Professor James didn't follow.

The dimly lit place teemed with sweaty and dirty laborers having a beer or something stronger. The denizens became quiet, scrutinizing the overdressed stranger. A bald bear of a man with an eyepatch shouted, "The Temperance Society meets down the street!"

Edgar smiled and raised both hands, surrendering to the joke. "Always need a drink or two before the meetings!"

Folks laughed and resumed their conversations.

Through the dim light, Edgar could see a pile of sandwiches on a table in the rear of the place, but he had a feeling they had been there since lunch and were probably stale. He noticed many folks eating chops, stew, and other dishes, so he knew they had a working kitchen.

He emerged from the place a few minutes later with a couple of items wrapped in newspaper and carrying a tin pail with a lid. He climbed onto the wagon and said, "I got us fresh biscuits—still hot— ham, cheese, and a bucket of ale. Shall we eat on the way, or wait until we get to the church?"

"Let's wait," said Professor James, shaking the reins. "Without Marie, the reverend has lost his cook and may be hungry. Did you purchase enough for three?"

"There's plenty."

They drove the wagon to the reverend's church and found Reverend Green readying the place, opening the windows around the chapel. When they asked him to join them in a meal, he looked grateful. They gathered around a table the minister had set up on the dais.

"I am internally and eternally in your debt," he

quipped. "Haven't eaten a full meal since Marie left."

They finished eating and passed around the bucket to polish off the ale. Edgar lowered the bucket from his lips just as a group of colored men arrived, all carrying guns.

Chapter Twenty-Three

As Saphne approached her family's house, she could hear the ruckus through the front door. She took a deep breath to prepare herself for what she would find within and pushed open the door. Inside, her two brothers ran pell-mell through the small house, screaming and shouting. Otis, the seven-year-old, held a dead rat before him by the tail, chasing Tom, his four-year-old brother, and the source of the shrieking. By the unlit fireplace, their mother sat, mute and oblivious.

"Get out!" yelled Saphne, holding the door open. "And don't come back 'til suppertime!"

Tom ran through the doorway, followed by his tormentor. Outside, Otis threw the rat's body into the road, and the two boys collapsed onto their ill-kempt lawn, laughing.

Saphne shut the door and regarded her mother. The woman sat in a rocker staring into the empty hearth. Saphne's father had built the rough fireplace from salvaged bricks when he constructed their home, back when Saphne was a little girl. Since his death, it became her mother's haunt—where she felt most comfortable. Her mother's world had shrunk to either the bed or here. Next to the rocker, an unlit kerosene lamp sat on a small wooden table with a chipped marble top—a table Saphne had secreted away from Garraty's rubbish. It had been hell to carry home, but a sight better than the wooden box it had replaced.

Despite the warmth of the day, a woolen blanket lay across her mother's lap. The middle-aged woman wore a gray nightdress and had a nightcap pulled over much of her black hair. A once handsome woman, she had become gaunt over the last year, eating only when prompted by Saphne or one of the boys. Before her, on the fireplace mantel, sat a daguerreotype of her late husband, Saphne's father. A black bow hung from one corner of the picture frame. The flowers Saphne purchased yesterday sat in a green bottle next to the picture.

"Momma?"

No response. She rarely spoke.

Saphne sighed and went into their little kitchen. On the wood stove rested a cast iron pot half full of pork and beans. She made it two days ago, and they had been eating it ever since. She lit the stove to reheat the food. Saphne removed the mess the boys had left on the kitchen table and set clean plates and spoons for them to use when they came home to eat. She boiled some mustard greens. Not knowing when they'd be back, she decided to stir the greens into the pork and beans. She filled a small ceramic pitcher with fresh water and set it on the table along with two tin cups.

Saphne stirred the cast iron pot and pulled it away from the direct heat. Otis would serve his brother dinner when they returned. In the meantime, Saphne decided to attempt to feed their mother herself. She dished the beans and greens into a bowl, poured a glass of water, and took these into the other room.

"Here, Momma, I got ya some food," Saphne said. She moved the lamp and set the bowl and cup on the small marble-topped table.

No response. Saphne pulled a stool near to her mother and sat. She scooped a tiny portion and put the spoon to her mother's lips. The woman took the food into her mouth and chewed. Saphne felt the tight muscles in her neck and shoulders relax. Sometimes getting her mother to eat was impossible—they'd force food into her mother's mouth where it would just sit. This time, it seemed, things would be easy.

As she fed her mother, she spoke. "Momma, I've met a man who's sweet on me. Says he loves me. He's from Harvard, which is a big important city up north. He's a professor-man. I'm sweet on him too." Saphne lapsed into silence until she finished feeding her mother and wiped the older woman's lips with a well-worn towel. "He says he's willin' to move near here to be with us. He knows about you, Otis, and Tom. Says he'll care for us all. I told him to take tonight to search his heart, just to be sure. So, tomorrow I could have some mighty big news. I'll be sure to tell ya as soon as I know."

Saphne got to her feet and bent to kiss her mother's forehead.

As if by magic, the older woman came to life. Her eyes focused on Saphne, and her eyebrows arched with concern. Her mother put her hand on Saphne's cheek, next to the swollen and blackened eye.

"Oh, sweetie," she said, "did your professor-man do this?

Saphne cried and put her hand over her mother's. "No, Momma, it's from something else." She could not bear to explain why she would be heading off to work for the man who raped her.

Her mother gently patted her cheek. "I'm glad it weren't him," she said and went back to staring at the empty hearth. "I'm glad."

Chapter Twenty-Four

"Gentlemen, thank you all for coming." Reverend Green addressed the two dozen armed congregants standing before the pulpit. They had returned to the Blandford Baptist Church to volunteer for the hunt.

Edgar studied the men from where he and Professor James sat on the dais. They represented a cross-section of the community—from prosperous merchants to poor tenant farmers. In the front sat Wendel Washington, the Virginia Lancet editor, who nodded a hello to Edgar when their eyes met. Edgar recognized some of the men from the previous night's meeting and others he had seen around town. Many looked stern and resolute, others anxious. Edgar figured he numbered among the latter. The visit to the madwoman unnerved him, as Professor James had warned. Moreover, he already encountered the beast and knew what they faced.

"In a few minutes," said the reverend, "you will receive silver ammunition for tonight's hunt." He pointed to the six-foot table where they had eaten. It now held numerous small wooden boxes filled with silver bullets. The two gunsmiths sat behind the table. "Our good friends, Tobias and Moses, have lent their expertise to our endeavors, but in the process, an accident occurred last night. Leroy Jenkins tragically died. We add his name to the list of those we have already lost due to this menace.

"Let us bow our heads in prayer."

Edgar saw the others lower their heads and clasp their hands. He felt compelled to do the same.

"Oh, Lord," intoned the reverend, "I beseech your protection, for these, your soldiers, who are preparing to do battle with the forces of evil. And I ask you to join us. Let loose the lightning of your terrible swift sword."

The reverend recited Psalm 23.

" 'Yea, though I walk through the valley of the shadow of death,

I will fear no evil; for thou art with me;

Thy rod and thy staff, they comfort me.'

"We ask all this in Jesus' name. Amen."

A chorus of "Amens" and "Hallelujahs" came from the men as they raised their heads. Some of those who appeared anxious a minute ago now looked calmer.

Edgar didn't feel any different—scared but also determined. He would face the creature, but this time with the right weapon. Edgar imagined Saphne showering him with kisses after he alone dispatched it. The absurd fantasy made him realize Saphne prompted his involvement in the hunt as much as anything. He wanted the monster gone and her safe. Other dragons awaited, such as Garraty, but one monster at a time, he told himself.

"Now," announced the reverend, "let us hear from Professor James. He and I will be coordinating the hunt from here in the church." Reverend Green stepped back from the pulpit and ushered Professor James to take his place.

Professor James stood, smoothed back his hair, and stepped before the other men.

"You all know the danger we face and the terrible cost to this community it has been." He looked at Wendell Washington and the rest of the men. "Some of you know that cost personally. Now is the time for action."

More shouts of "Uh-huh!" and "Amen!"

"We have the means for its destruction," continued Professor James, "but we must be careful. We are dealing with a supernatural creature with incredible strength and viciousness.

"You will be broken up into four groups of six. My associate, Doctor Gilpin, will lead one group. Tobias, Moses, and Wendell Washington will be leading the others. I have given them additional information that may prove useful on the hunt. Each group will be assigned an area. Check back here periodically in case there's a sighting.

"Take care to only use these silver bullets when you have a clear shot. The amount of this ammunition is limited. Do not blindly shoot at shadows or rustling in the dark. Nevertheless, if it shows itself, do not hesitate to shoot."

"That's right!" "Amen!" and "That's what I'm talkin' about!" arose from the men.

"This poor soul has been cursed," said Professor James, "but you need to harden your hearts. Once transformed, the beast has no conscience and will take your life if you do not act first.

"We may not encounter it tonight. My research has shown that this is a late-stage lycanthrope. Its transformation is no longer tied to the full moon—it can happen at any time, on any day, but these creatures prefer to hunt at night. We need to begin the hunt now and may need to continue for weeks. Sooner or later, it will show itself. Perhaps, if we're lucky, we can put a stop to this before it takes another life."

The chorus of affirmations arose from the men.

"We have a difficult road ahead," Professor James raised his right hand into the air, "but now we have the weapons we need to destroy it." He made a fist and swung it before him. "And with God's help, we shall prevail!"

The men stomped their feet and shouted their encouragement.

Tobias called the men over to the table with the ammunition. Moses told them to remove all other bullets from their guns and to be sure to check the chamber.

"Each of you will get several rounds," continued Tobias. "If we don't get it tonight, return here to the church to drop off your ammunition. That way, if different people show up on other nights, we can equip 'em."

The men queued in front of the table, presented their weapons to the gunsmiths, and received ammunition according to their gun. When Edgar presented his derringer, Tobias and Moses burst out laughing.

Moses held the little gun aloft for all to see. The laughter became infectious, and soon the whole room roared. Edgar realized they needed to defuse the tension they all felt before the hunt.

Edgar had reloaded the derringer back at the farmhouse, and Moses now opened the gun and removed one of the small-caliber bullets. "Get a load of this!" Moses exclaimed and held up the bullet between two fingers. More laughter.

Someone shouted, "The gun is the measure of the man!"

"Then here," Moses said, still chuckling. He placed a large pistol on the table, and it landed with a macho thud. "You need a grown-up weapon for tonight. Got me a rifle I can use instead."

Edgar thanked him and received a handful of ammunition. He considered commenting on the brass casings, but he realized only the silver bullet inside would be striking the wolf. He nodded his thanks and stepped away to load the pistol.

"You need a hand with that?" someone asked, still laughing. Edgar shook his head, smiled, and loaded the revolver himself.

"Don't forget Junior," said Tobias, tossing Edgar the derringer. Edgar caught it with one hand and thrust it into his pocket.

Chapter Twenty-Five

Doctor Victor Potok sat at his desk, looking wistfully at his dinner of fried chicken, greens, and mashed potatoes smothered with yellow gravy. On most nights, he would tuck into the meal. The kitchen provided decent fare for the staff, which made these night shifts more tolerable. But Potok's stomach had been churning for the last half-hour since he'd argued with those two visitors over the treatment of Marie Dubois. Disgusted, he threw his wine-stained napkin in the center of the plate. *Those damned Yankees have ruined my appetite.* He lifted his half-full glass of wine and downed the contents.

He should have turned those troublemakers away when they showed up. He tried to accommodate them and see where it got him? No good deed goes unpunished, Potok told himself. Still, those two could cause some trouble for the facility. What should he do? he wondered, his stomach doing flips. Prudence dictated he should follow the wine with a chaser of sodium bicarbonate and water.

Instead, he decided to have a look at Marie Dubois. Perhaps they had exaggerated. If not, he could make some immediate changes, so if anyone came snooping around tomorrow, she would be in different circumstances.

In the foyer, he saw the abandoned greeter desk

and figured Rose had returned to her room. The doctor went to the main entry and unlocked it. Across the way, he could see a group of colored orderlies eating and chatting in the cafeteria. One of them, Louis, stood and came to the cafeteria door.

"Can I help you, Doc?" he called. "You done with supper? You want that I should take away your plate?"

"No, don't trouble yourself, Louis. I may have more chicken later. I just want to check on the new woman. Seems our visitors expressed some concern about her state."

"You want that I should go with you?"

"No, it's not necessary. Go back to your meal."

Louis nodded and rejoined the other orderlies.

The doctor went to the women's ward and let himself in. Most of the lights on the ward were extinguished, but the room remained a hive of activity. The nurses scuttled from one bed to the next, doing their best to get the women to sleep or at least to quiet down. Doctor Potok appreciated the facility's protocol to medicate as a last resort; still, how could people sleep in this din? Lack of sleep would drive anyone crazy.

A large colored woman, with huge pendulous breasts visible through her nightdress, bounded off one of the beds and blocked his way. She peered at him through the gloom and screamed, "It's Master come to have his way!"

"No, you silly woman!" countered Potok. "I'm doing my rounds, as I do every night." His words came too late to have any effect. The room erupted into utter pandemonium. The head nurse, Miss Beechem, a large good-tempered white woman, stood at her desk beside the next set of doors.

"Evening, Doctor," she shouted over the commotion. "You're a bit early tonight. Before we got all our chicks to roost."

"Yes, well, I just—" Potok stopped. Why do I owe her an explanation? he asked himself. He turned back and cast his eyes around the dimly lit chaos. "Administer laudanum all around. I want them quiet when I get back."

The woman gave her head a curt nod. "Very well, Doctor." She clapped her hands and shouted, "All right, ladies, we're all going to have a drink of water and go to sleep!"

Potok opened the next set of doors and locked them behind him. He made his way up the stairs to the topmost floor. Upon entering the unit, he saw the two colored nurses playing cards at the desk halfway down the hall. Seeing him, one nurse swept everything off the desktop into a drawer, while the other approached him.

"Yes, Doctor?" This one, who he knew to be Gretchen, kept her eyes averted and curtsied.

"Put the cards in the trash. If I catch either of you playing again, you'll lose your job. Understood?"

"Yes, Doctor." Her eyes remained downcast.

"Take me to Marie Dubois."

Gretchen led the doctor to room three and opened the door. The rank smell inside the room caused him to step back and place a handkerchief over his nose and mouth. "My God," he mumbled. He entered and stepped across the tiled floor to the coffin-shaped Utica Crib.

Marie's forehead had become swollen and cut from smashing against the bars. Blood ran in little rivulets down either side of her face. As the doctor approached, two eyes opened on her bloody visage and regarded him. Could it be malice he detected in her eyes? Whatever lurked in the trapped woman's mind, she didn't speak. "She has soiled herself," he said aloud. The visitors had been right; she wasn't being treated well. "And she appears to have quieted down."

"Only just. She's been screamin' off and on for hours."

"I want her cleaned, put into a straitjacket, and moved to one of the padded cells on Level Two. Shall I send an orderly to help you?"

"No. Inez and I can manage all right."

Inez, now at the door of the room, heard the directive. "Yes, Doctor," she added, "we'll be fine."

"Get to it then. Right away," Potok told them. "And no card-playing. You hear?"

Both chimed, "Yes, Doctor."

****

A few minutes later, Inez entered the room with a towel, a clean nightshirt, a diaper, and a straitjacket. She saw Gretchen, hose nozzle in hand, turn the spigot and send a blast of what Inez knew to be cold water onto Marie, who remained trapped in the crib. Marie screamed and thrashed about in the cage but could not escape the blast of cold water.

Gretchen grinned at Inez. "Wanna try? It's fun."

The use of a hose was a novelty. Inez set the items on a table and took the nozzle, blasting Marie anew. Marie continued to scream and thrash, but the water kept coming. After a while, the old woman quit moving or making any noise. Inez turned off the spigot. The water slowed to a trickle and stopped.

"What's wrong?" asked Gretchen.

Inez pointed at Marie. "Is she all right?"

"Oh, I'm sure." Gretchen marched over to the Utica crib and unlocked the lid using one of the keys from a leather cord around her neck.

Marie sprang to life. She grabbed the keys with one hand and yanked hard. The sudden action caused Gretchen's head to smash onto the side of the crib. The nurse collapsed into unconsciousness, but not before Marie pulled the keys free.

Before Inez could comprehend things, Marie leapt from the cage and dashed from the room. The door slammed shut behind her.

After making sure Gretchen was OK, Inez ran to the door. Locked. She reached for her set of keys and realized she had swept them into the drawer with the deck of cards.

****

Marie ignored the nurse pounding on the door. Unintelligible shouts and screams came from the other rooms. She ignored these too and ran for the stairs, then stopped. The water cleared her mind but left her sopping wet and ice cold. She noticed the nurse's desk and ran back to rummage through drawers. She found keys but nothing else she could use. Marie shivered. *Where would there be dry clothes?*

Behind the desk stood a door marked with letters. The other doors all had numbers. While Marie couldn't read, she knew the difference. She tried the knob. Locked. She found the right key and entered the nurse's supply room, where they also kept their personal belongings.

A few minutes later, she emerged, dressed in a

nurse's uniform and cape and carrying a pilfered handbag. The nurse locked in her former room continued to pound on the door and demand to be set free. Marie shook her head and moved on. She approached the exit and located the key to open it.

Descending the stairs to the ground level, she saw the door to the first-floor unit and paused. Worried she would be found out, she decided to try another way. She moved around the stairwell and happened upon a steel door, also locked. Marie tried the same key as before and discovered it worked. The door led outside into darkness.

Enough light shone from the few lit windows in the facility for her to follow the gravel path around the building, past a pile of construction debris, to the main drive. She headed away from the asylum.

"Nurse?"

Marie turned toward the voice and saw a man with a lantern standing in front of the building. He held the light aloft, but she had gone too far for it to provide much illumination.

"Yes?" she answered.

"Is there a problem?"

Marie turned and continued walking away. "'Not well," she said in a loud voice, hoping he did not notice her accent.

After several steps, Marie breathed a sigh, relieved the man was not following her. But as she continued along the gravel drive, the weight of evil plaguing the town descended upon her shoulders. *What could she do?* Her warnings went unheeded. She could make her way back to New Orleans. To stay risked being returned to the cage. But could she ignore everything and run away? A bolt of lightning shot across the sky, and she jumped in fright. A booming clap of thunder followed. Marie felt the madness creeping up on her, fighting to take hold. Another blinding flash of lightning rent the sky above, followed by a deafening clap of thunder.

Marie decided she had to get to the church. It might not be too late.

Rain poured from the heavens.

Chapter Twenty-Six

The sunshine of the day gave way to storm clouds as sunset drew on. Now, in the dark of night, thunder rumbled in the distance. Without moonlight, Edgar couldn't see, and he didn't know the area. He realized Professor James had made a mistake appointing him as one of the group leaders. Edgar ceded leadership to one of the locals, Doc Jordan.

Doc, a local dentist, seemed to know his way and led them through the dark fields and woodlands. Their only lights were blackout lanterns, but they traveled with the lamps shuttered to not draw attention to themselves.

There continued to be some gentle ribbing of Edgar at the outset for having a small gun. But now, an hour into the hunt, the group moved along silently, aside from the occasional snap of a twig underfoot. Such sounds would make them halt and wave their weapons. They'd also raise the shutters on their blackout lanterns and shine the lights this way and that but would soon realize they had made the noise themselves and continue on.

As they traversed a field, a flash of lightning illuminated much of the area around them, followed by a tremendous boom. In the brief light, they spotted a barn and made for it at a jog. More lightning lit their way. Edgar appreciated the light but realized he and the men could attract a strike, being exposed in the field. He quicked his pace, and this time the others followed his lead.

No sooner had they entered the barn than the sky opened in a deluge of rain. The sharp distinctive scent of ozone from the storm mixed with the equally distinctive scents from the barn.

Horses nickered and cows lowed, nervous at the arrival of strangers and from the storm, but they soon quieted. The men looked through the open barn door at the deluge, illuminated by another flash of lightning.

"Perhaps a flood will drown the damn thing," said Doc.

"Don't count on it," said Edgar. "I met the creature last night, and it didn't seem troubled by anything. Professor James read something about werewolves having difficulty crossing running water, but I saw it splash through a stream without a care."

"*You what?*" asked Doc.

He and the other men peppered Edgar with questions.

"You fought it off?"

"How'd ya do it?"

"What's it look like?"

Edgar saw all the men gathered around him in the next flash of light and realized he had regained some of his lost prestige. Edgar proceeded to tell them of the attack on Cicero the previous night and how he'd saved himself by climbing a tree. He mentioned his little sidearm did not affect the creature, even when fired point-blank.

This time no one made jokes.

"I hope Professor James is correct about the silver

bullets," said Edgar.

A few of the men said, "Amen," but these sounded weak.

The downpour subsided, and the men prepared to go. Doc mentioned they could thank Jasper Tremblay, a Klan member, for this respite from the rain. "It wouldn't do for us to be found in his barn," he added.

After Edgar's story, the men wanted to stay near wooded areas, deciding it gave them a measure of safety to have the trees around. The rain had cut the late August heat a bit, but it remained oppressively hot. The rain also seemed to invite more mosquitoes. The whine of their approach and the sting of their bite made the search party slap themselves and curse.

So much for silence, thought Edgar. He wondered at the efficacy of these hunting parties. They could only cover a small bit of the Petersburg area at any one time. If the beast had preternatural senses to go along with its strength and size, it might be able to smell or hear the group coming, even if they managed to stay quiet. Still, they had to do something. Perhaps they or one of the other groups would get lucky. He considered the possibility of a trap but discarded the idea. Who in their right mind would volunteer to be the bait?

"Hold on, there!" commanded a man's voice from the darkness.

The group stopped as directed.

Those in the search party with lanterns opened the shutters just as the shutters on other lanterns opened and shone on them. The light revealed an armed band of white-clad men on horseback. The Klan moved their horses to encircle the search party.

Chapter Twenty-Seven

Garraty rode his horse toward the black men. He was the only Klansman with his face uncovered.

"Just what the hell do you darkies think you're doin'?" It had been Garraty's voice that commanded they stop. He now rode between Edgar and the other men and forced them to move to avoid being trampled. "Now, why would we allow an armed bunch of you folk to go rampaging through the countryside, raping white women and pillaging law-abiding white folks' property?"

"Beggin' your pardon, Mister Garraty," spoke Doc, after shedding his hat. He shuffled forward toward the mounted Klansman. "We're huntin' the bogeywolf, I'm sure you've heard tell. He's also gone after white—" Doc Jordan didn't finish his sentence as Garraty kicked him across the jaw. The dentist flew backward and landed on his rump. His rifle went flying and slid to a stop in front of another Klansman.

The white-clad man swung off his horse, took the rifle, and returned to his saddle.

Garraty rode again through the remaining black men. "You will surrender your weapons. Any further backtalk will cause you to be dangling from a rope." To emphasize his threat, he showed them a coiled lariat. "Now!" he shouted.

The black men complied. One by one, the weapons

landed on the ground in front of Garraty.

Edgar held on to his weapon until everyone else surrendered theirs. Disgusted, he threw his revolver onto the pile and looked at Garraty with hatred burning across his features. That was a mistake.

"You," growled Garraty. He tossed the lasso over Edgar's torso and cinched it tight, pinning Edgar's arms to his chest.

Garraty chuckled and rode his horse around Edgar, wrapping him further in the rope. "This here's the reason why you others have forgotten your place!" he announced. He continued to circle Edgar and now spoke to his confederates. "This boy has stirred 'em all up! Filled their heads with Yankee trash and notions that have caused them to become a threat to our community. Well, they say you should remove the head of a snake, and that's just what we're gonna do."

Garraty got off his horse and pointed at a tree limb. "George, take your rope and throw it over that branch." Garraty stuck his face next to Edgar's.

"You and my cook arrived together last night. Did she cook-up somethin' special for you? She sure did for me. Tell ya what, while you're hanging from this here tree, I'm going to get me another taste tonight. She's a little bruised, but I don't mind bruised fruit." Garraty leered. "I think it tastes all the sweeter."

Edgar's lower arms had been free when first lassoed, and he had shoved his right hand into his jacket pocket. Now the pocket raised in the direction of Garraty's chest, and the derringer fired twice.

The shots didn't sound particularly loud—more like firecrackers.

Garraty dropped his lantern and his end of the rope.

He looked at the splotches of red blooming on the front of his white robe. Bloody bubbles formed on his lips. He raised his head and looked at Edgar with surprise.

Garraty toppled forward. Without any arms out to slow his fall, he planted his face onto a large, exposed root with a satisfying thump.

The black men dove for the pile of weapons on the ground. They swung these up in all directions, prepared to fire.

Their captors had fled.

Chapter Twenty-Eight

Edgar freed himself from the rope and extended a hand to help Doc to his feet. Instead of thanking him, the dentist shook his head and said, "Boy, you're in it so deep, you got to part your hair to breathe."

"I'd no recourse," said Edgar, still rattled by what had happened. He prodded Garraty with his shoe, but the man did not respond.

"Oh, he's dead all right," said Doc. "I saw where you shot him. You best be getting a move on."

Edgar looked around at the other men, visible in the light from the lanterns dropped after the shooting. The colored men stared, dumbfounded, as though they couldn't believe Garraty could be killed.

"They weren't silver."

"What?" asked Doc.

Edgar produced the derringer. "They were ordinary bullets."

Doc retrieved the revolver Moses gave Edgar. He pressed it into Edgar's hands and said, "Skedaddle."

Edgar nodded, but before leaving, he aimed the gun at Garraty and fired a silver bullet into the man's skull.

"What the hell?" said Doc

All the men were staring at him. "Just to be sure," said Edgar. "If Garraty's the creature, I don't want him rising from the dead."

Someone toward the back of the group said, "Amen," and the rest of the men echoed the sentiment.

Garraty's horse stood a few yards away. Edgar went to the creature, patted its neck, and removed the white bedsheet covering it. He handed the sheet to the dentist and mounted the horse.

The dentist threw the wadded sheet onto Garraty's body before looking back at Edgar. "White men hang horse thieves," observed Doc.

"They can only hang me once." Edgar made a rueful smile. He slapped the ends of the reins against the horse's flanks and drove it into the woods. He needed to get away from the Klan as soon as possible. To keep from getting scratched by branches, Edgar bent over and let the horse go of its own volition.

They came to a road, and Edgar stopped the horse to get his bearings. The clouds parted enough for the moon to illuminate the road, and he realized it led to the Garraty estate. The Klan may have gathered there after the shooting. The smart thing to do was flee Petersburg this instant. He always considered himself intelligent. Top of his class, from grammar school through university. But despite the danger, he felt compelled to see Saphne and profess his love. Perhaps she would flee with him. Going to Garraty's was a risk he was willing to take. He slapped the reins against the horse's flanks and set off at a gallop.

He arrived to see the enormous house lit from one end to the other. Seven horses waited at the hitching posts out front—two of them still draped in white bedclothes. The sickly-sweet scent of honeysuckle perfumed the grounds.

Edgar pulled on the reins. The horse reared and

came to a stop. He spoke a few soothing words to the animal, apologizing for riding it so hard, and steered it to the back of the mansion.

Saphne had mentioned a cot on the rear porch, where she could sleep until she needed to prepare breakfast. Edgar tied the horse to a peach tree and crept toward the screened windows. He raised his head and peered inside. A couple of empty cots sat on the rear porch.

Perhaps she's helping wait on the Klansmen, he realized, *the men who want to kill me.* Edgar gritted his teeth and moved along the side of the house. He glimpsed into each window as he went, staying well back so as not to be seen through the glass. As he neared the front, men's voices came from an open window.

The Klan were gathered in a large parlor. No one wore hoods. Several had pulled off their bedsheets altogether. Saphne moved amongst the white men, serving them tall glasses of something on a silver tray. They didn't acknowledge her. Some men were yelling and stomping their feet in anger. Some paced around the room.

"What the blazes are we gonna do?" asked a white-haired man with a pointy beard.

"We're going to hunt that murderous Yankee darkie and tear him apart," said a well-dressed younger man.

"But he and the others got guns!" yelled a bald man with a shiny face.

The klansmen responded with shouts of frustration. Edgar knew armed black men defending themselves was their worst nightmare. Saphne served the last glass and left, carrying the tray.

Edgar moved along the side of the house, watching Saphne's progress within. She worked her way back through the house and joined two other colored women in the kitchen. Edgar waited, hoping she'd soon be alone. The minutes dragged on at an agonizing pace. After forever and a day, the other two women departed carrying small sandwiches and coffee. Edgar took this opportunity to approach one of the kitchen windows and tap.

Saphne glanced over from where she washed dishes at the sink, then returned to her work. Edgar tapped again, louder, afraid someone else might hear. This time, Saphne dried her hands on a dishtowel and came over to investigate. Despite everything, Edgar could not help but grin when she saw him. Saphne jumped, looking shocked, and bit the knuckles on her right hand. Her eyes welled with tears. She ran to the rear door and came outside.

Edgar raced to embrace her, but she pushed him away to arm's length.

"Aren't you glad to see me?"

"You're a fool, Edgar Gilpin. Don't you realize the danger in being here? Those men know you killed Mr. Garraty. They're going to get over their shock in a few minutes, pull themselves together, and hunt you down."

"Come away with me," Edgar implored. "We can send for your family, and they can join us."

Saphne moved away. "I can't, and I won't. I told you."

Edgar took a step toward her. She kept her distance.

"But you have my heart," he pleaded, his voice

cracking.

Saphne nodded but said nothing.

Edgar stood there, imploring her to come into his open arms. She refused. After what seemed an eternity, he dropped his arms in defeat. He swiped tears from his eyes with his sleeve. "Garraty has ruined both our lives."

"Go on now, 'fore I have to mourn your death. Some things are just not meant to be."

Saphne turned and went inside. He could hear her sobbing and moved to follow, but as he stepped onto the stoop, she shut the door in his face.

Chapter Twenty-Nine

Nigel drew a card and smirked at Sarah. They were playing euchre at the dining table. Edgar burst into the farmhouse without warning, looking possessed—dripping with sweat and his eyes red.

"Edgar?" inquired Sarah, standing.

Edgar ignored her and ran across the main room and into the hall. Sarah set her cards on the table and moved to follow.

"Hey, where are you going?" complained Nigel.

"Something's wrong," said Sarah.

"So *you* say. I was about to trounce you," Nigel showed his hand, but Sarah had turned to go. He threw his cards on the table and went after her.

In his bedroom, Edgar threw belongings as fast as he could into a carpetbag. He held it before the bureau and swept everything on top into the bag.

"Tell us what's wrong," pleaded Sarah, who put a hand on his back.

Edgar swung around and looked startled. "Garraty," he said and caught a breath. "I shot him. Killed him."

Sarah gasped. "What happened?"

"He and a group of Klansmen were about to lynch me."

"The Klan knows we're here," said Nigel, heading for his room. "We need to go."

"No!" cried Edgar.

Nigel turned to argue and saw Edgar's hands balled into fists, as though preparing for a fight.

Edgar shook his head and bared his teeth. He looked to be at the breaking point. "I can't ask you to risk your lives for me."

"You don't have to ask," said Nigel. "We'll not abandon you."

Sarah nodded. "I'm sure Professor James feels the same."

Edgar collapsed onto the bed and put his head into his hands. His back shook, and Nigel could hear a stifled sob. A few moments later, he sat upright, breathed in a ragged breath, and tried to compose himself.

"We must go," Nigel repeated.

Sarah pushed past him into the hall and went to her room. Nigel went to his room as well and threw his belongings into his luggage. He ran into the main room to pack Professor James's books and clothes.

Sarah appeared and pulled his arm. "Come quick," she said under her breath, clearly panicked.

She led Nigel to Annabelle's room. "I can't rouse her."

Annabelle lay sprawled across the bedspread, dead to the world. On her nightstand sat the large blue bottle of laudanum, a spoon, and an empty glass.

Nigel regarded Annabelle, whose usual pretty appearance and prim demeanor looked anything but. Slack-jawed, drool ran from her mouth. The unbuttoned top of her dress and corset fully displayed her cleavage. Her hair, often in a tight bun, splayed across the top of the bed. Since joining the group, he fantasized seeing her in bed, but not like this. Nigel used a corner of a bedsheet to wipe her chin clean, then threw the sheet over her bosom for modesty's sake. He patted her face, saying in a loud voice, "Rise and shine, Annie! We must away." No response. Now Nigel panicked. "Is she dead?"

"No. I felt her breath, but I can't bring her 'round."

"At least she's still dressed—well, mostly. Grab her things, and let's go." Nigel threw back the sheet, fastened a few of her buttons, and put Annabelle over his shoulder. He stood with a grunt. Sarah shoved Annabelle's belongings into a carpetbag and followed him into the main room.

Nigel stopped, and Sarah crashed into him.

"What's wrong?" asked Sarah.

"The wagon," said Nigel. "It's with Professor James."

Edgar moved around them and took the bags from the dining table. "I've got Garraty's horse," he announced.

"First time I feel obliged to that man," said Nigel of Garraty.

Outside, they decided Sarah would ride, holding Annabelle in front of her. They lashed together their belongings with an extra belt and draped them over the rear of the horse to improvise saddlebags.

"What of the werewolf?" asked Sarah.

"We've no choice," said Nigel.

Edgar displayed the revolver he'd gotten from Moses. "I've got this, with five silver bullets left. I'll use them on whatever monsters we encounter."

They struck off across the fields, worried the road would prove too dangerous.

Nigel felt déjà vu as he descended the hill in the dark, traveling the route of twenty years before. He prayed the results would be better. The rainclouds from earlier had cleared to reveal a full moon. The moonlight lit their way and helped them navigate the uneven ground and along fences until they found a gate, but it was slow going. Both he and Edgar craned their necks around now and then to check, half expecting a group of ghostly figures with torches to be riding them down.

At length, they came to the road and decided to remain on it to speed their progress. Nigel wondered if the Klansmen were enlisting others to hunt Edgar. If so, a few bullets, silver or not, would be inadequate. Nevertheless, they pressed on.

They approached a covered bridge which looked dark and forbidding. A good place for a trap, thought Nigel. At that instant, a horde of screaming demonic figures emerged from the structure and began diving for their heads.

Edgar hoisted his pistol from his belt.

"No!" shouted Nigel, too late.

Edgar shot twice at the screaming harpies swooping above them. One of the creatures exploded into pieces, the largest of which thudded onto the road before them. The rest of the creatures flew away, still screaming.

Nigel fetched the remains and held them so they caught the moonlight. He showed Edgar. "A barn owl," he pronounced. "Theirs is a common enough sound, but the gunshots might direct the Klan our way. Let's pick up our pace."

They soon passed several dark farmhouses. No one appeared to have been roused by the shooting. That didn't account for people already searching for them.

Further on up the road, they spotted a lit building. "The church," said Sarah, pointing.

Nigel noticed the fields around it lay studded with wood and stone markers. The colored cemetery.

The wagon and horse waited out front. Edgar and Nigel set Annabelle in the back of the wagon on the hay, still damp from the evening's rain. They then loaded their bags.

"If you don't mind," said Edgar, crawling under the loose hay on the other side of Annabelle, "I'll hide under here. The fewer people see of me, the better. Tell Professor James if he wants to stay and finish the job, I understand."

Nigel nodded and went inside to fetch the professor.

Several lamps burned along with large candles on either side of the altar at the church's front. Professor James and Reverend Green sat behind the table, on which a map of the area now lay spread. Both men had removed their jackets and draped them over the backs of their chairs. At present, Professor James's head rested on a corner of the map as he snored, while Reverend Green read the Bible.

The reverend looked up and flashed a weary smile. "I'm afraid you're a bit late for the hunt." His expression changed to worry. "Forgive me, Mr. Pickford, for not recognizing you at first. Is something the matter?"

Hearing the reverend speak, Professor James stirred. "I must have dozed off."

Reverend Green removed a pocket watch and shook his head. "It's been several hours. I felt you needed sleep since you got none the night before." He turned back to Nigel and repeated, "Is something wrong?"

Nigel hesitated about telling the reverend. Then he realized other men had seen Edgar shoot, so it wouldn't be a secret. He gave them an account of what happened between Edgar and Garraty. Nigel concluded by saying he and the rest of the group had agreed to help Edgar escape.

Professor James stood, as did the reverend. "Well," said the professor, his face creased with worry and fatigue, "it appears our time here is over. I'll not abandon my colleague." He slipped on his jacket. "I'm sorry we will not be seeing this through."

"Don't give that another thought," said Reverend Green. "You have provided us with the knowledge and means by which we can put an end to this scourge. We shall be ever thankful. I'll pray for your safe escape— and for the soul of Mr. Garraty, wherever it may be."

The reverend escorted them along the center aisle, with Nigel in the rear.

"I'm wondering," said Reverend Green, "how long should we maintain the hunt?"

Professor James stopped and considered this. "Keep it up for at least a month, a full cycle of the moon. Even though the moon has less to do with its transformation at this point, it may still prove to be a factor. If there are no further attacks, perhaps the creature has been driven off. That, or conceivably, the individual died as a human in other circumstances." He lowered his brows and gave the reverend a knowing look, conveying it could well have been Garraty.

"Yes, of course," said Reverend Green. "I

understand. I shall also pray this whole sorry thing is over, or will be as soon—"

Shouting occurred outside, and without warning, the door to the church burst open. A gray-haired dark-skinned woman raced into the room. The woman wore a nurse's uniform, but her wild expression and unkempt hair looked incongruous. Nigel caught a glimpse of Sarah on the church steps making a helpless gesture.

"Madame Dubois!" said Professor James.

Nigel recognized the crazy woman.

"*Prenez garde!*" The woman shouted in a hoarse voice, fixing her eyes on Reverend Green.

"Warn us about what?" asked Professor James, taking her hand.

The woman shook herself free and advanced on the minister, shouting, "*Prenez garde! L'heure entre chien et loup.*"

Reverend Green backed into Nigel.

Nigel screamed and recoiled. He shoved the minister away.

Professor James's voice sounded uncharacteristically sharp. "Mr. Pickford! Do not give rein to base prejudice!"

Nigel didn't hear.

Upon contact with Reverend Green, a rush of images and sensations flooded Nigel. He felt himself racing through the woods, power like he had never known filling his body. Feet flew over the damp ground, and he launched himself over a fallen log. His command of muscles and sense of smell and hearing became extraordinary—heightened beyond anything he'd ever experienced. Yet inside existed an emptiness, a hunger driving him on. Flashes of previous prey shot through his mind, frightened women, men, and children, all screaming. A tidal wave of bloodlust pushed aside every other feeling. An instinctual drive arose within him to howl, to gnash his teeth, to rend, to tear, to swim in the warmth of the kill.

"Mr. Pickford?"

Nigel felt nauseated. He stared at the reverend's back and whispered, "It's you."

Chapter Thirty

Reverend Green froze. After a moment, he turned to look at Nigel. His eyes went wide, and his mouth hung open in shock. He slowly shook his head.

"It's you!" repeated Nigel, louder.

Reverend Green shook his head with vehemence, as if willing this not to be so. His face broke out in a sweat. Behind him, Professor James's face blanched. He looked just as shocked as the reverend. Marie Dubois, on the other hand, smiled and nodded. "*Loup-garou*," she uttered in a hoarse whisper.

"Of course!" said Professor James in a stunned voice. "Marie has been trying to warn us." He faced the minister. "You must've had some hold over her that has driven her mad."

"No!" yelled Reverend Green. He glanced from one to the other with eyebrows raised, imploring them to accept his denial. The reverend buckled in a convulsive spasm. Still bent, he raised his head and looked at Nigel with glowing red eyes and a mouth full of canine teeth. "No!" he snarled.

The half-man half-monster blocked Nigel's way. Beyond it, Professor James and the old woman stood at the church door. "Get out!" shouted Nigel to the professor.

Professor James shook his head. "I'll not leave—"

Nigel waved his arm to cut him off. "Tell the

others! *Go!*"

Professor James grabbed the woman's arm, but once again, she shook herself free. She shoved the professor outside and slammed the door shut. Marie turned and pointed. "*Loup-garou.*"

Nigel backed away. Now what? he asked himself. Can I escape? Nigel glanced around and considered trying to dive through one of the open windows. If so, might the creature just follow him? Then what?

The transformation from man to wolf accelerated. An audible cracking of bones and cartilage occurred as the reverend altered before Nigel's eyes. Reverend Green winced in obvious pain, grabbed the back of the rear pew, and screamed. As he did so, he tore the bench from the floor. Continuing to shriek in pain, he threw the entire pew behind him. The heavy wooden bench flew through the air and collided with Marie, crushing her against the door. A rivulet of blood ran from the old woman's open mouth and off her chin. Her eyes, wide with shock, lost their light, and her head and shoulders slumped forward over the remains of the pew.

Reverend Green's face morphed into a wolf's snout with fangs becoming ever more prominent. Hair crawled out of the man's face and on the back of his misshapen hands. The reverend's black shirt, pants, and shoes split open, no longer able to contain the large creature. The transformation complete, the werewolf dropped to all fours and howled—the sound deafening in the confines of the church.

In a flash, Nigel weighed the merits of ducking beneath the pews, but he had a mental image of the beast trapping him there, helpless and cowering, with no place to go. Moreover, he'd just seen how the monster tore a pew free from the floor. *I'll not go that way*, he decided. *I'll not be easy prey.*

Nigel sprinted to the front of the church and grabbed the two glass lamps off the altar. He threw each at the advancing wolf. The first was batted away with the back of one paw. It struck a wooden pew and burst into flames. The wolf easily dodged the second lamp, which clipped several pews on the other side of the church and spread flames there as well.

Out of desperation, Nigel tipped over the table, a three-foot wall that he realized offered no real protection. With slow, deliberate steps, the huge black wolf continued to approach, its malevolent red eyes fixed on Nigel. The creature's jaws opened, and its wet tongue lolled out. Saliva dripped from the tongue and left a shiny trail on the wooden floor.

Nigel could hear pounding against the door in the rear of the church, but the others could not get in.

Protection, I need protection!

An idea struck him. Nigel grabbed the reverend's suit jacket off the back of a chair and wrapped it around his left arm. With his free hand, he hoisted the chair and held it before him, hoping to drive the creature back like a lion tamer.

The wolf bounded forward and leapt over the table, jaws held wide.

Nigel shoved a chair leg into the creature's mouth. The beast's momentum drove Nigel back against the altar as its teeth sank into the wooden leg and jerked the chair from Nigel's grip. The chair flew back over the pews and smashed to pieces on the rear wall near the door. The wolf's hind legs kicked the table into the pews, causing several to fall over like dominos.

Do I have a chance?

Nigel held his padded arm before him to block the attack, and the wolf sank its teeth into the appendage. The crushing pressure of its powerful jaws caused an agonizing cry of pain from Nigel. The beast snarled through bared teeth as the fiery coals of its eyes burned brighter.

The creature savaged the padded arm, yanking its head back and forth, trying to get at his flesh. Nigel flew through the air, hitting the altar each time the beast swung him one way then the other. Landing on top of the altar, Nigel made a mad grasp for the foot-high silver cross that had toppled over.

He clenched it in his right hand. With all his strength, Nigel brought the marble base of the cross down upon the beast's head. It landed with a sickening thud. On impact, the werewolf huffed a fetid breath into Nigel's face. It blinked its eyes a few times, then attacked with new fury. Again and again, Nigel struck the monster with little effect. He persisted until the base of the cross broke off. The werewolf seemed infuriated by his defense.

Its front claws tore at Nigel's clothing. The creature's hind legs scrabbled against the dais. Its jaws snapped open and closed as its head twisted in different directions—going for Nigel's throat. Nigel continued to force his padded arm into the snarling orifice of teeth. It hurt like the devil, but he persisted—though he knew he could not keep this up much longer.

Nigel realized he had one chance. Summoning every ounce of strength, he shoved his padded arm hard into the wolf's mouth and stabbed the sharp broken end of the cross into the creature's abdomen. The beast yelped in pain. A loud sizzling sound occurred along with the stink of burning flesh. Nigel stabbed and stabbed again. Each time the wolf howled in pain and attacked anew. Scalding hot blood from the creature coated his right hand and forearm, but he managed to keep his grip on the cross.

Nigel felt the power of the beast's attacks begin to slacken. This time, he drove the cross upward under its ribs. The creature jerked back, yelping. Nigel lost his grip, but the cross remained embedded in the werewolf, where it hissed and glowed white hot. The creature's chest burst into flames. Front paws flailed at the fire, then slowed to a stop.

The malevolent red eyes dimmed. The wolf stared at him with the same imploring look Reverend Green had worn before he transformed. With a human voice, it uttered one word, "No—" and toppled backward.

The creature fell across the dais, still on fire.

Chapter Thirty-One

Nigel fell to his knees, exhausted. His left arm hung useless at his side. His clothes were now shredded rags, and his body torn where the werewolf's claws raked him. But most of the blood covering him belonged to the beast. Nigel gulped air, rancid with the burning creature, knowing he was going to live.

Professor James, Edgar, and Sarah at last managed to get the church door open. They shoved the pew aside, causing Marie's body to slump to the floor with a thud. Edgar vaulted over the woman and broken pew and ran up the aisle. Bits of straw clung to his clothing. As he ran, Edgar held before him the pistol containing the silver bullets.

"Too little, too late," said Nigel with a grimace.

In front of Nigel, the creature lay engulfed in a fiery blaze. Flames spread across the front of the church and set the podium alight. The whole place stank of sulfur.

Edgar put the pistol between his belt and his back. Professor James joined him, and together they tried to move Nigel away from the fire. But as soon as the professor lifted Nigel's left arm, Nigel screamed in pain.

"Grab him from behind, around the chest," Professor James told Edgar. But before they could depart, the professor launched into a fit of coughing.

When he recovered enough for them to move, he picked up Nigel's legs. The three lumbered away as flames spread to where Nigel had just lain. As they left the church, Nigel tried to convey what happened.

Outside, they saw Sarah had pulled Marie from the building and was crouched near the body. Sarah stood and shook her head, indicating Marie was dead.

Sarah approached Nigel and put her hand to his bloody cheek. There was only care in her touch. "I'm glad you're still with us, Mr. Pickford."

Nigel made a wan smile and passed out.

****

Professor James and Edgar set the unconscious Nigel on the damp hay in the back of the wagon, next to Annabelle. The two men coughed and wiped their eyes—aftereffects of the smoke.

"Are they going to be all right?" Sarah asked.

Professor James stopped coughing and surveyed the two. "For the present. It's a warm night, so the damp shouldn't be a problem. As for the future, I have any number of concerns…" His voice trailed away as he saw a group of bobbing lights in the distance. In a few seconds, he could discern a half-dozen figures running toward them.

Sarah and Edgar turned to see.

"Trouble?" asked Edgar. He removed his pistol while staring at the approaching men. He returned the gun to his belt. "It's my group from tonight."

The men ran to them and gestured at the church. They shouted: "Why aren't you fighting the fire?" "We should form a bucket brigade!" and "Where's Reverend Green?"

Doc, the dentist, simply yelled, "What the hell is

going on?"

"We were preoccupied," said Professor James. He took the dentist's lantern and held it above Nigel.

"My Lord Jesus," uttered Doc. The other men quieted when they saw Nigel's torn and bloody appearance.

"Mr. Pickford dispatched your werewolf, single-handed. Unfortunately, the one cursed with the disease was Reverend Green."

"No..." Doc uttered in disbelief. The rest of the search party made similar protests.

Professor James gave an account of the events, dispelling all doubts.

"Shouldn't we try to save the church?" asked Doc.

"You can try. Given its source, you may wish to let it burn itself out."

The dentist gave his head a shake. "Helluva thing. We'll try to save the house. You folks get on outta here." He looked at Edgar. "There's gonna be hell to pay if the Klan gets hold of you. Head north to Richmond. If asked, we'll tell 'em you went south. Better yet, we'll say you died in the fire. Leave Garraty's horse to help prove it."

Edgar and Professor James nodded their thanks. Sarah added her appreciation.

Doc approached Edgar. "I admit being too flabbergasted to say anything proper when you put the bullets in Garraty." He grabbed Edgar's hand between two of his and pumped it up and down. "As far as I'm concerned, you folks got rid of two monsters this night."

After Doc shook Edgar's hand, the five other men formed a queue to do the same.

****

Nigel awoke many hours later and discovered he had on clean clothes. His left arm hung in a sling, and he could feel numerous bandages beneath his clothes. He sat in a wheelchair on an unfamiliar railroad platform. By the feel of the air and the angle of the sun shining under the awning, Nigel judged it to be late afternoon or early evening.

"Where am I?"

Annabelle had her back to him, staring at the empty track. She turned around and gave him a warm smile. "Delighted to see you've rejoined us, Mr. Pickford. We are in Richmond and will soon be heading home to Boston. We decided it would be best to put some distance between us and the events of last night. The train is due any minute."

An image flashed through Nigel's mind of the snarling wolf lunging for him. He shivered, despite the day's heat. He shook his head clear and focused on the much more pleasant memory of Annabelle's bosom he had glimpsed the previous night. *I wonder if she has any idea*, he speculated, smiling back at her.

Edgar, Professor James, and Sarah surrounded his wheelchair. The professor and Sarah wore traveling clothes. On the other hand, Edgar had on black pants and a wrinkled denim shirt, looking more like a farmhand in his Sunday best than the well-dressed doctor of physics he usually presented to the world. He looked similar to other colored men waiting at the far end of the platform.

"Can you walk, Mr. Pickford?" asked Professor James.

"Yes," said Nigel, "I think so." Nigel pushed back

the foot stands with his feet and stood from the chair. "I do feel a little woozy," he confessed.

"That would be Annabelle's laudanum. You don't remember us administering it to you?"

Nigel shook his head.

"Perhaps it's for the best. Your arm is fractured in several places," continued Professor James. "I have set it, but it will be some time before you will be fighting monsters again."

"Thank God for that," Nigel mumbled.

"God may well have had a hand in dispatching the werewolf, given your use of the cross."

"Handy," said Nigel. "I would have grabbed anything."

"And fortuitous the cross was silver." Professor James lowered his brows and said, "You may want to retake your seat before I give you some information which may prove upsetting."

Not in a mood to argue, Nigel plopped onto the wheelchair, grateful someone had set the brake. "Lay on, Macduff," he groaned.

"I've dressed your wounds and assessed your injuries. I'm happy to report it appears the beast's teeth never broke your skin."

"He seems to have done enough damage."

"Indeed," said Professor James, "and that's what concerns us. Some of the literature indicates the lycanthropic disease is spread through the wolf's bite. Other sources state anyone surviving an injury is at risk."

"Meaning, I may become a werewolf?" he asked in a stunned voice.

"We don't know." Professor James paused to

scrutinize him. Nigel made an impatient gesture with his one good hand for the professor to continue. "Furthermore," said Professor James, "you were drenched in wolf's blood. No doubt some of it got into your wounds."

Nigel felt himself becoming even more light-headed. He massaged his temples with his right hand. "So how will we be sure?" he asked after some consideration.

Professor James looked at the others, nodded, and focused his gaze on Nigel. "In the early stages of the disease, the moon appears to be the catalyst. We will need to keep you under lock and key come the next full moon. Should this prove to be true—well, we'll cross that bridge should we come to it. In the meantime, for what little comfort it may provide, know you are a member of our team and deserving of our loyalty."

Everyone nodded.

Moved by this, Nigel lowered his head and felt close to tears.

There came a rumble and the blast of a locomotive's whistle. People crowded onto the platform as the train pulled in. With a hiss of steam and a screech of metal on metal, the train pulled to a stop.

Passengers disembarked, some exiting the platform, others directing porters who carried their luggage. Stevedores rushed to the baggage cars, unloaded trunks, and set larger cargo onto flatbed carts. All became a flurry of commotion.

Annabelle looked at Nigel as he raised his head. She smiled again and offered him a silver-headed cane. "A gift from us," she said. The others nodded. "We didn't know if you would need a cane or not, but its silver head seemed apropos."

Touched, Nigel smiled and said, "Thank you." He grabbed the head of the cane and stood. "Well," he glanced at them all, "shall we board?" No sooner had he said this than he let go of the cane, and it crashed onto the wooden platform. He collapsed back into the chair. His face drained of color, and he broke out in a clammy sweat.

"Is he ill?" cried Annabelle, looking from Nigel to Professor James for an answer.

"I don't know," confessed the professor.

"His eyes get glassy like this when he is having one of his visions," said Sarah, touching Nigel's sleeve.

"What do we do?" implored Annabelle.

As quick as it had occurred, color returned to Nigel's face, but he gasped for air as though he had just run a mile. "Do not board this train," said Nigel in a staggered cadence between gasps.

"We must," said Annabelle. She added, whispering, "Edgar is wanted for murder back in Petersburg. And we may all face recrimination with the death of the reverend and his housekeeper. We must be away."

"No!" Nigel barked. "The train will crash into another later this evening. We can take the next."

"But every minute I'm here presents a risk," said Edgar. "For me, which is worse?"

"I don't know." Nigel heaved a sigh. "I didn't see you in particular."

"What about all these people?" asked Annabelle, casting her eyes around the crowded platform.

"We must warn them," said Sarah.

"No use," said Nigel. "No one will believe you.

Monique said I'd be cursed to utter prophesies no one will believe."

"*We* believe you," said Annabelle. She looked around for confirmation, and all but Edgar affirmed this. After a few seconds, he shrugged his assent. "That and other things indicate you are breaking free of this curse. We must try."

Edgar looked around at the throng of people milling around the platform. "Shouldn't we avoid calling attention to ourselves?"

"We can't just let people die," persisted Sarah.

Professor James gestured for calmness with his hand and looked around. "You all have valid points. Edgar, you may wish to stand apart, as you have the most to fear from unwanted attention. The ladies and I shall raise the alarm."

Nigel watched from his wheelchair and hoped, for once, the warnings would go heeded.

Annabelle, still limping, moved in front of a bulldog-faced woman in a brown velvet dress who had a pudgy boy of about five in tow. "Ma'am," said Annabelle, "please don't board the train. There's danger ahead."

The boy stopped in his tracks and looked at Annabelle with his round cheeks framing a worried frown. He moved his gaze to the large woman who had hold of his hand. "Mama?" he asked for reassurance.

The mother pushed Annabelle aside so hard she fell to the platform with a shout of surprise. The mother jerked the boy forward, causing him to trip over Annabelle.

"Ouch!" cried the child.

The mother and tearful child boarded the train.

Professor James and Sarah fared no better.

Sarah stopped a young couple who walked arm in arm. "Please," she said, "catch another train. There is danger of a crash."

The woman put a hand to her mouth and made a startled cry. The man stepped before Sarah, "See here, what's the meaning of this?"

"We have knowledge of an impending crash."

The man shot a glance at the crowd of other passengers busy boarding the train. He put a protective arm over the woman's shoulders and led her on. "Stay away, you lunatic!" he told Sarah.

Professor James approached a natty gray-haired gentleman in a white linen suit and carrying a lacquered bamboo cane. Behind him stood two women, one of similar vintage as the man, and the other a much younger woman who bore some resemblance to the other two.

"Sir," Professor James said as he tipped his hat, "I beg you and your family to consider taking another train. There will be a crash later, putting your lives at risk."

The old man moved with remarkable speed. He whipped his cane above him and brought it crashing down onto the professor's hat. "Help, help!" the old man shouted. Sarah and Annabelle led Professor James away from his attacker.

Someone must have already informed the station master. He came running from the terminal, his face beet-red and contorted with anger. "Just what the hell do you folks think you're doing?"

Professor James removed his damaged hat. "My apologies, sir. We should have come to you straight away. You must cancel this train."

The old man shouted, "Says there's going to be a crash."

The station master puffed his chest with incredulity. "I think not," he pronounced. "Who gives you the right to spread fear and rumors among the passengers?"

A police officer approached and slapped his billy club on his palm. His nose and cheeks featured a spider web of red veins from drink.

Professor James persisted. "My associate has had a vision of death and tragedy. We are trying to save people's lives."

Annabelle chimed in. "It's true."

"We've never known him to be wrong," added Sarah.

The policeman had heard enough. "Shut your mouths right now, or I'm arresting y'all for disturbing the peace. *Understood?*"

After a long pause, Professor James nodded. "We understand," he said in a resigned voice. He ushered the ladies to step away, and they all slunk back toward Nigel.

As they retreated, they overheard the station master ask the officer to keep an eye on the group. The officer said he would.

For his part, Edgar tried to warn the colored passengers, but they were just as skeptical. He looked over at his comrades and shook his head. Having seen the confrontation with the policeman, he went around the side of the building to wait.

"Alas," said Annabelle to Nigel, "You were right. It's terrible knowing the inevitable."

"One would think they'd err on the side of caution," added Professor James.

Sarah looked at Nigel with pity. "I think this predicament could drive one mad."

A conductor called for final boarding. Several harried passengers raced to catch the departing train. The locomotive blasted its whistle. There came the hiss of steam, the squeal of metal, the pungent scent of coal smoke, and the chugging sound of the engine. The train pitched forward and picked up speed. As each car went by, Nigel felt worse. He looked at the others. A pall hung over them.

"Would any of you like a strong drink?" he asked with a sardonic smile.

****

When the train departed, the group remained the only people on the platform except for the policeman who watched them from the station's double doors. The group moved to a shaded area, Nigel in his chair and Professor James and the ladies on a bench. Edgar needed to remain inconspicuous, so he waited along the station's far side, out of view.

An oppressive silence hung like a blacksmith's anvil over the group. No wonder, Nigel thought, so many will die…

After a while, Nigel looked over at Professor James and said, "Why did the minister write to you, inviting us, when he was the werewolf?

Professor James gave him a little smile, as though he were a pupil who had posed a perceptive question. "I've been wondering the same thing. Perhaps we all have."

Sarah and Annabelle nodded.

"The only thing I can surmise is part of him wanted to be caught, to be stopped." Professor James took a deep breath and exhaled audibly. "As a man of the cloth, he must have been at war with himself—that is, if he were aware of the monstrous force at work within him.

"The disease, in its late stage, becomes increasingly dominant. His creature-side must have recognized the threat you posed when you accused him and took over, transforming the minister before our eyes."

Considering this, the four of them lapsed into silence once more.

****

Around the corner, Edgar waited for the next train in the hot evening sun. Sweaty, thirsty, and edgy with fear, he would now and then snatch a peek to see the police officer still keeping a watchful eye on the others. *Damn,* he muttered, returning to the discarded wooden crate he'd been using for a chair. Edgar closed his eyes and tried to calm himself but imagined the officer and a group of Klansmen storming around the corner to capture, torture, and kill him. His eyes flew open, and he immediately ascertained the best escape route. Edgar realized he might be able to clamber over a pile of large wooden crates to get over the brick wall. Just possible, he figured, unless they had guns.

All this swam in his head as he kept a lookout, keyed-up, ready to bolt at a moment's notice. So when Saphne came around the corner of the station, Edgar jumped out of his skin.

Chapter Thirty-Two

As soon as Saphne sent Edgar away from Garraty's place, tears welled in her eyes. She choked off her emotions with tremendous effort until she got back into the kitchen, and then the dam broke. *What have I done?* she wailed. Saphne swept away the tears and ran back outside. Too late. Edgar, astride his horse, faded away into the darkness. She covered her mouth and bit her hand to keep from crying his name—she couldn't call for fear of attracting the attention of the Klansmen in the front room.

Saphne breathed in a lungful of honeysuckle-scented air and tried to think. Through the open windows at the front of the house, she could hear the voices of the Klansmen, shouting and debating their next move.

Garraty was dead. Her employer, her rapist, her reason for being here, no longer existed. Who knows what would happen to all the servants over the next few days and weeks? She had turned Edgar away for what?

Saphne tore at the front of her white apron top. The ties bit into the back of her neck then snapped. She tried to do the same with those around her waist, but they would not break. She fumbled with the fabric ties until they came free. She threw the apron to the ground and ran from the Garraty mansion.

Halfway into the tobacco field, she stopped and

looked around. *The bogeywolf.* She'd forgotten the danger in fleeing. *Was I ever any safer in that house?* Saphne asked herself. She knew the answer and resumed her flight.

Having spent their fury in the thunderstorm, the earlier clouds were now breaking apart and moving on. The intermittent moonlight made it difficult to see. Despite this, Saphne found the path through the woods and made her way toward Petersburg. When she came to her home, Saphne entered as quietly as possible, not wanting to disturb her brothers in the back bedroom.

Her mother had fallen asleep in the rocker by the unlit fireplace.

"Momma?" Saphne said as she touched her mother's arm. The older woman stirred but did not open her eyes. "Momma?"

The woman's eyelids fluttered and opened. She smiled at her daughter. Saphne could not remember the last time a smile crossed the woman's lips. "Hello, Dearheart," her mother said. "Fell asleep thinking about what you told me yesterday." She took Saphne's hand and gave it a squeeze. "Honey, all I gots to say is follow your heart. Lightning has struck. Your feelings for this professor-man be a gift. They're like what your father and I shared. Your words inspired me. I shook the dust off my bones, got up, and did some housework last evening after I put the boys to bed. Plum tuckered me out. Could say I'm outta practice."

"Oh, Momma," Saphne sobbed, "you don't know the half of it." At last, she told her mother about the rape and Garraty's death. She recounted the offer Edgar made that evening outside Garraty's house and her refusal. With tears in her eyes, Saphne said, "Mama, my heart is torn in two."

Her mother rose from the rocker and hugged her. The sudden transformation tonight made Saphne's tears swell into a torrent.

"You better get your things and go," her mother told her, wiping Saphne's eyes with a small handkerchief. "The longer you wait, the longer you'll have to go to find him."

Saphne protested, citing worry for her mother and siblings, but her mother would hear none of it.

"Look at me," she said. "I've been soul-sick with the loss of your father. But tonight, my soul got repaired. That, or I got me a shiny new soul. I want you happy. I got a little money in a tin can you don't know about, and I can take in laundry or mending like I used to." She made little shooing motions with her hands. "Get on, now. We'll be okay."

****

Saphne decided to go to Reverend Green first. Edgar might even be at the church. If not, the reverend would know where to find him. At the very least, the minister brought the group here, so he'd know their address if she needed to go up north.

As she ran along Jerusalem Plank Road, carrying a small cloth bundle of her belongings, Saphne recalled getting her mom's blessing. This made her heart soar. She felt if she could just run faster, she'd take flight like a bird.

Saphne stopped in the middle of the road and sniffed. The air smelled of smoke. Wood smoke was commonplace but not in August and not in the middle of the night. She noticed a glow in the distance and ran toward it with a sense of foreboding.

When free of the trees, Saphne saw the Blandford Baptist Church engulfed in fire. Yellow and orange flames danced above the remains of the structure, as though happy for its destruction. She could feel the heat on her face, a quarter-mile away. With a burst of energy, she sprinted the rest of the way. A small knot of white people watched from the other side of the road, next to their church, doing nothing to help.

As she got closer to what remained of Reverend Green's Baptist church, she saw a group of colored men trying to deal with the fire. A bucket brigade snaked off to a nearby creek. It seemed the men abandoned trying to save the church and instead threw water onto the small parsonage—which hissed as each bucketful of water landed.

The fire's roar surprised her. Saphne ran to Moses, who stood closest, and shouted, "Where's Doctor Gilpin and the others?" He shook his head and came nearer. "Where's Reverend Green?" she asked.

Moses jerked a thumb in the direction of the burning church.

Hearing this, she looked at the conflagration and collapsed.

****

Saphne regained consciousness flat on the ground with the dentist kneeling over her, rubbing her wrists and looking worried.

"Moses asked me to tend to you. Thought we was going to lose someone else for a second there," confessed Doc, "but then I realized you'd just fainted. You never seen a fire before?"

Saphne forced herself to sit. "Doctor Gilpin and the others—they in the church when it caught fire?"

"Yes—"

Saphne felt faint again. The dentist grabbed her shoulders.

"—hold on, they got out. All except for the reverend. That professor said Reverend Green was the bogeywolf all along. *Can you believe it?*"

The news seemed beyond comprehension. Saphne and her family started attending this upstart church several years ago. Petersburg already had two big Baptist churches for coloreds, but she liked Reverend Green. His sermons focused on love and compassion, not fire and brimstone, and his church had welcomed her. Here they'd been in the jaws of death for years and hadn't even realized it. *What about Edgar?* She needed to know about him. "Did the bogeywolf harm anyone?"

"Like your Doctor Gilpin?" Doc asked with a faint grin.

Saphne grabbed his arm as worry plowed her brow into furrows.

The dentist put his hand over hers and patted it. "He's fine. One of the white fellas looked worse for wear. Killed the creature single-handed, but not without receiving some wounds. The creature did kill that poor woman." The dentist pointed a finger just beyond her.

Saphne turned her head and noticed the draped body about five yards away, feet protruding from a canvas tarp. She scooted away. "Who's that?"

"Marie, the reverend's cook and housekeeper. Seems the reverend killed her when he became the monster."

"Where are they? Doctor Gilpin and them others."

The dentist pointed in the direction she had come. "I told 'em to skedaddle to Richmond, where they can catch a train north. Your Doctor Gilpin shot Garraty and needs to make himself scarce."

Saphne nodded her head to indicate she knew.

"They just left. I'm surprised you didn't run into 'em on the road."

"I saw no one 'til I got here."

The dentist looked at the fire. "Helluva thing. All those deaths, and him organizing us to search for the creature. Here he was, the bogeywolf, under our noses all along." The man sighed and stood. "Well, I got to get back to helping. You going to try to catch up to 'em?"

"I'm gonna try."

Saphne stood but grabbed the dentist's shoulder to steady herself.

"You okay?"

Saphne nodded. She let go of him and retrieved her bundle from the grass where it had fallen. "Thanks for doing for me, Doc."

"Pullin' teeth is more my area. Glad you're all right. Good luck to ya." He waved goodbye as he turned and headed for the bucket brigade.

Saphne returned to the road and retraced her steps. Part of her felt bad for leaving the men without helping, but she couldn't pass on the chance of reaching Edgar and the others before they boarded a train. Richmond lay miles away. Harvard, she guessed, lay a good deal farther.

She tried to run but could not sustain it for long. Still, she pushed herself to go as fast as she could. After a bit, she rounded a bend in the road and saw a group of white-clad horsemen carrying torches a short distance away. She considered jumping into the bushes but figured they'd seen her already, and hiding would seem all the more suspicious. She continued toward them.

The Klan member in front raised his arm, and the horsemen behind him pulled to a stop. "Halt, you!" he said to Saphne.

Though he wore a hood, Saphne recognized Roy Amblin, owner of the largest general store in the white part of town. She served him lemonade an hour ago in Garraty's drawing room.

"Yes, sir," she said, stopping and lowering her head to show her respect.

"Do I know you?" asked Amblin.

"Yes, sir, I worked for Mista Garraty. I served you and the other folks who came by tonight. Just heading home when I saw the fire and went to go have a look."

"What fire?"

Saphne pointed back at the direction she had come. "The Baptist church for coloreds is afire," she said.

Amblin's horse snorted and pawed the road, anxious to get on its way. Amblin pulled on the reins and leaned toward Saphne. "We're looking for a colored Yankee. You seen him?"

Saphne shook her head. "No, sir. But there is a whole lot of colored folk at the church trying to put out the fire. Maybe you should try there."

Amblin snorted, not unlike his horse. He glanced back at the others and waved his arm. "Let's go!" he shouted. He dug his heels into the horse's flanks, and the horse bolted forward right at Saphne. She jumped clear and watched as Amblin and the other night riders rode past and disappeared down the road.

Now Saphne pushed herself to run with all her might. When she got to Petersburg and moved through its dark streets, she worried how the men at the church would respond to the Klan. She felt bad for directing them that way, but what else could she do? She prayed Doc and the others would not send the Klan toward Richmond. Still, the Klan might figure it out on their own—unless the men said Edgar died in the fire. She hoped Doc, Moses, and the rest were good liars.

Saphne ducked from sight at the approach of any traffic she encountered, but when she crossed the Appomattox into Colonial Heights, she could run no more. Her legs were like rubber, and her throat parched as a desert. A rain barrel stood next to a nearby house, and Saphne stopped to drink her fill. Richmond still lay thirty miles on. She decided to take a chance and waved down a wagon headed north, a two-horse vehicle driven by a solitary colored man. He had a large load in the back of his wagon covered with a tarp.

"You headed to Richmond?"

"Who wants to know?" asked the man.

"Name's Saphne Taylor. I'm trying to get to Richmond before my fiancé takes the train north. We had a fight, and I needs to put things right." Saphne hoped the Lord would forgive her stretching the truth.

The man nodded. "I had been fixin' to have a long boring ride. How can I say no to a pretty lady in need of a hand? Climb on board."

Saphne threw her small bag of belongings under the seat and climbed aboard next to the driver.

It turned out Marcus, the teamster, had a load of cotton bales headed to Richmond. For the price of holding up her end of the conversation, she traveled in relative comfort, though the hot sun followed them throughout the day.

When they arrived at the Richmond station, the station clock read half-past six. She expressed her gratitude for the ride and climbed from the wagon.

"Happy for the company. You tell your fiancé from me to forgive you. If he don't see the light, you look up ol' Marcus Brown in Colonial Heights. You hear?"

Saphne waved goodbye and went inside. A mill of people clustered around the ticketing windows, but otherwise, much of the station looked empty. Saphne guessed she had arrived between departures, but she really didn't know, not having ridden a train before. She checked all the people in the building. No sign of Edgar. Worried, she decided to try outside on the platform.

Chapter Thirty-Three

Upon seeing Saphne, Edgar sprang to his feet but became immobilized. He wanted to embrace her. Instead, he just stood there with hands hanging at his sides. *Is she real? A phantom?* With all he'd seen and experienced over the last year, he wondered.

"Edgar?" Saphne's voice quavered. She carried a red and white checkered cloth bundle and wore the same dress he'd seen her in at Garraty's the night before. The area around her left eye still looked bruised, but she now regarded him with both eyes wide.

A wave of self-consciousness washed over Edgar. I look like a farm-hand—a murderous farmhand. *What right have I to hope she could love me?*

Saphne stopped a short way from him and set her bundle on the ground before her. In a quiet voice, she asked, "Did you mean everything you said last night?"

He nodded. "Every word."

With abruptness, all inhibitions fell away. He sprang toward Saphne, and they fell into each other's arms.

She felt very real.

When they parted, they straightened themselves, and Edgar, smiling from ear to ear, offered her his erstwhile chair. She made room for him on the crate, and the two sat together, holding hands. Saphne put her head on his shoulder, and Edgar nuzzled his face in her thick black hair.

"After refusing your offer," Saphne spoke, "I was heartsick. I ran outside to catch you, but you'd gone. I kept runnin'. Why should I stick around serving Kluxes? I asked myself. When I got home, I woke Momma and told her everything. She said, 'Child, you best go find that man. We'll be all right,' she told me, 'especially if he's a man of his word. If not, you'll know soon enough and come on home.'

"I went to the church, or what's left of it, and Doc told me you folks lit out for Richmond. Started runnin' until I could run no more. A farmer with a wagon brought me the rest of the way. I figured I'd missed ya and would have to find my way to Harvard. I got lucky. When I came onto the platform, Professor James recognized me and directed me around the side of the station. And here I am.

"So." Saphne straightened, turned, and met his eyes. "I got to ask you again, are you a man of your word?"

****

When Edgar and Saphne came around the building an hour later, Edgar still wore the same wide grin. He wondered if he'd ever stop smiling. The two stepped onto the central platform, arm in arm. Edgar noticed the policeman was gone. *Thank God.*

They approached his friends and colleagues. Professor James, Annabelle, and even Nigel wore broad smiles, mirroring his own. Sarah, however, became pale and turned away.

Edgar's smile faded. *What's that about?* He decided to follow-up with her later.

****

The warm evening light faded to darkness. The platform became more crowded as the arrival of the next train neared. Three and a half hours after the previous train, now in the glow of lamplight, the next train pulled into the station. A repeat of the seemingly choreographed hubbub occurred, with exiting passengers, loved ones being met, luggage and freight being hauled away on carts, all changing places with the new people, tearful goodbyes, and the baggage of the boarding passengers.

Professor James had purchased new tickets. This time, the Eidola Project, the little band of academics and misfits, scrambled aboard. All but Edgar and Saphne, who had to ride in the colored car, had a large cabin to themselves, and Nigel took a window seat. It wouldn't be long, he knew, before they'd be delayed on a siding for hours so the wreckage ahead of them could get cleared from the tracks.

As the train left the station, a beautiful blonde woman with piercing green eyes remained on the platform. She waved a white handkerchief goodbye and blew kisses. Nigel realized the woman was staring at him. His stomach turned.

Monique smiled at his reaction.

She hadn't aged a day.

Once their eyes met, she stopped her charade and broke out in a laugh. Then she disappeared in a cloud of smoke and steam.

A peek at the first Eidola Project Novel

Almost a month after Molly's disappearance, a full bladder forced Sarah Bradbury awake in the middle of the night. Try as she might, sleep would not return. She could not deny the inevitable—she needed to pee.

Sarah groaned, pushed away the ratty quilt, and sat up. For the thousandth time she wished her father would allow her a chamber pot, but she'd spilled one once, four years ago, when five-years-old, and that was the end of that. Pitch-black darkness filled her room, so she fumbled around on the small table next to her for a lucifer.

Sarah located one and struck it on the rough surface of the unpainted tabletop. Sulfur filled her nostrils and she sneezed, nearly dropping the burning matchstick. After lighting the wick in the old metal lamp on the bedside table, she shook the lucifer to extinguish its flame. She then raised the little metal arm on the kerosene lamp, which caused a small glass globe to lower over the burning wick. The lamp provided faint light, but enough to find her way. She pushed her red hair back from her narrow face and stood.

Easing open the bedroom door, Sarah crept down the hall past her parents' room, hoping beyond all measure she hadn't woken them. She tiptoed into the wider area of the house that served as kitchen, eating area, living room, and entryway. She lifted the metal latch on the door with the greatest of care and eased outside. Dew covered the rough boards of their front porch and the well-worn path through the yard to the outhouse. The moisture caused dirt and grass to adhere to the bottom of her feet as she trudged along.

The previous day's overcast sky looked rent apart, as though some celestial demon raked its claws first one way across the night sky, then the other. Patches of stars shown between the many small clouds. For a moment the full moon appeared, then scuttled behind a cloud, causing its outer edge to glow.

Sarah pulled open the outhouse's wooden door and held the lamp before her, peering within. Empty. One night a raccoon found its way in there, and they both had a fright until the critter scampered out. Sarah did not wish to renew the acquaintance.

She stepped inside, pulled the door shut, and twisted the peg that held the door closed. Sarah put the lamp on the floor, hiked up her nightgown, and sat on the seat—a plank with a hole in it. A pile of newspapers sat next to her, and after relieving herself, she tore off a piece of one sheet to wipe herself dry.

Sarah retrieved the lamp and twisted the peg. The outhouse door swung open on its own, and she gasped.

"Momma?" Sarah asked as she held out her lantern.

No. A ruined version of Molly stood in the doorway. Before her disappearance, people often commented on the sixteen-year-old's beauty, but in the last twenty-eight days birds pecked out her pretty blue eyes, and maggots now swam in the sockets. Molly's head hung to the left at an odd angle. Her skin looked mottled with patches of gray, blue, and black. A beetle crawled out of Molly's half-opened mouth and darted back in.

Sarah's heart leapt to her throat. Recoiling, she lost her footing, fell onto the outhouse seat, and dropped the lantern to the floor. She bent to retrieve it; thankful the glass globe did not break. Sarah looked up and saw an empty doorway.

Impossible, she told herself. *Must've dozed off, had a nightmare, and woke up when I dropped the lamp.*

Her heart still pounded in her chest, and Sarah took a deep breath to calm herself.

Holding the lamp before her once more, she edged out. Nothing unusual. She made her way around the side of the house, but as she turned the corner to the front, there stood Molly.

Sarah turned and ran. Over by the outhouse, she looked over her shoulder and saw she wasn't being followed. She stopped.

If Molly were a spirit, nothing prevented her from appearing somewhere else.

Sarah shivered despite it being a warm night. She rubbed her arms, feeling the goosebumps beneath her fingers, and looked back toward the house.

What does she want? Soon, curiosity overpowered her. Sarah crept back toward the front of the house and peered around the corner. Molly still waited there, facing Sarah, but neither said anything. The supernatural figure turned and shuffled across the matted grass of Sarah's front yard and went out onto the road leading from the farmhouse.

Sarah dashed up onto the porch to where her father left his boots under the awning. She put them on over her bare feet but did not bother to lace them. She clomped after Molly. The moon emerged from behind a cloud, and now Sarah could clearly see Molly walking ahead. After about a mile, Sarah stumbled into a pothole and fell. This time Molly waited for her.

They headed down Old Mill Road. Molly stopped

and pointed, so Sarah came up and looked where indicated. She held the lantern before her, but no more kerosene remained in the lamp and the flame became a thin blue line which guttered out. A canopy of trees blocked the moonlight, and she could make out nothing ahead in the darkness. When Sarah looked back, Molly had disappeared.

Sarah wondered for a while what to do, then she used the heel of her right boot to carve a line across the dirt road and found enough rocks to make an arrow of them on the shoulder. She hoped the markers would be visible in the daytime.

When she got home, her father waited for her with a switch in his hand. He slapped it against his palm a few times for effect. "You fixin' to run off like Molly?" he asked, despite Sarah's young age. "You got a boy you're seein', same as her?"

He commenced to beat her backside raw. Between tears and shouts of pain, Sarah tried to tell him what happened and he beat her all the harder for lying.

From her parents' bedroom, her mother emerged. Heavy-set, like her husband, with a perpetual sheen to her face. Her hair, a wild rat's nest, often stayed uncombed throughout the day. She regarded the beating with mild interest, then complained about how Sarah had tracked dirt into the house.

Whatever Sarah said didn't matter, so she quit saying anything.

When her red-faced and sweaty father spent his fury, her mother put a hand on his damp back. "Come, Honey, sit down at the table. Looks like you worked up an appetite this morning."

Later, when Sarah left the house to go to school,

she did nothing of the sort. Her backside ached and she wasn't sure she could sit at her desk. It even hurt to walk, but she did it anyway, compelled to retrace the steps she traveled last night.

The farms and homes along the way looked as always and were mundane in their familiarity. Fields appeared bright green with early summer growth. Corn, rye, barley, and pumpkins, all popular local crops, flourished in the morning sunshine.

Eventually, Sarah turned down Old Mill Road and left the farms behind. The road led into a wooded area—thick with second growth that grew back once the mill, which rotted away long ago, closed.

Will I be able to find the spot? What will I find?

A half-mile along, Sarah spotted the line she scraped across the dirt road and the rough arrow made of stones. She surveyed the gooseberry bush blocking her way. Sarah weighed her options. Brave the thorny bush or find some way around it. She chose the latter and managed to find stinging nettles instead. Her right calf stung and began to break out in a blistery rash. She tried rubbing soil and spit on the affected area, achieving some relief, and pressed on until she stood where she figured her markers lay on the other side of the brush.

Sarah started walking away from the road and noticed a terrible smell that hung heavy and rancid in the air. Sarah placed a hand over her mouth and nose, trying to use it as a filter. A few feet beyond, she found Molly's corpse lying face-up on some green leafy foliage. The remains of the girl looked exactly as last night, including the beetle in Molly's open mouth.

Seeing this in the light of day with the added smell

of putrefaction became too much for her. Sarah vomited.

After a while, nothing more would come up, yet she still gagged. She needed to move away from the site and the terrible scent. Now what? Go to the police or tell Molly's father?

Sarah decided Mr. Scott, Molly's father, deserved to know first. She retraced her steps back to the road, careful to avoid the patch of nettles.

The Scott's farm, like many New England farms, was lined with stone fences—people needed to do something with all the rocks they dug up. Molly's father used much of the farm for pasture instead of growing crops, but the animals she saw as she approached the house looked poorly. A thin shabby horse and a similar-looking mule stared at her with impassive eyes. Four Holstein cows lowed in pain, imploring her to milk them as they crowded around the gate to the fence.

Sarah knocked on the door and looked through the nearby window. Bertrand Scott slept at the kitchen table, next to a bottle of gin. After many knocks, she managed to rouse him. Bleary-eyed, the man struggled to his feet and staggered to the door, unlocked it, and swung it wide.

Seeing her, he growled, "What do you want?" His breath stunk of gin, and a filmy line of dried saliva ran along the inner edge of his chapped lips. He grimaced in the morning sunshine and held his right hand to his head in evident pain. "Go away," he snarled.

The man teetered back to the chair at the kitchen table, plopped down, and massaged the sides of his skull.

"I saw Molly last night," Sarah told him.

Mr. Scott sat up, suddenly alert.

"She's dead," Sarah added.

Mr. Scott came at her, and Sarah flinched, afraid he would hit her. Instead, he grabbed her shoulders and gave her a little shake. "My girl—dead?" he asked.

Sarah gulped. "Yes, sir."

"How do you know?"

"Her ghost visited me last night."

Molly's father let go and turned away in disgust. "Go away."

"I know where to look. I marked it last night where she showed me, out on Old Mill Road. I went there this mornin' to check—makin' sure it weren't a nightmare. She's there all right."

Mr. Scott turned back and looked at her. "What was she doing way out there?"

"I don't know. Perhaps she'll tell me next time."

"You're crazy."

"No, sir, I thought maybe so, but I just come from where she's layin'. I could have gone to the sheriff, but I thought you should know first."

The man's eyes bore into her, but she held up under the scrutiny. At last, he stood and went to the sink. He stuck his head beneath the pump's spout and worked the handle until water ran over his head. Eventually, he stood up and pushed his sopping hair back from his face. "Let's go."

Outside, Mr. Scott retrieved his horse and hitched him to the buckboard wagon. He climbed onto the plank seat and motioned for her to do the same. When she climbed up next to him, he stared straight ahead and said in a threatening voice, "If this is some sort of sport, our next stop *will* be the sheriff's."

Molly's father shook the reins and they rode off.

Every bump and pitch to the wagon awakened fresh pains in Sarah's raw backside. By the time they reached Old Mill Road, tears clouded her eyes and ran down her cheeks.

Sarah swiped the tears from her face and studied the roadbed ahead. The shadows cast by leafy trees above made it difficult to see details in the road as they went along.

"Slow down, will you?" she said.

At last, she found the spot, more by gut instinct than anything else. She yelled for him to stop. The two climbed off the wagon and went around the gooseberry bushes as she had done before.

When they found Molly's body, Mr. Scott let out a wail and dropped to his knees. He picked up one of her rotting hands and held it to his chest.

Later that morning they drove the wagon into town to present Molly's remains to the sheriff. The sheriff came out of the jail, followed by Mr. Scott and Sarah, and drew back the canvas draped over Molly's body. He turned a little green.

The sheriff threw the tarp back over Molly and retreated a few steps. He looked up at the sky for several long moments then leveled his gaze at Molly's father. He put a hand to his holstered gun. "Bertrand, I have to ask you to step into a cell on suspicion of murder."

Bertrand Scott, already ashen, turned whiter still. "What?"

"You heard me. I've had doubts about you from the start, out there in the boonies with your daughter.

You and Molly fought, no doubt, and you did something you probably now regret. You couldn't live with yourself after what you'd done, cooked up this crazy story, and got this girl here to buy into it."

Bertrand struggled to speak. His mouth worked up and down like a fish out of water. Tears ran down his cheeks. At last, he found his voice, as he clenched both his eyes and his fists, but only one sound came out, a wracking heartfelt moan.

The sheriff glanced at Sarah and back at Bertrand Scott. The lawman became suddenly conciliatory. "Step inside, Bertrand, and we'll sort this thing out. Don't make me have to pull my sidearm or cuff you."

Bertrand let out a deep breath and sagged as though deflated. He lowered his head and shambled into the jail. The sheriff ushered him through the door in the rear of the office that led to the cells.

When the sheriff came out of the back room, Sarah tried her best to protest, but the man cut her off and growled, "Get on out of here before I stick you in the lodge too!"

The sheriff's threat made Sarah feel somehow guilty as if she were responsible for everything. She turned, walked outside, and saw the wagon and the bedraggled horse. When the sheriff emerged, she said, "I don't think I can manage the wagon, but I'd be willing to walk the horse back to Mr. Scott's farm."

"I'll put him up in the livery. You get yourself on back to school where you belong."

"Yes, sir," said Sarah and walked away, but instead of school, she returned to Mr. Scott's farm and tended to the animals.

In fact, she continued looking after them while

Molly's father sat in jail.

Sarah needed to testify at the court hearing the following week. Her parents accompanied her, and all three sat in the gallery. When the bailiff called her name, Sarah squeezed past her folks and the other people on the bench until she got to the center aisle. The bailiff led her to the witness box and there he told her to place her right hand on the Bible he held before her. The man recited the pledge to tell the truth. Sarah nodded.

"Say, I do," Judge Phineus Newbold said with a kind smile as he looked down from his seat at the thin red-headed girl.

Sarah recited the two words with all the solemnity she could muster. When asked, she told the court about the apparition of Molly—to the titters and guffaws of many.

"And how did Miss Scott's body get into the woods?" asked Albert Schmidt as he waved his right hand in a little flourish. The man oiled his hair so that it shone and his huge waistline made him an imposing figure.

"I don't know," said Sarah, "but you can ask Molly yourself. I've had the feeling all week she wants to speak."

This time Albert led the guffaws until the judge gaveled the room back to order.

"Well," the prosecutor said with a snide grin, "let's hear from her."

Sarah closed her eyes and took deep breaths for several moments. Her breathing became labored, and she sat back on the chair and moaned.

The judge pounded his gavel several times. "That's

enough of this," he proclaimed.

Hugh Marsten, the defense attorney, stood up. "Begging the court's indulgence, sir. If her story is true, it could exonerate my client."

Judge Newbold looked over at Schmidt, who still chuckled. "No objections, your honor," said Schmidt. "I enjoy a good performance as much as anyone."

"I'll let this go on for a minute or two, provided it doesn't turn into a sideshow," grumbled the judge.

Sarah opened her eyes with a start. She looked at Bertrand Scott. "Father," she said in Molly's voice, "what are you doing here?" She looked around with panic. "What? Where am I?"

"You're in a court of law," said Judge Newbold, "and may I remind you, Sarah Bradbury, you are under oath. Are we to believe you are now Molly Scott?"

Sarah looked at the judge with shock. "What are you talking about? Wait—I remember…" Sarah turned to face the people in the gallery. "I snuck out of my house for a buggy ride with John Hyler. I'd never done anything like that before, but I thought with the sheriff's son, there would be nothing to fear."

John Hyler bounded to his feet from where he sat in the rear of the courtroom. "This is crazy!" shouted the young man. "The girl's a lunatic!"

The judge pounded his gavel. "Bailiff, please help the junior Mr. Hyler find his seat. I'm starting to take some interest in this testimony after all."

The sheriff, John's father, moved down the center aisle in the courtroom, adding his protests to his son's. "You can't be serious, Phineas. The girl is clearly disturbed."

The judge held his gavel out toward the sheriff.

"Quiet, Charley, and be seated before I have you arrested for contempt."

He turned back to Sarah. "Please continue."

"It was a warm May night, and I wore my favorite blue dress and my late mother's brooch. I crawled out my window and met John in his surrey. We drove off, not saying much, but enjoying the beautiful evening. After a while, John stopped the carriage. We were on Old Mill Road. He grabbed me and started kissing me, putting his hands all over."

Sarah became more distressed as she relived the event. Her arms beat at the air before her, attempting to drive the man away.

"He said everyone knew I was loose, and he wanted his turn. I fought him off as best I could. In the process, Mother's brooch got torn off and rolled beneath the seat. I screamed and cried as he had his way.

"When he finished, he climbed off me and turned the carriage around. We headed back, but I couldn't stop crying. He hit me while he drove the horse on faster and faster. Finally, I said I was going to tell his father and he went berserk. He swore and threw me from the racing carriage. My head struck the ground first, breaking my neck.

"John stopped and went back to where I lay on the road. He dragged me out of sight, through some bushes, and left me there to rot."

Sarah stood up and pointed to the sheriff's son. "John Hyler, you're a rapist, a murderer, and a coward. My mother's brooch is still beneath the carriage seat where it fell."

A word about the author...

The supernatural always had the allure of forbidden fruit, ever since my mother refused to allow me, as a boy, to watch creature features on late-night TV. She caved in. (Well, not literally.)

As a child, fresh snow provided me the opportunity to walk out onto neighbors' lawns halfway and make paw prints with my fingers as far as I could stretch. I would retrace the paw and boot prints, then fetch the neighbor kids and point out that someone turned into a werewolf on their front lawn. (They were skeptical.)

I have pursued many interests over the years, but the supernatural always called to me. You could say that I was haunted. Finally, following the siren's call, I wrote *THE EIDOLA PROJECT*, based on a germ of an idea I had as a teenager.

Ultimately, I hope my books give you the creeps, and I mean that in the best way possible!

robertheroldauthor.com

P.S. Please consider posting a few lines (or more) as a review. Reviews are golden to writers.

Acknowledgments

No author is an island (apologies to John Donne), and in the process of writing a book, one incurs many debts, artistic and otherwise. My deep appreciation and gratitude to the following people who helped to make this book happen:

To Laura Peterson, Scott Wyatt, Ulrike Rylance, Sandy Nygaard, Cheryl Hauser, & Z. D. Gladstone, for your incredible feedback and support along the way.

To members of the Puget Sound Sisters in Crime (they allow "misters"!), thank you for your community and devotion to craft.

To the alphas of beta readers: Ruth Herold, Gerry Hall, Amy Johnson, Freda Cook, & Debby Ingram—thank you for your keen eyes & sound judgment.

To Professor King Davis, Ph.D., of the University of Texas at Austin, who is leading a project to digitize the records of the Central State Hospital archives. Thank you for your invaluable assistance in providing insights on the hospital in 1885. Please forgive my playing fast and loose with a lot of the facts!

To Al Runte, for his tremendous support and his knowledge of railroads of the era.

And finally, to Ally Robertson, for her kindness, encouragement, and assistance in the editing process, all of which were legion.